HOMEGOING

HOMEGOING

Frederik
· Pohl

A DEL REY BOOK
BALLANTINE BOOKS ◆ NEW YORK

A Del Rey Book
Published by Ballantine Books

Copyright © 1989 by Frederik Pohl

All rights reserved under International and Pan-American Copyright Conventions. Published in the United States of America by
Ballantine Books, a division of Random House, Inc., New York,
and simultaneously in Canada by Random House of Canada Lim-
ited, Toronto.

Library of Congress Cataloging-in-Publication Data
Pohl, Frederik.
  Homegoing.
  "A Del Rey Book."
  I. Title.
PS3566.036H6 1989   813'.54   88-7413
ISBN 0-345-33975-4

Text Design by Alexander J. Klapwald

Manufactured in the United States of America

First Edition: April 1989

10 9 8 7 6 5 4 3 2 1

HOMEGOING

Chapter
• 1

At this time John William Washington, who is usually called "Sandy" by his old nursemaid and his six friends, is biologically twenty-two years and eleven months old. He thinks of himself as roughly a twenty-two-year-old, although time-keeping in the Hakh'hli interstellar ship does not go by Earth years. His age doesn't really reflect the elapsed time since his birth anyway. Time dilation has cooked the clocks; the ship has spent much of its time traveling at relativistic speeds. Sandy is an excellent physical specimen—not counting such minor problems as deafness (but that is easily remedied by the hearing aid his shipmates have made for him) and a certain squatness of form. He stands only five feet five inches tall, but he masses two hundred pounds—on Earth he would have weighed that, though in the gravity of the Hakh'hli ship he weighs thirty percent more—and he is strong enough to support his own weight in each hand, with his arms outstretched. But Albert Einstein had been right about that, as about many other things. Everything was relative. Among the Hakh'hli on their huge inter-

stellar spaceship Sandy is as frail as a puppy, and his other nickname among his peers—the one they use when they are mad at him—is "Wimp."

A tiny voice in Sandy's dreams cried, "Unclasp, unclasp, Sandy-Wimp." It wasn't a dream; it was the voice of his cohort-mate Polly, filled with mixed affection and irritation. The reason it was faint was that Sandy's hearing aid had come loose again during the night. "We've got work to do this morning!" she bawled, her sour but pleasant breath stirring his hair. He winced away from her. Polly was not the biggest of the six Hakh'hli in Sandy Washington's cohort, but she was sometimes the bossiest.

Sandy let go of Demmy with one arm and Helen with the other, sat up, stretched, and yawned. He readjusted the hearing aid, gazing around. The whole cohort slept in a tangle on the matting in one corner of their exercise room, and it was not uncommon for him to wake up with Bottom's immense right leg pressed across his back and, say, Titania's two-thumbed claw in his mouth. But this time he was on top, and he jumped off the pile before the inevitable morning rough-housing started.

They splashed and rubbed themselves clean while one of them went for the morning meal cart—it wasn't anything like the great gobbets of roots and meat they would devour at the main midday meal, just the broth and wafers they called "cookies and milk." Being sleepy, they didn't talk much. The morning music was going, since the Hakh'hli disliked silence as much as any Earthly airport manager. It was playing Earth tunes on the special program for the cohort quarter, of course. Sandy hummed along with the Beatles in "Yesterday" as he pulled his clothes out of the locker. He leaned forward to kiss the picture of his mother that was stuck inside the locker door. Then, because it was a work day, he hurried back to the meal cart. They all ate quickly of the salty, steamy broth and the crunchy wafers. There was no special ceremony about eating—on work mornings they didn't take time for the Kitchen Game or the Restaurant Game—and when they were through they hurried out to the portal of their quarters. A sharp click, a shrill hiss, a deeper, louder thump as the pressure-lock door opened, and they walked through the pressure change. Sandy swallowed. The pressure change from their quarters, maintained at an Earthly 1000 millibars, to the Hakh'hli 1200 wasn't supposed to hurt his ears any more, but it did. His Hakh'hli cohort, of course, didn't even notice the difference.

Obie daringly hunched himself out into the corridor for a quick look in both directions. "ChinTekki-tho isn't here!" he crowed. "He's late! Maybe we'll get the day off!"

"Maybe your turds will fly! Get back in here," Polly commanded, and cuffed him at the base of his stubby tail when he did.

"But it's *hot*," Obie whined, lifting himself on his springy legs to present his tail to Sandy for comforting. It was there to be licked, and Sandy obliged. Everyone knew that Polly was right. Obie shouldn't have gone out of their quarters without permission. That wasn't allowed any more. But the whole cohort resented Polly's bossiness, and besides Obie and Sandy were best friends.

Polly took it upon herself to lecture. "The reason the ship is hot," she said severely, "is that the navigators had to bring us in close to this star so that we could do the course-change maneuver. That could not be helped, and anyway it is getting cooler now."

"Praise the navigators," Obie said instinctively.

Helen echoed, "Praise them a lot!" She was simply sucking up to Obie, of course. She was pre-positioning herself for the time, obviously not far away, when Obie would come into sexual season. Then it would be his whim that could spell the difference between rejection and a successful coupling in amphylaxis.

But Obie wasn't listening. He was daringly peering out

into the corridor again, his spirits completely restored, and it was he who cried, "Here comes MyThara!"

They flocked to greet her. Especially Sandy, who, grinning with the unexpected pleasure of seeing her instead of the teacher, hurled himself on her back as soon as she was within the portal. She shook him off, limping a little. She pretended to be angry. "Get off me, you! What ith the matter with you, Lythander?" Sandy winced; the full name meant she was really angry. "I call that improper conduct for a Cheth who will thoon be carrying out urgent work. Chin-Tekki-tho cannot come today, therefore I will conduct you to your job. Come along, all of you!"

Weeping amused tears, the cohort followed her into the corridor and across the ship. The whole Earth-mission cohort liked old MyThara, though it was only Sandy who looked on her as the closest thing he had ever had to a real mother. Her full name was Hoh'My'ik perThara-tok 3151. The "Hoh" and the "ik" had to do with her family bloodlines. "My" referred to her status—she was a mature adult, but not a Senior. Thara-tok was her personal name; "per" referred to her age—now approaching the end of her life, as Sandy well knew but tried not to think about; and the number distinguished her from any other of her lineage and generation— it was something like the batch number of her particular set of stored, fertilized eggs. Sandy sometimes dared to call her Thara-tok, but formally, to young adults like those of the cohort, she was MyThara.

With the time before the Earth landing growing so short, even Sandy and his cohort had to take a turn at doing ship-work. Sometimes the work was harvesting, pulling out the food plants and cleaning their tubers of soil, separating the stalks and the leaves; before that it was picking the blossoms from the plants when they were in their flowering phase, or collecting the round, pale globes that came when the plants had fruited. Tuber-pulling was dirty work, but not as dirty as what they had to do when the harvest was complete. Then they had to get ready to seed the next crop—pour in the buckets of sludge from the recycling stations and mix them into the soil. The Hakh'hli food plants were marvels. Every part of them was edible, and every part could be prepared and eaten in a hundred different ways. But they left nothing in the soil. So all the nutrients had to be put back—once the remains of the food had gone through the garbage bins or the alimentary systems of the ship's crew and turned up as sludge in the bottom of the recycling tanks.

Even that kind of shipwork wasn't as bad as cleaning out the pens of the hoo'hik, the four-legged, hairy, pale, docile, hog-fat food animals. The hoo'hik were as big as Lysander himself and affectionate. They did smell bad. Especially their droppings did. But sometimes one of them would nuzzle up to Lysander, even when he was loading them to the slaughterers—they would even gently pat and stroke the slaughterer himself with their stubby paws as they waited dumbly for the blow that would end their lives. The hoo'hik weren't much like the dogs and cats Sandy saw on Earthly TV. But they were the closest things to dogs and cats around. There were times when Lysander wished he could have had a young hoo'hik as a pet. But of course that was impossible. No such things as pets were allowed on the big Hakh'hli interstellar ship.

Unless Lysander Washington himself could be considered one.

"Hurry up, hurry up," MyThara kept calling as the cohort dawdled, gazing wistfully into every compartment and corridor that once had been theirs to roam and now was denied. The Hakh'hli they passed gazed back, because the Earth-mission cohort was now more newsworthy than ever on the ship. They would not normally have had much status. By Hakh'hli standards they were only "cheth," which was to say that they were adult, but not very. In the normal course of Hakh'hli life none of them would be considered worthy of serious responsibilities for another half-twelve years at least, but the times were not normal. The Earth-mission cohort didn't have time to grow older and wiser, because the time when they would need to act that way was almost upon them. Consequently, the other Hakh'hli thought of them the way a Japanese cynic in World War II might have regarded an eighteen-year-old kamikaze volunteer. The serious, even vital, job they were going to do entitled them to a certain amount of respect—but they were still kids, and feather-headed ones, at that.

Their shipwork job that morning was to help rig netting in the nurseries. When the ship reached its orbit around the planet called "Earth" it would turn off its motors. Then everything in it would immediately lose weight. At that time the nets the cohort was putting up would be essential, so the newborn Hakh'hli infants, happily springing about the nursery, would not bash their infant brains out against the unforgiving walls.

"Up top, Sandy," Demetrius commanded when they had looked over the situation. "You're the lightest."

"You've given me the hardest part," Sandy complained. Whoever was on the upper part of the walls would have to hang on with one or more limbs and, with whatever limbs were left over, catch the heavy balls of elastic fiber as they were tossed up to him.

"Serves you right," Helen croaked malignly. "It's about time you did some real work." And then, because she was the next smallest to Sandy, though the margin was wide, she was sent to clamber up the far wall to catch his return throws.

So as not to waste the time the cohort organized one of their informal games—they just called this one "Questions"—and tossed hard ones back and forth. It was Helen's idea, so she got to choose the category. "Middle names," she decreed.

"Of American presidents?" Bottom ventured. He was always the most diffident one. He was the fattest and shortest, too. Everyone laughed at the clumsy way he hopped about, but when he made a suggestion, if anyone listened at all, they generally found it was a good one.

"That's okay," Sandy said eagerly, adjusting his hearing aid to make sure he didn't miss anything. "Let me start. How about Herbert Hoover?"

"Clark," Demmy said at once. "His middle name was Clark. Herbert Clark Hoover, 1929–1933. He was president during the stock market crash, 1929, which led to the Great Depression, apple sellers, breadlines, unemployment, miniature golf—"

Polly hurled the ball of cord at him. "Just say the name," she snapped. "Go again."

Demmy giggled as he caught the cord, his eyes weeping with pleased vanity. He tossed it to Sandy, who listened as he fastened a loop of it to the wall studs. "All right. How about Richard Nixon?"

"Milhous!" Polly cried at once, already ready with her next stumper. "Calvin Coolidge." She licked her little tongue in and out in satisfaction, confident she had stumped them. But Bottom fooled her.

"It was Calvin!" he said triumphantly. "Calvin *was* his middle name; his first name was—was—"

"Was what?" Polly demanded. "You didn't answer the question."

"Yes, I did," he bellowed.

"You didn't!"

"You silly slabsided sapsucker," Bottom hissed at her, vain of his Earth slang and the way he pronounced his *s*'s. "I did, too!"

"Not really, no. *I* said his name was Calvin. You have to say what his other name was, or else you've lost and I go again and—*oof!*" she gasped as Bottom leaped at her, butting his triangular head right into her belly.

9

♦

That put a stop to rigging nets for a while. Helen leaped down to join the fray, but Sandy stayed where he was on the wall. These free-for-alls weren't particularly dangerous for his friends. The young Hakh'hli weighed twice as much as he, and they were pretty evenly matched with each other. Sandy was a different case. He had neither the mass nor the elephant-hide skin to take that kind of brawling lightly. Nor did he have the muscle, for that matter. Any one of the Hakh'hli youths could have wrenched his limbs off as easily as a lover plucking petals off a daisy; and there had been times when they were all much younger when some had come close.

It wasn't that Lysander Washington was a weakling. Nobody on Earth would have called him that, but the Hakh'hli were something else. They knew it. Even when one of them was mad at him, they didn't let it get to the stage of physical violence. For one thing, they knew what would happen to all of them if anything bad happened to the one human member of their cohort. For another, they were not ungrateful to him. They were in his debt. They knew very well that if it hadn't been for the fact that this Earth human, Lysander Washington, had needed some kind of companions to grow up with— not human companions, of course, because there weren't any of those on the ship, but as close to human as a Hakh'hli could manage—all of them would very likely still be unhatched eggs, frozen in the ship's vast cryogenic nursery.

While the others were roughhousing, Sandy slipped down from the wall and tucked himself into a corner, behind a squatting bench. He was protected from the combat by the rows of empty infants' nests—none of the baby Hakh'hli who would occupy them were out of the incubators yet. Comfortable and glad to be off the perch on the wall, Sandy pulled a pad and stylus out of his pocket. He tucked his head down in case of flying objects and began writing a poem.

Writing poetry was not an unusual activity among the

tions had the confusing habit of transmitting historical films, and, even worse, some of the films were golden oldies without any discernible clue to when they had been made. Togas, the Hakh'hli were sure, were out. So were plumed hats and swords. Business suits seemed safe enough, but—well, what kind? Single-breasted or double? Wide or narrow lapels? A tie? A stiff collar? Cuffs on the pants? A vest? And, if so, a vest that tamely matched the jacket, or one in red or yellow or plaid?

Then, of course, there was the vexing problem of what the clothes were to be made of. The best of the television pictures from Earth showed colors and sometimes even surface textures, but there were subtleties no one on the interstellar ship understood. The wisest scholars, poring over nearly a century's worth of transmissions, had learned much and deduced even more by collation and comparison, but they could not say whether a particular garment should be single thickness or double, or whether they were lined or not, or how, exactly, they were held together. This was far more important for Sandy than for the rest of his cohort, of course. The six Hakh'hli who were his constant companions wore Earth clothes, or at least something like Earth clothes— shorts, suitably modified to accommodate their huge, long, folded legs, and short-sleeved jackets and now and then even caps. Shoes were out of the question for the long Hakh'hli foot, but sometimes they were willing to wear something like sandals. Lysander, on the other hand, dressed human all the time. He had even been required to practice "tying a tie" in front of a mirror, as Earth males had been seen to do. But nothing in his previous life had prepared him for the ordeal of selection that was now confronting him. "I can't wear those things!" he cried. "How do I excrete?"

"The thcholarth thay it ith betht to remove the pantth," MyThara soothed. "You'll work it out all right, Lythander."

"I'll look like a fool!"

"You will look very handthome," MyThara promised, key-ing the final selections into the machine. "The Earth fem-aleth will lick your tongue, I promithe." Sandy, pretending to scowl at her on the outside, felt his heart leap inside him at that thought, as she finished, "Now get ready for the midday meal."

Since the food cart had not yet arrived for the midday meal, the cohort had begun a game of basketball, both to keep themselves busy and to relieve some of the strain of their bubbling young glands.

Their notion of basketball wasn't exactly regulation. There were only three on a side, plus one as referee—although until Lysander was through with his wardrobe chores they wouldn't be able to have a referee at all. And the ball didn't bounce exactly the way it did on broadcasts of the Knicks and the Lakers, and they didn't have anywhere near the room for a regulation-size court. But they did the best they could. Sandy Washington urged the others to play as often as he could, because it was the one sport he could, sometimes, beat them in. They were stronger by far, but he was quicker.

He persuaded Obie to drop out to become referee—easily enough, because Obie didn't much like the game—and plunged in. It was not as good as the games they used to have in the old days, before the Earth-mission cohort were cut off from the dozens of others they had grown up with, when their teams had, sometimes, a dozen players on each side. But it was a good game. The ship had been cooling down a little, now that they were well past the close approach to Earth's Sun that they had used to slow the ship down. That was both good and bad for Sandy Washington. The good part was that the rest of the cohort didn't sweat as much. The bad part was that they didn't tire as rapidly.

He did, though. Long before the midday meal cart arrived he dropped out. While the players were shuffling around and Obie was getting back into position, Polly came over to him, limping and rubbing her immense thigh where Obie had kicked her on his way in.

"He *hurt* me," she complained.

"You're bigger than he is. Punch him out," Sandy advised.

"Oh, no!" She sounded shocked. She didn't say why, but she didn't have to; by now everybody could see that Obie was getting close to a sexual season, so her reasons for keeping on his good side were obvious. "Why don't you go for the food cart, as long as you aren't playing?" she asked.

"I went yesterday. It's Helen's turn."

"But that will break up the game," she explained irritably.

"I don't care," he said, and turned away.

Then Sandy went off in a corner to watch TV on his personal monitor. It was the rule that at mealtime the cohort could watch anything they liked, just so it was in the English language for the practice. The old movie Sandy chose was called *The Scarlet Pimpernel*. It was certainly not the one he enjoyed most, and he could not pretend that it contributed to his education about Earthly ways. The costumes were all wrong, and exactly who was on whose side in that complicated drama of the French Revolution not even the Hakh'hli scholars had been able to figure out. But Sandy watched it over and over with fascination, because it was about a spy. And that was, after all, the task the Hakh'hli had decreed for him.

Chapter
· 2

There are some 22,000 living Hakh'hli aboard the vast
interstellar ship but there is only one of Sandy Washington. So
sometimes he feels outnumbered. It isn't just that he is alone.
He is also—not counting food animals—by a long way the
smallest grown-up living thing on the ship. An adult Hakh'hli
may mass anywhere from 350 to 750 pounds, depending on age
and the purpose it was bred for. Power plant and outside-of-
ship workers, for instance, are almost as big as the oldest Major
Seniors, though for occupational reasons they seldom live anywhere near as long. Though all Hakh'hli have the same basic
body pattern—short, supple forelimbs; long, pointed face like a
collie's; huge hindlegs as powerful as a kangaroo's—some of
the specialized types have stronger hands or shorter tails or even
no tails at all. The Hakh'hli hand has three fingers, plus two
thumbs and a stubby, hard-clawed digit called a "helper." It
looks quite like a human hand, but with the helper emerging
from what would be the heel of the hand in a human. If the
Hakh'hli on the ship are diverse, the many times as many

Hakh'hli on their home worlds are far more so—partly because they have more various purposes to meet, partly just because there are so many more of them. In all, there are in excess of one trillion Hakh'hli on the planets of their native sun and of the two nearby star systems they have colonized. No Hakh'hli on the ship has ever seen any of those other trillion. Nor have any of the trillion seen that ship, not since it began its voyage, 3000 Earth years ago.

Long before *The Scarlet Pimpernel* came to its heart-melting conclusion (the refugees safe, Leslie Howard triumphant, The Girl melting into his arms) the food cart arrived with their one great midday meal.

Sandy hung back from the rush. He had never learned to eat "properly," and all his friends in the Earth-mission cohort had regretfully concluded that he never would. His diffidence in rushing the food cart proved it, for a proper Hakh'hli didn't eat. He gobbled.

Sandy's cohort tore into the midday meal with gusto. They made a lot of noise doing it, too. While Sandy picked daintily at his slab of meat, his friends were snapping great chunks out of the carcass and stuffing lumps of tuber and fists-full of the flavored wafers in after. The long, powerful jaws crunched. The throat muscles gulped and swallowed. Sandy could see successive wads of lightly chewed dinner chasing each other down the throats of his friends. None of the Hakh'hli actually snatched from him the morsels he had cut away for himself, but he didn't expose them too openly. While they chewed they sucked in great quantities of the broth of the day, a sort of fishy consommé with lumps of wafer material floating in it. They sounded like half a dozen sump pumps going at once.

There was no such thing as dinner-table conversation among the Hakh'hli, nothing more than "Pass the broth bowl *now!*" and, "Hey, that bit's *mine!*" Sandy didn't even try to talk to them. He just sat patiently, cautiously nibbling at his own meal while he waited for the feeding frenzy to subside. In a few minutes it had. The great gobbets of food hit their respective stomachs. The Hakh'hli circulatory system rushed blood toward the digestive organs to meet the need for action. The chewing faltered and stopped, and one by one the Hakh'hli eyes went vacant, the Hakh'hli limbs went slack, and within five minutes every one of the Hakh'hli in Sandy's cohort was stretched out unconscious in "stun time."

Sandy sighed and walked slowly over to the food cart. Amid the wreckage there was still a fair-sized chunk of the hoo'hik meat, nibbled-at but undevoured, and several handfuls of the flavored biscuits.

He took what he could carry and wandered over to his personal carrel to finish his meal in peace. Having nothing better to do while his cohort was unconscious and digesting their meal he did what he liked best to do anyway. He watched a film.

The best part of Lysander Washington's life was also the most important part, because it was watching the old recorded television programs from Earth. He had to do that. Everybody in his cohort did, because that was how they learned Earth language and Earth ways. He also loved it. The way he liked best to do it was to curl up next to Tanya or Helen or even, if she was in a good mood that day, Polly, enjoying the smells of their scales and the warmth of their bodies, at least ten degrees hotter than his own. Together they would watch documentaries and newscasts, because they were instructed to, but when they had free choice it would be "I Love Lucy" and "Friends of Mr. Peepers" and "Leave It to Beaver." They weren't good recordings. They had been recorded originally from up to a dozen light-years away; in fact, they were the electronic signatures, picked up by the ship's always-scanning sensors, that had first alerted the Hakh'hli to the fact that there was intelligent, techno-

logical life on some planet of that little G-2 star their telescopes had located.

The old family-style television sitcoms were always fun,
but they made Sandy a little wistful. Sometimes he wondered what his life would be like if he had grown up on Earth,
with human companions instead of Hakh'hli. Would he have
played "baseball"? (Out of the question on the ship. They
didn't have the room. Or the players. Or a mild enough gravity to be able to hit a ball as far as Duke Snyder and Joe
Dimaggio did.) Would he have "hung" around with his
"pals" at the "malt shop"? (Whatever a "malt" was. None
of the TV chefs had ever made one, and the Hakh'hli experts
hadn't been able to decide even if it ought to be sweet or
sour.) Would he—maybe—have had a *girl*?

That was the biggest question in Lysander's mind. To
have a girl! To touch one (the touch was "like fire," "like an
electric shock"—how could those things be pleasant? But it
was said they were), even to kiss one (kisses sweeter than
wine! Whatever wine was), even to—

Well, to do whatever it was that humans did when they
were in sexual phase. Exactly what that was he wasn't sure.
He knew what the Hakh'hli did; he'd watched the other
members of his cohort often enough when they were sexual.
Did humans do the same? Unfortunately he couldn't know.
If there were porn channels for TV on Earth, the ship's receivers had never picked one up. It was apparent that human
males and females kissed. They did that a lot. They took off
each other's clothes. They got in bed with each other. Sometimes they got under the covers and the covers moved about
quite a lot . . . but never once did they throw the covers back
to show what made those busy lumps go bump.

Every night Lysander dreamed. Almost all the dreams
were the same. They were populated with female humans
who knew exactly what to do—and did it. (Though he never
could remember, when he woke up, exactly what it was they
had done.)

Sooner or later, the Seniors promised, Lysander would be back on Earth, with all its nubile female humans. He couldn't wait.

Sandy switched off the film he had chosen—it was called *Jesus Christ, Superstar,* and it was too much of a puzzle to watch alone. From his private locker he took out the photograph of his mother and looked at it. She was so beautiful! Slim, fair, blue-eyed, lovely—

The only thing that troubled Sandy was that although he knew from Earth films that men often carried pictures of their mothers and displayed them in moments of great emotion, he had never in any of those films observed that one of the mothers had been photographed in the nude. That was a puzzle that none of his cohort, or even the Hakh'hli scholars who had spent their lives trying to understand the ways of Earth people like himself, had been able to help him solve. It seemed improper to him. It was more than improper, it was confusing—because when he looked at his mother's picture, so fair, so bare, so inviting, he had exciting, unbidden thoughts that, he was nearly sure, were not at all appropriate to the situation.

He could not understand why that was.

He was not going to understand it today, either, he decided. His meal finished, he carried the crumbs back to the messy cart and returned to the carrel to get back to work on his poem.

Sandy didn't remember drowsing off and wasn't aware the he had until he woke with Obie standing over him. "You're turning into a real Hakh'hli," Obie told him, approving of the after-meal nap. "What've you got there?"

"It's just a poem I wrote," Sandy said, covering it up.

"Come on, let me see it. We always show you ours."

"It isn't ready," Sandy protested, getting up just in time to see Polly lumbering toward them irritably.

"Lysander," she accused, "you didn't clean up after the meal. Next thing you know we'll have bugs here, and then we'll have to get the hawkbees in."

Sandy was stung by the injustice. "Why are you blaming me? Why am I always the one who has to clean up?"

"Because you're the one who doesn't sleep. You know that."

"Well, today I did sleep. I didn't have time to clean up."

"You had time to write a poem," Obie pointed out treacherously. He turned to Polly. "He won't show it to me, either. He says it isn't finished, but it looked finished enough to me."

"Let's see the poem," Polly commanded, pinching her thumbs together in a meaningful way. Resentfully Sandy passed it over as the rest of the cohort, yawning and stretching, straggled toward them.

> Oh, my
> almost   forgotten
> terrestrial   homeland!
> I dream of you each day
> and think of you asleep
> and wish the experience
> of treading upon your
> soil would come, O
> Earth!

> Also
> it has the
> pretty old
> moon

"It's an attempt to write a Hakh'hli poem in the English language," the poet explained nervously.

"Hum," Polly said, not committing herself.

"I think that's pretty hard to do," Bottom commented.

"Maybe it's not worth doing at all," Helen put in. "It's

21

not the same thing as a real poem, you know. Those wriggly little characters are just *ugly*."

"Besides," Obie, the astronomer, added, thumping the notepad with his clenched fist, "you've got it all wrong. The proportions are inaccurate. The Moon ought to be a lot smaller."

"I couldn't fit enough words in that way," Sandy said defensively.

"Then you just should have made the Earth bigger, of course. And both of them are flattened out more than they ought to be. They look more like the one they call 'Jupiter.'"

Sandy snarled, "It's a *poem*. It's not an astronomy lesson!"

"Yes," Polly said severely, "but you ought to get it right. Also, how can the Earth be 'forgotten'? You couldn't forget it. You weren't ever there to remember it, were you? We picked your parents up in space."

"That's poetic *license*," Sandy said stubbornly.

Polly lashed her tongue at him in reproof. "Poets don't have license to tamper with the facts," she informed him. "Hakh'hli poets don't, anyway, and it doesn't make any difference if Earth poets do, does it? Now, no more of this! I vote we watch some films until MyThara comes back."

But the films the cohort chose to watch were not a kind that Sandy liked. They were all about wars and terrorism, and all those other nasty things humans were known to have done to each other in the twentieth century. When MyThara returned the cohort was quarreling about them. She paused in the door, frowning, as Bottom told Sandy judgmatically, "I think that your Earth governments are fools."

Sandy said sullenly, "You don't understand, is all. They probably had their reasons for what they did."

"What reasons, Sandy? Killing each other? Destroying farms, when neither side has enough food to live on? Spreading poisons? This is not a government of wise leaders who have been bred and trained for the purpose, like our Hakh'hli

Seniors. Have you ever seen such outrageous things here on the ship? The hoo'hik tenders attacking the extravehicular workers, for instance?"

"The hoo'hik tenders would be slaughtered if they did," Obie put in. "Those extravehiculars are *tough*."

"That isn't the point! The point is that such a thing could not happen here on the ship. Hakh'hli do not behave so wantonly."

Sandy stuck to his defense. "It's a lot easier to govern a few thousand people than a couple of billion."

"Oh? Indeed?" Bottom licked out his tongue sarcastically. "And on our Hakh'hli home worlds, where there are a thousand times a billion, have you ever heard of such warfare?"

"I don't know anything about what's going on in the Hakh'hli home worlds," Sandy said belligerently, "and neither do you. When was the last time this ship had any communication with them?"

But that was going too far. Even his friend Obie twitched resentfully, and MyThara gasped, "Thandy! How can you thpeak tho?"

"But it's true," he said, and then clamped his mouth shut. He didn't mind giving offense to his cohort-mates, but MyThara was someone he loved dearly.

"Dear Lythander," she said seriously, "you shouldn't talk lightly of the wortht tragedy in our hithtory. Don't you remember what you have been taught?"

He gave her a repentant look. "I'm sorry, MyThara." He knew perfectly well that every Hakh'hli in the ship mourned the long-ago day when the Major Seniors of the time, after bitter soul-searching, had made the decision for the ship to go on with its mission even after it had lost contact with the Hakh'hli home worlds.

Obie put in loyally, "He's just nervous because it's getting close to the time for visiting Earth. He even wrote a poem about it."

"Oh? Show me the poem," MyThara requested. When she had read it she flung her stubby arms around Sandy and gave him an affectionate lick. "It ith a *beautiful* poem, Lythander. May I have a copy? Oh, thank you! I will keep it in my own netht ath long ath I live. But now, pleathe, it ith work time. We will thtart with buddy thythtem, ath uthual. Lythander, you go firtht with Polly and talk railgun."

The seven in Sandy's cohort had a whole planet to learn—Earth language, Earth customs, Earth ecology. Plus all the things every young Hakh'hli had to learn as part of his normal socialization. Plus, for each of them, the harder lessons of his own specialty. Demmy's was agronomy. Bottom's was aerosol and food chemistry. Polly's was piloting and magnetic engineering. Tanya's was genetic manipulation. Obie's was astronomy and stellar navigation. Helen's was chelation, vitrification, and crystal-bonding—in other words, the processes involved in containing toxic and radioactive materials. What Sandy had to learn was easier, but larger. He had to understand something of all the other's skills, as they all did, for there was always the chance that somehow in the actual Earth mission one of them would be lost. But Sandy had to learn a little more than the rest, because he would be the one to make first contact with the Earth people, and he had to know what to say.

Polly was not Sandy's favorite to learn from, since she got rough when he was slow to grasp his lessons. As soon as they were alone in her own carrel she commanded, weeping with anticipation of his getting it wrong, "Explain the purpose of the railgun."

"All right," he said in resignation, "but no pinching, okay?"

"Maybe not. Get on with it!"

Sandy hunkered down crosslegged beside her—not too close—and began. "In return for all the good things that the Hakh'hli will do for the Earth humans, we ask only a few favors, for example that they help replenish our supplies of some stock things of no great value to them. We ask for oxygen, carbon, and hydrogen in particular. To get these to us, you will show them how to construct a sloping rail system, magnetically driven, which will accelerate canisters of water and solid carbon—they call it 'coal'—to the ship's orbit.''

"Why do we need those things?''

"They are fuel,'' he said promptly. "All of those elements are to fuel the lander, which is driven by hydrogen peroxide and alcohol fuel, and additional hydrogen is also wanted for reaction mass for the main drives. Do you want me to tell you how the railgun works?''

"I exactly do, Wimp. In detail, and no mistakes.''

He inched a bit farther away, cocking an ear to listen to the background music. It was one of his favorites, an Earth song called "The Man I Love.'' He could not help fantasying some female human singing it to him, but he said nothing because Polly would simply have ordered it turned off. "The railgun is to be built somewhere on the Earth's equator, to take advantage of the planet's rotation—''

"Which is pretty slow,'' Polly put in scornfully. The Hakh'hli ship day was only seventeen and a bit Earth hours long.

"Yes, but their gravity is only about seven-twelfths normal,'' Sandy pointed out, "so that makes the launch easier. The railgun will be six what they call miles long, ending at an elevation two miles over the surface. It will be best if they build it on the 'west' slope of a mountain. Every twelfth of a twelfth-mile along it there will be a magnetic hoop, each of which is charged in succession. The magnets will be superconducting-wound and will probably require the construction of a whole electrical power plant to supply them—''

"Not nuclear, though. We don't want to encourage them to do nuclear.''

"Polly,'' Lysander said carefully, "these are my people we're talking about, not hoo'hik. They will do what they want

25

to do." He ducked away as her thumbs reached warningly toward him, but he was saved a pinch as MyThara called out.

"End of period. Thwitch partnerth now," she ordered. "Lythander, now you will go to Oberon for athtronomy."

By the time of the eighth twelfth-day they were all exhausted and ready for the evening "cookies and milk."

That was not a time of relaxation, though. On MyThara's orders, they spent it practicing fast food. Demmy and Tanya took their turns at working the counter, and the others collected their "money" and lined up with their orders. "Cheeseburger, small fries, vanilla shake," Sandy ordered, calculating the cost in his head and pulling out two "dollar bills" and seven "quarters."

Demmy looked at him angrily. "You should give me three 'dollar bills' and three 'quarters,'" he complained, but Sandy stood his ground.

"I want to get rid of some change," he explained. He'd seen that in one of the taped sitcoms. Demetrius scratched his thumbs across his belly irritably, but he took the money, counted it out, and produced twenty-two "pennies" in change.

"I want to get rid of change, too," he said, weeping triumphantly.

Well, that wasn't fair. The counterpeople weren't supposed to get rid of change, Sandy was quite sure. But he didn't want another fight with Demmy, so he took his tray over to a table and sat there, examining the food. The "hamburger" was all right; it was simply ground up food animal. The "cheese" was another matter. From the cooking programs on Earth television it was known that "cheese" was something you made by letting milk sour and then doing a number of things to it. No one had determined just what sort of microorganisms did the souring, though, and so, as always, Sandy carefully lifted the slice of "cheese" off his meat and deposited it on the side of the plate. The "bun" was not a real bun—all the experiments at producing something edible out of ground carbohydrates had failed. It was simply a slice of tuber, shaped like a hockey puck and warmed; not really bad. The "fries" were more of the tuber, cooked in hot grease, and Sandy had developed a real taste for them. (He never bothered with the "ketchup" or the "mustard." Whatever the real things were like, the Hakh'hli imitations were horrible.)

The "shake" was the real daunter. It was made with hoo'hik milk, that much was clear. The rest was incomprehensible. This time it was flavored, unfortunately, more or less like the "cheese."

Sandy forced it down, hoping he wouldn't get sick. There was no stun time after so light a meal, and that was fortunate. Just as they were finishing, ChinTekki-tho, their principal tutor, came in. Polly daringly stopped him to display Sandy's poem before he could speak to the group. He didn't reprimand her. He seemed in a very good mood. He complimented Sandy. "No, it's quite a good poem, Lysander. That is, considering. It's very difficult to write a good poem in a bad language, after all. However," he added, "that is not why I am here to intrude on your evening snack. I was unable to be with you this morning because final plans are being made. Soon you will appear before the Major Seniors!" There was a stir of excitement in the group; no one got to see the Major Seniors! "Meanwhile, I have 'watches' for you."

"Watches?" Polly said doubtfully, but already he was passing them out, metal things on straps that the cohort examined curiously.

"You put them on your arms to tell time," he explained. "From now on, you are all to begin reckoning your days in Earth time. The research section has informed me that it is

27

now twenty-three 'minutes' past four 'A.M.' on what is called 'Wednesday, July twelfth' in your landing site, and the watches have been set accordingly." He paused while the cohort studied the dials, then added softly, "On Monday, July twenty-fourth, you will land on the Earth."

Chapter
◆ 3

The Hakh'hli ship is bigger than any human spacecraft ever dreamed of being, and not a lot smaller than a twentieth-century supertanker of the sea. It is in the shape of a stubby cylinder, 1,100 feet long and 450 feet across. That adds up to something like 175,000,000 cubic feet of volume, two-thirds of which is devoted to fuel storage and the engines that drive it across interstellar space. The ship's average density is a little less than that of water, mostly because so much of the fuel-storage space is given to hydrogen; if it were somehow deposited gently on a terrestrial ocean it would just about float. The inhabitants of the ship, 22,000 Hakh'hli and Sandy Washington, have an average of not quite 1,000 cubic feet of space apiece, but that includes not only their living quarters (mostly communal, anyway) but whatever space they need for recreation and for work. It isn't a lot. It was even worse, a few twelves of days ago, when the big ship was cutting near the Sun to change its orbit. Then much of the "spare" space was allowed to heat up so that the vast coolers could keep the rest of it bearable.

The Hakh'hli are glad now to be able to reenter the formerly closed off spaces. Even so, they are fairly crowded, at least by Earth standards. But that does not bother any of them, since none of them have had any personal experience of what Earth standards are like.

Of course the cohort were excused from the next morning's shipwork—being given an audience by the Major Seniors took precedence over any routine duty. The bad part of that was that ChinTekki-tho first put them through a long twelfth-day of interrogation and rehearsal, since it was unthinkable that any of them should say or do the wrong thing.

It was still hot in the common room, and they were all a little irritable from trying to adjust to the queer Earth time ChinTekki-tho had insisted they adopt. Obie was a distracting influence, too. Even Lysander could smell that Obie was close to entering his sexual phase, and more than once ChinTekki-tho had to reprove one or another of the females for showing more interest in Obie than in the lecture. "You must all pay very close attention!" he demanded. "Especially you, Lysander!"

ChinTekki-tho's *s*'s were as sharp as any of the cohort's; he was the best of the ship's experts on Earth languages and customs, which was why he was their tutor. But he wasn't always fair. "I *am* paying attention," Lysander said, aggrieved. "I'm not the one who wants to get laid."

"I hope that is true," snapped ChinTekki. "Now observe!" He displayed a section of the Earth on the screen, pointing to a land area. "This is where you will land. It is a northern area, easily accessible to your landing craft as you come in over the Earth's pole—"

"It's called 'Alaska,'" Tanya put in, showing off.

"We know it is called Alaska," the tutor said irritably. "Because of its location it is a cold part of the planet. It will probably be covered with the solid-phase water they call 'snow.' So you will all need appropriate clothing. Then, Lysander, after the ship lands, you will go out alone among the natives, carrying a radio. Your mission is to learn what things are like on Earth now, since we are no longer receiving as many broadcasts as heretofore. You will report to your cohort, who will remain with the ship. They will instruct you on what to do. When you speak on the radio you will speak Hakh'hli only, no English. Do you understand why all this is necessary, Lysander?"

"Yes, of course. It appears that we must be very careful in dealing with human beings because—" He hesitated, then finished sulkily. "Because some of them behave very badly."

"Not just some, Lysander. Very many of them. I am sure there are good ones, but by and large they are spoilers. You know what they have done to their planet—to your home planet, Lysander! What would our ship be like if we permitted such uncontrolled emission of dangerous pollutants?"

"It would be *awful*," Polly volunteered smugly.

"That is true, Hippolyta," said ChinTekki-tho, "but I am addressing Lysander. Do you know why your human people need our help, Lysander?"

"With verifiable accuracy and no uncertainty at all," Sandy said, using English words but the Hakh'hli locution just to show his independence. But it did not pay to be too independent in the presence of any Senior, so he hastily went on with the familiar recital. "The human race has raised the heat-retaining capacity of its atmosphere, released acid-forming compounds into the ambient air, cluttered up its low-orbit space with debris, saturated the surface waters with reduced and organic materials, discharged long–half-life radionuclides into the environment, and permitted deforestation and soil erosion."

"Also," Demmy chipped in eagerly, "eutrophication. You forgot eutrophication of the lakes."

"No, I didn't. That's part of what I said about reduced

and organic materials, isn't it, ChinTekki-tho? Of course it is."

"Yes, it is," the teacher agreed. "But you left out something even worse. Also, your human people are combative. They have weapons. They fight wars among themselves, even, with much killing."

"I have seen the broadcasts," Lysander said shortly.

"Yes, you have. So you know that we must be very cautious in approaching them. If it turns out that there can be a peaceful meeting between humans and the Hakh'hli, then we will reveal ourselves. But first we must be certain, and that is your job. We cannot risk the ship."

"Praise to the ship," cried Obie, and all the females immediately joined in.

"Yes, praise to the ship," ChinTekki-tho echoed. "Now, what is your story, Lysander?"

"First off," Lysander said rebelliously, "my name isn't Lysander, not when I'm on Earth it isn't."

"A good point," the tutor said with approval. "Go on."

"My name is John William Washington. I am twenty-three years old. My home is in Miami Beach, Florida, but my parents, who were named Peter and Alice, were killed in an automobile accident. I am a college student, but after my parents' death I was very upset and I took some time off from school to get away. I have been traveling in Alaska, because I always thought it would be an interesting place to visit. I have been off by myself, mining gold, and I am now getting ready to go back to Miami Beach, but I have lost my way."

"Yes, that is all right," ChinTekki-tho said approvingly. He paused, looking them over thoughtfully. Then he asked, "Are there any questions?"

Tanya put up her hand, Earth style. "*Why* don't we get as many transmissions anymore, ChinTekki-tho? We're getting tired of all these old movies."

"That is not known, Titania. There are certain electromagnetic signals being received all the time, so it is certain that the Earth people have survived their difficulties. To some degree, at least. But the signals we have detected do not seem to carry data. We don't know what they are. Anyone else?"

Obie piped up, "Why can't we see the friends who trained with us now?" He was referring to the thirty and more other Hakh'hli youths who had been brought up with them and then, just a few twelve-days before, had been removed to another part of the ship.

"The Major Seniors have decided to segregate you," ChinTekki-tho explained. That was, really, the only explanation that was need for any Hakh'hli, but he added graciously, "After all, you six—seven, I mean, Lysander—are special. You are the ones who will land first on this planet."

"But there were many attractive females in the rest of the group, and all we have left here are these three," Obie complained. All three of the females hissed angrily, but the tutor overrode them. "That's enough, Oberon! Now we will go to the chamber of the Major Seniors for your audience. However, there is one thing more. To prepare yourselves for your mission, you must all only speak English even among yourselves from now on—except to the Major Seniors, of course."

Because the Major Seniors weren't ready to see them, Sandy and the rest of his cohort had to wait in the compression room for one hour fifty-two minutes by their new watches. At first they were all subdued, because of the solemnity of the occasion. Lysander rubbed his ears ruefully; the compression still hurt, in spite of what had already been done to his ears to relieve it.

The subdued atmosphere didn't last long; the occasion was too exciting. Obie and Helen began roughhousing, as usual, and Polly had to sit on them to calm them down. That was normal enough, though. Going into the big part of the ship was always an adventure for them. At least it was an adventure when it wasn't simply drudgery, as when they had to take their turn at shipwork. But there wasn't much that was interesting in the compression room. It was just a room. It had benches to squat on, and the ship's screens to watch for entertainment, but what those showed was seldom really entertaining. True, once a twelve-day the whole ship was allowed to view a recorded Earth movie, selected out of the many thousands on file. That was interesting even to the cohort, because in these movies the dialogue was dubbed into Hakh'hli by some of the English-speaking scholars, and it was always amusing to hear a cheth female voice speaking the lines of, say, a hard-bitten infantry sergeant in World War Two. The rest of the time the screens were slaved to the standard ship's circuits, and all you could get on any of its channels was the check-shots of the engines and farms and pilotage and housekeeping functions, and maybe now and then a boring, a *really* boring, look at the sun they had just circled and then perhaps a shot of the planet they were aiming at. That would have been interesting enough, except that Sandy's cohort had their own screens, which were a lot better. They had all the recorded stories and documentaries and gleanings of half a century's eavesdropping on the planet's radio and TV transmissions. Although they had been watching those recorded transmissions for three-twelfths of every day for all of their lives, the old broadcasts were still exciting, simply because they were from Earth.

There was nothing like that in the anteroom. It wasn't very big, either, and the faint odors that arose from Obie were very distracting to the females. It was a lucky break that Tanya found one channel with a sports event. The ship's wrestling championships were under way. Somewhere in the Hakh'hli recreation space two huge Hakh'hli were competing in the quarter-finals. The cohort immediately chose up sides and rooted for their favorites. Even an Earthman might have been able to follow the action, if any Earthman but Sandy Washington had been there to see it, because the sport was actually an Earth innovation. It was copied from Japanese sumo wrestling and consisted of two Goliaths falling on each other.

And it was certainly exciting. Obie told Sandy enthusiastically, "If your Earthies never gave us anything else, that would be good enough." But Polly disagreed; and Tanya disagreed with Polly; and while the bout was going on on the screen, naturally another fight broke out among the cohort.

When at last the Major Seniors had reached the point in their deliberations when they were willing to grant audience to Sandy's cohort, the fight had long since been quelled. Obie was still bleeding slightly from a cut below his eye, but Demmy had torn a strip off his undershorts for a bandage— wearing human-type clothing had its uses, after all—and the whole cohort looked presentable enough as they lined up before the six huge Major Seniors. The Major Seniors were being genial, anyway, so they probably wouldn't have said anything even if they had noticed. "And how are our *Earthlingth* today?" the Fourth Major Senior asked—in Hakh'hli, of course. Sandy noticed that she had managed to weep a benign tear of welcome.

The Major Senior had spoken to the group at large, but everyone knew the question was directed mostly at Sandy. "We eat and excrete very well, ancient female," he said respectfully, in the same language. And then he added, using the English words when there was no Hakh'hli equivalent, "We are studying *automobile* driving, *credit cards* and late twentieth-century popular music, and yesterday we played *basketball* twice." He enjoyed speaking Hakh'hli when he had just been told it wasn't to be allowed anymore. It nettled him that his peers spoke better English than he did Hakh'hli. They had all had their vocal systems fiddled a little—surgically as infants or genetically before they were even born. They could make all the sounds of English easily enough, while when Sandy talked Hakh'hli too long his throat got sore from the clicks and glottal stops.

"Satisfactory, satisfactory," the Major Senior muttered affably. "This First Major Senior will inform you now and not later."

The First Major Senior always did, but all the same there was a little whiffling snort of resignation from the nostrils of almost everyone in the cohort. When the First Major Senior "informed" anyone, he started way back and left nothing out. Addressing Sandy directly, he did so again.

"*Earth* person Lythander Washington," he said, his eyes gazing vacantly toward the gray ceiling of the audience room, "your female parent and your male parent were abandoned in spacecraft when your *Earth* persons engaged in one *war*. In course of this *war* much damage was done by both particle and photonic beams, and by kinetic impact of either solid objects or of chemically or atomically explosive blasts. Your parents could not return to their home. Although we rescued them they were in damaged state and not well. We were unable to keep them alive, but you were already one quickened ovum, near to term, and we were successful in preserving you alive. We supplied you with living necessities and companionship while we—"

"Ancient male," Sandy said experimentally, "I have already received this information." He didn't think it would make the First Major Senior stop, or even blink, and it didn't. All that happened was that Polly sidled away from Obie's side long enough to give Lysander a quick, savage pinch from behind. The Fourth Major Senior looked up with thoughtful interest as Polly returned to crouch near the almost-tumescent Obie.

"—investigated certain nearby stars, including *Alpha Centauri*," the deep voice rolled on. "That star was of no use or interest. We have now returned to system of your own planet. You are now adult and educated. Confirm that this information is verified and not in error."

"It is verified, ancient male," Sandy said, rubbing his bottom. Polly's two-thumbed hand gave nasty pinches. He was aware that all the females were beginning to move toward Obie.

"We have been observing your planet since first approaching this system. There are certain facts of interest. First, those electromagnetic signals which originally attracted us to this system, and which increased exponentially in energy and in number all through our first approach, are now quite sparse. We do not have good, complete, recent information either by *radio* or by *television*. This may be because your *Earth* people have become either numerically few or technologically backward, due to that *war*. Alternatively, it may be for some other reason."

The First Major Senior paused for a moment, interlacing his six-fingered hands across his belly meditatively. No one spoke. The Fourth Major Senior absentmindedly left her elevated seat and waddled in the direction of the cohort, her eyes on Obie.

"One second new fact of interest," the First Major Senior said then, "is that there are no indications of powered vehicles anywhere in this solar system. From this we conclude that that inability of your *Earth* persons to enter into space since they blockaded themselves still continues and has not been overcome."

There was a nasal sigh from all the cohort at that. "Oh, pellets!" Demmy whispered, and Bottom kicked him. None of the Major Seniors showed any sign of hearing. Apart from the First, the others were gazing interestedly at the Fourth, who was sniffing Obie's spine. Her hip pouches were visibly swelling.

"We will, however," the First Major Senior said, "be able to make landing with one of scout craft by using one polar entry window. Most of debris remains in the plane of that *Earth* equator. Significant quantities are orbiting in other trajectories, but our analysts have identified one number of time periods during which approach can be made. Fuel costs will be very high, since no use can be made of rotational speed of planet and power must be applied all through descent phase; and similar costs will be encountered on return flight. However, that landing is feasible."

Daringly, Polly moved between Obie and the Fourth Major Senior. The Major Senior half raised herself on her hind legs, glaring at Polly, who sidled resentfully away.

The Fourth Major Senior addressed the group of her peers. "Excuse us and do not be offended," she said decorously, and led Obie away with a grip on the back of his neck.

"Yes, of course," the First Major Senior said to her back. "Well, I think that is all that need be said in any event. You Lythander, you remember that, though you are *Earth* human, you are also Hakh'hli. We Hakh'hli gave you life. We Hakh'hli wish only to help your *Earth* humans to correct errors of their own folly. But we must go with caution, and so we require you to carry out your mission fully and exactly and not without success. Will you, Lythander, do this?"

"I will," said Sandy, hoping the interview was over.

No such luck. The Second Major Senior stirred herself. "You must be clever and true and not disloyal, Lythander," she said severely. "Your *Earth* people are vain, idle, careless, and deceitful. They are spoilers. They have spoiled their planet. You must be like us and not like them in your actions on this *Earth*."

"All right," Sandy growled, shifting from one foot to another.

The First Major Senior shed a consoling tear. "What these people do on their planet is their guilt and not yours, Lythander," he said generously. "You need not swallow your own spit over this matter. Now you may all go."

There were no rough-and-tumble games in the waiting room this time. There was only waiting—waiting for Obie to finish his amphylaxis with the Fourth Major Senior and return from their lek. And the waiting was not at all pleasant, because all three females of the cohort were simmering.

By the time Obie came back, looking chipper and pleased with himself, they had reached the boiling point. "Oberon, you're a hoo-hik turd!" Polly thundered, and Helen and Tanya chimed in. "How could you?" Helen whined, and Tanya complained, "And with an old Major Senior!"

Obie was unrepentant. "You all saw what was going on, didn't you? Why didn't one of you squeeze in?"

"Against a Major Senior?"

Obie twitched a shrug. "There'll be more chances," he said generously. "And, wow, she was *big*. I never did it with a Major Senior before! It was all I could do to hold on."

"Were there lots of eggs?" Bottom asked enviously.

"What do you think? I mean, her being as big as she is? She was just beginning to lay when I left—and, listen, somebody's got to take them in for freezer tagging. You don't expect *her* to do it, do you?"

There wasn't, really, any particular reason why any one of them, rather than any other, had to perform that task. But, as Obie said, it had to be done. All the females were jealous of the Fourth Major Senior, both the other males were jealous of Obie, Obie himself was too full of himself to consider such a task—one way or another, it was Sandy who wound up twirling the sticky baton to catch each of the egg masses as they emerged from the swollen ovipositor of the Fourth Major Senior.

He had never done that before. It was kind of interesting to do. They looked like that Earth thing called "caviar," with a salty-sour smell that disturbed him.

As was customary, he wrapped them in transparent plastic and carried them through the halls to the sorting section, all the Hakh'hli he met scattering out of his important way. He lingered while the sorters gently coaxed the masses apart into dishes of warm water; watched while each one was weighed and sniffed and tested and labeled with the codes of Obie and the Fourth Major Senior. He waited until he saw them put into trays and frozen before he left.

Sandy did not know why the whole process was so fascinating to him. He only knew that it was. For all that time he was absorbed, and on the way back to the cohort's quarters he felt stirrings in his groin and a warmth flooding through his body and, oh, how impatient he was for the day when he would land on Earth, with its countless millions of nubile, human females.

Chapter

◆ 4

Although on the ship's plans the seven-twelfths of its cubage given over to the propulsion systems is described as "fuel storage," that isn't quite right. The three drive motors take up no more than a twelfth of a twelfth of that space, and the real fuel takes even less. The fuel for the Hakh'hli drive comes in three lumps. Each one, now, is about the size of a Hakh'hli's head. They are small, but they are heavy. Each one masses something like four by ten to the fourteenth grams. Although they are matter, they are not normal, baryonic matter, which is composed at root of nothing but up and down quarks. The fuel of the Hakh'hli ship is what Earth physicists called "strange" matter, because it is made up in equal parts of up, down, and strange quarks combined. It is the most violently energetic substance known. What takes up most of the space in the "fuel compartment" is simple hydrogen gas, there for no other purpose than to be fired out of the ship's nozzles at near light speed when driven by the energies of the strange matter. What takes up the rest of the space is the containment for the

41

fuel itself. Those basketball-sized fuel elements need bracing to keep them in place, because they are heavy. They weigh as much as all the rest of the ship combined, and, since they are what they are, they could not be kept in a galvanized-iron tank. Strange matter has to be held by electromagnetic fields, which themselves have to be braced against the fabric of the ship. Fortunately for the ship's designers, the fuel core weighs nothing at all when the ship is at rest—because nothing does—and when the drive is in operation the back-pressure against the core is exactly equal to the drive thrust that moves the ship. Newton's laws of equal and opposite motion hold good here, too. When the core is activated the strange quarks boil off to heat the hydrogen working fluid and shove the ship along as it accelerates, and the masses are in balance. There is enough strange-matter fuel to last for a long, long time. It has been powering the ship for 3000 years, and it is good for 10,000 more before it is used up. In fact, it never will be used up. One of the strangest things about strange matter is that the more you use it, the more you have left; and that is a problem that has been worrying the Hakh'hli on the ship for some centuries.

Sandy had never seen the drive engines. No one on the ship did except for the specially bred drive engineers, who managed to live (though not very long)) in the residual radiation that would have killed anyone else, human or Hakh'hli, in hours. Sandy had never desired to be one of them. What he did desire was to be allowed to pilot the great interstellar ship itself. Naturally there was no chance of that. Sandy wasn't supposed to pilot the landing ship, either, when the time came for him and all his cohort at last to brave the garbage barrier that surrounded the Earth and drop down onto its surface. Piloting the lander was Polly's job, though any of the others could take over. But the flight simulator that all the members of his cohort trained on—ah, that was another matter.

What made it possible for Sandy to sneak in a few lessons

was that flight-simulation took place right after the midday meal and its consequent stun time. Since Sandy was physiologically exempt from stun time he could get there before any of the others. It helped, too, that the instructor in charge was not the smartest Hakh'hli on the ship. The reason he was there was that he had actually been in the crew that was preparing to land somewhere in the Alpha Centauri system. They never did land, because there wasn't anything big enough to land on, but he was the closest the Hakh'hli had to an experienced lander pilot. Although he had never been authorized to let Sandy try his hand at pilotage, he had never been ordered not to, either. With a little wheedling, Sandy got past him and again took his place in the simulator capsule.

Sandy had brought cushions with him and used them to wedge himself into the kneeling-seat that had never been designed to accommodate a mere human anatomy. For a quarter of a twelfth-day—no, he corrected himself; for about twenty minutes, in the Earth reckoning of his new wrist watch—he was able to go through the whole sequence, from the magnetic-repulsion "launch" of the capsule from its recess in the side of the great interstellar ship, through the course-correction that brought it over the Earth's pole in a descending slant, through the dodging of space debris and the buffeting of atmospheric entry, and to a good, or at least not catastrophic, landing on a level, snow-covered plain between high mountains. The simulator made it all real. When the "lander" lurched away from the mother ship—pistons gave it a realistic jolt as it happened—the screens showed the black of space, and the green planet underneath, and the great ship shrinking rapidly away. When he "turned" the lander, the same pistons gave his capsule enough of a twist to match physical sensations with the slipping images on the screens, and they filled in again to suggest the terrible jolting of atmosphere entry.

A session in the lander simulator was as good as any

Earthly video game for a young adult, or actually a lot better. It wasn't good enough, though. When Sandy had to get out to make way for the first real space cadet from his cohort he was sulking. "I don't see why I can't fly it down," he complained to Polly—unwisely, because she gave him a pinch.

"Because you're too little, and too clumsy, and too dumb!" she told him. "Now get out of the way so I can check out!"

He glowered after her as she climbed in. Obie touched the small of Sandy's back in sympathy. "I'd let you fly if I could," he said. Sandy shrugged morosely; they both knew that Obie's time for influencing anyone else in the cohort had passed with his brief sexual phase. "Well," Obie said helpfully, "do you want to do something else? I'm last on the list; we've got at least a twelfth and a half before my turn."

"Do what?" Sandy asked.

"We could watch an Earth film," Obie proposed. "There's a 'Star Trek' I'd like to see again. I like those funny spaceships."

"No way," Sandy said positively, because Earthly ideas of nonexistent spaceships weren't what interested him; if he were going to watch films on his free time he wanted something with prettier girls in scantier clothing. Or alternatively—

He looked around thoughtfully. The four other waiting members of his cohort had started a Questions Game—name all fifty-three states of the U.S.A. in order, left to right, from Guam to Puerto Rico—and were conspicuously shunning both Sandy and Obie. The communications screen was being ignored. "Well," he said slowly, "there is a film I'd like to see again. Only it isn't from Earth. It's Hakh'hli."

It took Obie a lot of juggling to find the old records Lysander wanted, but when they appeared on the screen even the other members of the cohort gave up their game to cluster around. That wasn't particularly welcome to Sandy. What

was dragging. "Very bad and not at all good," the instructor pronounced. "You crashed this ship. You do not at all bring credit to your cohort." And while Bottom, the next in turn, was getting into the still-warm kneeling seat and buckling himself in, Obie had to stand silently through a lengthy criticism of the way he had failed to deploy his trash deflectors, missed his angle of approach over Earth's pole, and decelerated too rapidly on landing.

As soon as it was over he growled to Sandy, "Let's get out of here."

Sandy had no objection. "Where?"

"Anywhere," Obie said sulkily. "Listen. We're outside our quarters, aren't we?"

"Well, of course we are."

"So why don't we do something about it? As long as we're out we can look around."

"Look around where?" Sandy asked eagerly, already convinced.

"Anywhere we haven't been lately," Obie said, meaning anywhere they weren't authorized to be going.

"I don't think we're supposed to do that," Sandy said thoughtfully. It wasn't an objection, just a matter of putting all the evidence on the table, and Obie regarded it as such. He didn't answer. He just led the way out of the simulator chamber, and they stood for a moment in the corridor, looking around.

Sandy proposed, "We could go see some of the things they're making us to take to Earth."

"No, wait a minute!" Obie cried. "Listen, we can do that later, but maybe they've got some funny new freaks in Genetics! Let's go see!"

It wasn't what Sandy had had in mind. Genetics was a place of stews and stinks, and he didn't usually like to go there for personal reasons. But when he tried to explain that to Obie they were already on the way there, and anyway Obie was puzzled. "Tell me again what you don't like, Sandy?"

"I told you. They've got my mother there."

"Oh, Sandy," Obie said sorrowfully, twitching his thumbs in disagreement. "It isn't really your mother, you know." And actually Sandy did know. What the Hakh'hli had taken from his mother's body after her death was no more than a few microorganisms and cell samples. If they kept them alive as cultures, that was just science.

But Sandy couldn't see it that way. To him they weren't cultures, they were his mother—not alive, but not exactly dead, either. "Really, Sandy. The samples they've got in there aren't *her*. They're just *cultures*. All the rest of her fed the titch'hik long ago."

Sandy flinched. He disliked the thought of his mother's body being eaten even more than the thought of parts of it being preserved. It wasn't that Hakh'hli burial customs bothered him particularly. All his life he had been aware that the ultimate fate of every living being on the ship was to be tossed into the tank of the things, more like a limbless starfish than anything else on Earth, called titch'hik; the titch-'hik swiftly consumed all the flesh from the bones; then the titch'hik were harvested and fed to the food animals, the hoo'hik, as a valuable protein source; the bones themselves, ground up, went into the nutrients for the plants and to the hoo'hik as a calcium supplement—nothing was wasted. But when it was your own *mother* you were talking about it was *different*. Especially when you knew quite well that somewhere in Genetics there were flasks of cultures from her very own maternal body, kept on hand for experiments in gene-splicing.

Obie stopped halfway up the spiral ramp to the Genetics level. "You're serious, aren't you?" he said.

"Yes. I'm serious."

"But it's silly! They've got a lot of my own ancestors in there, too, you know."

"They can't have, or you wouldn't be here," Sandy pointed out sullenly.

"Well, I mean, at least from the same batch of eggs in the freezers. And I've certainly got children there, you know. Not even counting the ones with the Fourth Major Senior," he finished with a touch of offhanded pride.

"It's not the same."

"It *is* the same," said Obie, getting irritated. "Are you coming or not?"

Sandy shrugged and followed, still reluctant. But as it turned out he was spared. They were met at the Genetics doorway by a Senior who told them severely, first, that certainly there were no new organisms created by Genetics at that time—didn't they know that all of Genetics was preparing for the influx of new creatures from Earth to study and add to their gene pools? So how could they manage to breed funnier-looking or more efficient plants and hoo'hik and titch'hik at such a time? And, second, he pointed out, they had no business there in any case, did they?

They retreated hastily. "Ah, well," Obie sighed. "You didn't really want to anyway. I know! Let's go see what they're making for us!"

The laboratory rooms were hot, and not just because they had been in the part of the ship that had been allowed to heat up in the solar passage. Things were being *made* here, and there were furnaces and ovens to make them in.

Sandy was entranced. In the first chamber two old Hakh'hli were tending a plastics blender, out of which fabrics were being extruded in a dozen colors and textures. "For you," the boss said proudly. "These will be socks, these will be underwear, this is a 'necktie.' But if you want to see something really interesting, go next door."

Next door was really interesting, as promised, and even hotter than the fabric room. Part of the heat came from a furnace. An elderly Senior was standing over a couple of technicians who were carefully maneuvering a crucible. They tipped the crucible, and tiny, shiny, orange-glowing droplets fell into a tall vat. Sandy couldn't see inside it, but he heard a sudden violent sputtering from within.

Then the senior reached inside—Sandy blinked, but evidently the water inside was still cool in spite of the molten droplets it had quenched—and pulled out a couple of fingernail-sized, irregular lumps of yellow metal. He tossed them back and forth, hissing in amused discomfort, then handed one to Sandy. "Gold," he said proudly, using the English words. "Ith for you. Ith to give tho can buy thingth."

"Yes, to buy things," Sandy nodded eagerly. How many lessons they had had in "buying" and "shopping" and "paying"! The little golden nugget almost burned Sandy's palm, but he held it with reverence because it was an Earth kind of thing.

"I think buying things is silly," Obie put in, curiously fondling one of the little chunks of metal. He glanced up, and his eyes sprang a quick tear of surprise. "Theseus!" he cried. "I didn't expect to see you here!"

It was obvious that the other young Hakh'hli hadn't expected to see them either. Theseus was one of the three or four twelves of young Hakh'hli who had trained with them through all their childhood and growth, then suddenly been taken away from them when the final half-twelve had been selected for the Earth mission.

The other thing that was obvious was that the goldsmith hadn't expected them to meet and didn't like the fact that they had. He excused himself and huddled over a communications screen as Theseus said suspiciously, "You two aren't supposed to be here."

"Why not?"

"Because it's orders not, that's why!"

"That's not a reason," Obie said stubbornly, sticking to their story. "We were ordered to stay in our quarters, that's all. Then we were ordered to go—somewhere—and nobody said we couldn't look around. What are you doing here?"

"I'm picking some things up," said the reject. "You'll be swallowing your own spit if they catch you here."

"Why? What's the big secret?"

"We're not supposed to discuss it," Theseus said firmly, and he and Obie inched nose to nose, glaring at each other.

It was never a good idea for Lysander to get between any two Hakh'hli who were about to get physical, but these two were his friends—well, Obie was definitely his friend, no doubt of that, and Theseus had at least been a comrade, before the group had been split up. He opened his mouth to try reason.

It wasn't necessary. A voice from the communicator squawked at them. "John William Washington! HoCeth'ik ti'Koli-kak!" It was MyThara's voice, and the fact that she called them by their formal names told them how much trouble they were in. Sandy darted a furious glance at the goldsmith for turning them in, but there was no time to argue. "I did not believe the Thenior when he called, but it'th true," MyThara went on. "You are both where you have no buthiness being! Meet me at onthe in your quarterth, Lythander! And you, Oberon, get back to the thimulator chamber where you belong!"

When MyThara got to the cohort's quarters, slower than Lysander because she was limping more than ever, she found him at his carrel, gazing at the picture of his mother. It wasn't entirely guile on his part. When he was in trouble he had always found solace in gazing at the only memento he had of the woman who had given him birth. But it wasn't entirely without guile, either, because he had learned early on that MyThara's wrath at any transgression could often be muted if he played on her sympathy.

"That ith *no uthe*, Lythander," she said sternly. "You have been very wicked today!"

"I know I have, MyThara," he said in penitence. But he added, anyway, "MyThara? Why is this the only picture I have of her?"

She hissed reprovingly at him, but he could see that she was taking the bait. "It ith not a Hakh'hli cuthtom to keep picturth of dead people." she reminded him.

"But I'm not a Hakh'hli!"

"Indeed not," she agreed, with sympathy creeping into her voice. "Well, thith ith the betht we could do. We found it in your father'th 'wallet.' It ith a good likeneth, though."

"You know what she looked like?" he asked eagerly.

"Of courthe," said MyThara, and added considerately, "She wath very beautiful. For an Earth perthon, I mean. You look like her, I think."

Sandy gave her a skeptical scowl. "What are you talking about? She's so skinny, and I'm so fat!"

"You are not fat, Lythander. That ith muthle."

"But look at the difference between us!"

"Of courthe there ith a differenthe. The differenthe ith becauthe you grew up here on the ship. Earth gravity ith only eight-twelfthth of ship normal. If your mother had come to uth ath a baby she would be a lot thtockier, too."

"Yes," Sandy said reasonably, "I see that, but—"

MyThara's patience had worn out. "Thandy! Don't think I don't know what you are doing."

"I beg your pardon?" he said, trying to look innocent.

She wrinkled her nose in sorrow, looking weary as well as disappointed. "Oh, Lythander," she said, shuddering in sadness. "How could you?"

"That's Lysander," he snapped, to hurt her feelings.

"Ekthcuthe—I mean," she said, angrily forcing out the sibilants, "excuse me. I am quite tired, dear Lysander, but I am also disappointed. May I tell you a tht—a story?"

"I don't see any way of stopping you," he said.

She looked at him sadly, but began her story. "Once, long ago, when I was only half-tailed, a hawkbee queen escaped.

52

She flew into the thpatheth between the wallth and laid eggth—"she was lisping badly again, but Sandy didn't have the heart to tell her—"and there wath a whole hawkbee netht that no one knew about. Then she laid queen eggth. When they hatched, the new queenth flew away, and new nethtth were thtarted, all out of thight. No one knew. Only people kept complaining. Where do all thethe hawkbeeth come from? What can they be living on, there aren't any bugth here, are there?

"And then—" She paused, looking dire. "And then there came a time when the pilot wanted to make a courthe adjuthtment, and he fed hith inthructionth into the thentral command controller machine—and it didn't rethpond! The ship didn't change courthe!"

"Golly," Lysander said.

His nurse waggled her tongue solemnly. "Golly, indeed," she said. "Of courthe, the backup thythtemth took over, and the courthe change wath made. But when they checked out the mathter machine, it hada hawkbee netht in it! The netht had short-thircuited itth relayth! And, oh, Thandy, you would not believe how hard it wath, for twelveth of dayth after that, to thcan every thpan of the ductth and ventth and pathageth! Everyone wath working an extra twelfth-day every day until it wath cleaned up and the latht wild hawkbee netht wath wiped out. Do you thee the moral of the thtory?"

"Of course," Sandy said promptly. "Or, no. Not exactly. What is it?"

She touched the tip of her tongue to his arm before she spoke. "The moral," she said, "ith that even good thingth can do great harm if they are done in thecret. Now do you thee what I mean?"

"Certainly I do," said Lysander, certain that she would go on to explain it anyway.

"Thertainly you do," she agreed. "The moral ith that you mutht *never* keep thecretth from your thuperiorth."

53

Sandy thought that over for a moment. "They keep secrets from me," he objected. "They didn't tell us why Theseus and the rest aren't allowed to see us any more."

"But that'th very different, ithn't it? You don't *need* to know thothe thingth. At leatht you don't need it now, and when you do, you'll be told. But the Theniorth need to know, becauthe they're the oneth who have to make the dethisionth, after all. You don't, do you?"

"No," Lysander said thoughtfully. "I don't make any decisions." But he wished, all the same, that at least now and then he did.

"Tho," she said, "when I am not here any longer, I hope you will remember what I've taught you."

"Sure I will," he said, and then did a doubletake. He scowled at her, half in anger, half in sudden alarm, and demanded, "What do you mean, when you're not here?"

She waggled her jaw, like a shrug. "The freetherth have reported that my latht batch of eggth wath mothtly infertile. Tho I've retheived orderth to report for a termination examination," she said.

Lysander was shocked. "MyThara!" he gasped. "They can't do that!"

"Of courthe they can, Lythander," she said firmly. "And I think I will fail it, my dear, and then, of courthe, it'th the titch'hik tankth for me."

And of course they could, so when Lysander finally huddled with the rest of his cohort for sleep that night his drowsing thoughts were not of his return to Earth, or even of scantily clad human females. They were sad thoughts. MyThara had been a part of his life as long as he had had a life. He did not like to think of her being terminated.

Some of the fun was going out of the adventure.

Chapter
◆ 5

The great Hakh'hli ship is powered by three main drive engines. Each one of them is capable of shoving the ship through space at 1.4 G. For the sake of simple engineering prudence that seldom happens; ordinarily two are running, at fifty percent thrust, at all times, while the third is available for maintenance and, when rarely necessary, repairs. The great advantage of a strange-matter drive is that you need never run out of fuel. The problem is all the other way. Strange matter breeds. When ordinary matter is introduced into a lump of strange, the strange matter converts it into itself. This does not mean that if you drop a speck of strange matter onto the surface of the Earth it will turn the whole planet strange; it isn't that easy. Strange matter repels the ordinary. To get past the force of that repulsion, the particles of ordinary matter must be fired into the strange matter with great energy; but that is what unavoidably happens in the Hakh'hli drive system. The result is that the longer the great ship flies, the more "fuel" it accumulates. The lumps at the heart of the Hakh'hli drive engines are each now six times as massive as when the motors first began to thrust. Because they are now so heavy there is that much more mass to accelerate and decelerate—which means more energy is needed—which means that the lumps are getting bigger faster. All the Hakh'hli need to feed it is ordinary matter, of which there is an infinity available in the universe; at every stop they tap asteroids, gas clouds, or the stellar winds for extra supplies—each particle of which adds one more particle to the mass of the ship. The Hakh'hli have known for centuries that they should soon divest themselves of some of that extra mass . . . but it is valuable mass. Like a miser clutching a bar of gold while he is drowning, they have clung to it. But they can't cling to it much longer.

As the cohort gathered for shipwork the next morning they felt two momentary shifts in orientation, like small earth movements underfoot; it was the navigators making small course corrections as the ship decelerated toward its parking orbit around the planet Earth. It meant that the end of their journey was near. They all chattered excitedly about it, all but Sandy.

When their tutor ChinTekki-tho at last waddled toward them, he took one look at Sandy and asked, "What's the matter with him?"

The cohort knew at once what the Senior meant, because all of them had noticed his gloomy mood. "It's MyThara-tok," Obie volunteered. "She has to take her physical."

"Sandy doesn't want her terminated," Helen added.

Polly finished spitefully, "He wants her to stay alive because he likes her better than any of us."

ChinTekki-tho waggled his tongue in deprecation. "It is good to love one another," he told Sandy, "but Thara-tok is getting old. She passed her eighteen-twelves of twelve-twelves of days long ago,"—it would have been the Earthly equivalent of fifty years or so—"and so she gets examined every twelve-twelves; that's the rule, Lysander."

"I know that," Sandy said sulkily.

"She may well pass," ChinTekki-tho pointed out. "I myself have passed five termination examinations. Many Hakh'hli pass as many as eight or nine of them; look at the Major Seniors."

"Major Seniors always pass," Tanya put in.

"They don't *always* pass," ChinTekki-tho corrected. "They *usually* pass, because, after all, they are Major Seniors; that's all."

"MyThara doesn't think she will," Sandy said. "I can tell."

The teacher inclined his head. "Then that is that, isn't it? It's nothing to be sad about. It happens to us all, sooner or later; otherwise the ship would be too full and everyone would die. And if the old and weak do not go, how would we ever take more eggs out of the freezer to start new lives?"

"And then where would any of us be?" Polly demanded. "You just don't think, Sandy."

The tutor reproved her. "Of course he thinks. Lysander is a fully intelligent being, even if he isn't Hakh'hli. He knows that MyThara-tok has many, many eggs in the freezer, and sooner or later some of them will be allowed to hatch and she will live again in them. He also knows that it is the Major Seniors who have made these decisions. He doesn't question the Major Seniors. Do you, Lysander?"

Lysander was shocked into a response. "Oh, no! Not at all! Only—" He bit his lip. "Perhaps special exceptions might be made for people as valuable as MyThara."

"And isn't that a decision for the Major Seniors, too?" the tutor asked kindly.

Sandy shrugged self-consciously. He was tired of this discussion, which had been going on ever since they woke up. "We're going to be late for shipwork," he said, evading the question.

ChinTekki-tho accepted the change of subject. "Well," he

said, "that's why I'm here this morning. What's your ship-work for this morning?"

"Tending the food animals, ChinTekki-tho," Bottom said respectfully. "The hoo'hik are cubbing."

"Yes," the tutor said thoughtfully. "Well, the herder will be a little short-handed today. I have a new instruction for you from the Major Seniors."

The cohort all raised themselves slightly on their hind legs with interest. The tutor gazed at them benignly. "As you know," he said, "Obie's season came upon him yesterday and it interrupted our meeting with the Major Seniors."

"We know that, all right," Polly said cuttingly, glaring at Obie.

"The Major Seniors have recognized that if this were to occur during your Earth mission it might increase the risk. Suppose Bottom or Demetrius did it while you were in the middle of some important negotiation?"

Polly gasped. "Oh, ChinTekki-tho! You aren't saying that you'll give the boys something to keep them from entering a sexual phase?"

"No, nothing like that," said the tutor, amiably crossing his legs. "The very opposite, in fact. The Major Seniors have directed that we bring on the male season now and get it over with. Then it will be six or twelve twelves of days before the problem comes up again."

"Really?" Bottom cried. "You mean we're going to do it now?"

The whole cohort was glowing until Polly cried, "But Obie just did it!"

"Of course," ChinTekki-tho agreed. "Naturally we don't want to do him again. One of you would probably get a reduced number of sperm cells, and you don't want infertile eggs, do you? So we will excuse Oberon today."

Obie looked downcast. All the females look horrified. Tanya gasped, "But then there's only two males and three of us—"

"We thought of that," the tutor said indulgently. "So I will accept a shot myself and join you."

Amid the shouts of joy Obie wailed, "But what about me?"

"You'll carry out regular shipwork, of course. Lysander, too. And, hear me, Lysander, when one is dejected for any reason it is good to work with the animals. I found that very soothing when I was cheth."

If Genetics had been full of smells, the food-animal pens absolutely reeked. Sandy didn't find it soothing at all. To get to the hoo'hik pens they had to pass the capped tanks filled with writhing, copulating, eating titch'hik, and that was not only unsoothing, it was hardly bearable. (What was it they were eating now—or whom? And what might they be eating a few days from now?) Sandy averted his eyes as he saw that other shipwork crews were respectfully lowering the two Hakh'hli corpses that were the day's crop into the tanks even as they passed.

Sandy shuddered. At least he could take some comfort in the fact that this time he and Obie weren't assigned to work with the bones or with the titch'hik. They didn't have to swamp out the hoo'hik pens, either, because four of the females had littered a few twelfth-days earlier, and it was time to pith the cubs.

"You," said the herder, grinning at Lysander. "You get the cubs out. No, don't worry," she added kindly. "The mothers won't hurt you. Just let them smell you first, pat them, don't get them upset. And bring me the cubs, one at a time."

Lysander peered down into the nearest pen. He had done this before, but he still felt uncertain about it.

The cow hoo'hik didn't shrink away as he approached. She only gazed mildly up at him, her forepaws protectively pressing two of the cubs to her teats. They were sucking away vigorously.

"Don't be all twelfth-day," the herder called irritably.

"Which one shall I get first?" Lysander asked.

"Any one! Hurry up, will you? I've got forty of them to do, and then there's all the milking—"

Lysander took a deep breath and reached down under the cow hoo'hik's belly, where the other half-dozen cubs were squirming blindly around, impatient for their turn. He picked one up at random, a wobbly little thing the size of his head that mewed and gasped worriedly as it felt his hands grasp it. He carried it over to the herder. "Turn it over," she ordered, picking up a thing like a huge needle. The handle of it was shaped to fit her hand, and it had a dial and a button. She checked the dial and waited impatiently for Lysander to hold the squirming body still. Then with one hand the herder grasped the cub's head, not roughly but firmly, and with the needle searched out a point at the base of the cub's skull, just where it joined the neck.

"Did you see that Earth movie last night?" she asked, making conversation as she worked. Sandy shook his head, wishing she would get on with it. "It was called *A Bridge Too Far*, and it was all about fighting and not being at peace. Oh, Lysander, you must be careful when you go there—"

Then she grunted with satisfaction. "There," she said. When she pressed the button there was a tiny, almost inaudible *bleep* of sound. The cub squawked and stiffened, and then relaxed.

"Now get another," the herder ordered.

It didn't help Lysander's mood that Obie, taking turns with him in carrying cubs to be pithed, seemed as depressed as he. Of course, the causes were different. Obie was simply sulking, thinking of what was going on back in the cohort quarters that he was not a part of, while Sandy's thoughts were all of MyThara-tok.

Still, the cubs were cute. They didn't seem hurt by the pithing. They cuddled in Sandy's arms as he carried them back to the mother, and she accepted them amiably enough.

They were shorter and paler than some of the other strains he had worked with. The geneticists were always varying the breed a bit, introducing new textures and flavors, but they all had the sunny dispositions that would last them right up until the time they licked the fingers of their executioners.

Even Obie was charmed by the cubs. He poked one of his thumbs at them as he carried them back to their mothers and giggled as the little things tried to suck on it. By the time they finished with the forty the first twelfth-day had passed, and when he joined Sandy for the wafers and broth he was weeping in amusement, humming along with the omnipresent music, his grievances forgotten.

But Lysander was still troubled. He pushed the wafers away. "Eat, Sandy," Obie said anxiously. "You aren't still upset about MyThara, are you?"

"I'm just not hungry."

"You *are* still upset about her," Obie diagnosed. "But our tutor explained all that to you."

"I know he did."

Obie nibbled quietly for a moment, absently listening to the background music. It was Hakh'hli music, very unlike the Earth tunes they had recorded and played in their own quarters. Earth music was waltzes, polkas, marches—rhythmic tunes tied to regular foot movements; but Hakh'hli didn't have the foot anatomy to dance or march. Obie remembered his own grievance and burst out, "And anyway, how do you think I feel? They're all doing amphylaxis back in the quarters, and here I am with you!"

"You did it already," Sandy pointed out. "I'm sorry, Obie. I guess I just don't like pithing cubs."

"What's the matter, Sandy? You've done it before."

"I didn't like it then, either," Lysander confessed.

"But we have to pith them," Obie said reasonably. "For their own sake, you know? It keeps them from being too smart."

Lysander blinked at him. "What do you mean, too smart?"

"Oh, too *smart*," Obie said vaguely. "Can you imagine how horrible it would be for them if they grew up with, you know, some kind of rudimentary intelligence? So you'd know that you were alive only so you could be killed and eaten?"

"They can't be that smart!"

"Not after we pith them, no," Obie said smugly.

"But— But— But it's *wrong* to kill intelligent creatures, isn't it?"

"They *aren't* intelligent. That's why they're pithed."

"But you're telling me they *would* be, if we just didn't pith them. There has to be a better way! Can't the gene-splicers arrange them so that they aren't intelligent?"

"Oh, Lysander," Obie sighed. "Do you imagine they didn't think of that? They keep trying. But it always spoils the taste of the meat."

When they straggled back to their quarters it was almost time for the big midday meal, and the other members of the cohort were happily playing a rough-and-tumble game of what they considered to be touch football. "How'd it go?" Obie asked jealously.

"*Oof*," said Tanya, as Polly plowed into her, knocking the tied-rag ball out of her hands. "Oh, it went just fine, Obie. Imagine! I coupled with ChinTekki-tho, and you never *saw* so many eggs!"

"I bet I saw even more when I did it," Obie snapped, but there was no point in being resentful. He hunkered down on his strong legs for added strength and then hurled himself across the room at Polly, now scrambling rapidly away with the ball.

"Want to get in the game, Sandy?" called Helen, in hot pursuit.

Sandy shook his head. "No, thanks." No one was surprised at that, since everyone knew he didn't belong in body-contact sports with the Hakh'hli, especially when their natural competitiveness was sharpened by hunger for the midday meal.

Sandy simply went over to his own carrel and sat there. He didn't turn on a flick. He didn't open his locker to gaze again at his mother's picture. He didn't even daydream about the landing on Earth, so very near, with its promise of human females and the almost certain prospect of glorious coupling. He just sat and glowered into space, thinking of MyThara's flesh being torn away by the titch'hik, while the game finished, and the food cart arrived, and the cohort flung itself, shouting and slobbering, on the meal.

Sandy didn't even approach the cart until the last of them had staggered, empty-eyed, into stun time. Then he sighed, got up, and surveyed what was left.

There was quite a lot, actually. The main roast had been torn apart, but there were human bite-sized pieces all over.

As he lifted one morsel to his mouth, Sandy stopped to look at it.

It was roast hoo'hik, of the tender kind that came from the very young cubs.

Sandy hesitated for a moment. But then he ate it and, still chewing, strolled back to his carrel to turn on an Earthly musical film with pretty girls in scant costumes.

Chapter

♦ 6

The landing vessel which will take the Earth-mission co-hort down to the surface of the planet is 150 feet long and shaped pretty much like a paper airplane. Its wings are retract-able. Once the lander is in the atmosphere the wings can be extended as needed for the various flight domains they will en-counter, stretching farther out and changing shape as speed is reduced. The lander's rockets are fueled by alcohol and hydrogen peroxide—once in air the atmosphere will supply the oxygen needed, and so the hydrogen peroxide load is only enough for maneuvering while still in space. This is important to the Hakh'hli. The fuel for the lander represents a serious expendi-ture of irreplaceable materials. The alcohol and peroxide it burns are lost forever to the ship's recirculatory systems, and must be made up from outside. Most of the weight of the lander is fuel, because it needs to carry enough for a two-way trip. The structure of the ship itself is comparatively light, due to excellent Hakh'hli technology, but even so the total launch weight of the craft is something over 200 tons. Landing on Earth is a piece

*of cake, because Earth's surface gravity is only 1.0. The landing
ship can handle twice that. The interior of the ship has squatting seats for a crew of eight. One of them has been removed,
and another refitted for Lysander's non-Hakh'hli anatomy—it
is a special, big one, meant for a Senior, but no Senior is going.
Because of that it is impossible for Sandy to reach the ship's
controls, but that doesn't matter. None of the cohort would trust
him to fly them anyway.*

When at last Sandy's cohort was sent off to tidy up the
lander itself for their flight they all fidgeted nervously on the
way. They had never been inside it before, and what little of
it they could see from the ports seemed so *small*. It was also
not located in a comfortable place for anyone, Hakh'hli or
human. When the lander was not in use, which was almost
all the time, it nestled in a recess in the outer hull of the big
ship. That was the bad part, because, like most of the outer
sections of the ship's shell, that part had been left uncooled
as the big ship made its course change around Earth's Sun.
As they came close enough to feel the heat everyone in the
cohort woofed in displeasure. "How do they expect us to
work in that?" Bottom demanded.

Polly said shortly, "Shut up." Then she paused, thinking
up some additional remark to put him down with, and found
one. She added, "Be glad you don't have to go outside."

They were all glad of that. Through the tiny observation
ports they could catch glimpses of the hulking lander outside. Around it were eight or ten of the heavy-duty Hakh'hli
who were bred for extravehicular duty. They wore spacesuits
that were only round balls with a protrusion at one end for
their heads and mechanical handling "arms" sticking out all
over. The interstellar ship's roll had been controlled to put
them in shade, at least, but that solved only part of the problem. The exterior hull of the big interstellar ship itself had
soaked up so much heat that it was still reradiating an invisible, constant glow of mild infrared, and the Hakh'hli out-

side were beyond doubt sweltering in their suits. It was not only hard work but dangerous—even a Hakh'hli bred for such things could stand just so much suffocating swelter—but it had to be done; their big job was to rig the stiff wire-mesh outer shell that would surround the lander and, when overlaid with foil, would intercept the worst of the micro-meteorites in Earth's trash orbits.

It turned out that the interior of the landing craft was even worse. Polly fussily checked the pressure gauges to make sure there was a seal and then popped the door. Out of it came a blast of hot air that reeked of alcohol and decay. "Oh, turds!" Helen groaned. "Do we have to work in *that*?"

They did, of course. Polly ordered Bottom in first to turn on the air circulators. When he gasped that they were beginning to work she kicked Demmy in the door. The rest followed.

Even with the air circulators working away it stank. There was a concentrated reek of stale and musty disuse. That was natural enough; the lander hadn't been used either at Alpha Centauri or in the previous visit to Sol—at Alpha because there was nothing to go to, at Sol because the Major Seniors hadn't liked the looks of things and so decided to give the Earth a little time to settle down.

The previous users had not been neat. Three of the seats had crusted stains on them, and in the cupboards of the landing craft there were shrunken bits of decay that might once have been food. "Slobs," Sandy gasped. "I'd like to tell them a thing or two!"

"Don't count on it," Bottom advised. "They've all been minced a hundred years. No one has made a planet landing in—well, when was it, Polly? Six stars ago?"

"Look it up on your own time," she ordered. "Come on, let's clean up!"

"Yeah, but hold on a minute," offered Demmy. "What about that alcohol smell?"

"What about it? It's clearing out, isn't it?"

"I don't mean about the *smell*, I mean why was it *here*? How could alcohol fuel get into the cabin? Does that mean there's a leak?"

"That," she said grimly, "is one of the things we're here to check. Probably it's just seepage, but we'll have to pull the seals out and check them."

Pulling the seals was the hardest job—a solid twelfth-day of difficult work—but thankfully there was nothing wrong; the fuel smell was simply the slow, centuries-long seepage of ancient fumes. The fuel compartment was as tight as it needed to be. Once that was done the cohort cheered up.

What they were doing was arduous and not very pleasant, no doubt, but it was for their own sakes that they were doing it. They were *going*! Even the heat became bearable as they turned to the easier, if nastier, job of cleaning out the waste left by the long-dead previous crew, because what would replace the old moldering garments and food remnants would be their own. "Let's have a game of Questions," Tanya proposed, beginning to cheer up. Sandy opened his mouth to suggest a topic, but Polly was ahead of him.

"Certainly not," she said. "That is *immature*. We should concentrate on our mission now, not childish things. Let's drill Sandy on his cover story."

"Oh, turds," Sandy said, but the others accepted the idea at once.

"Tell us your name," Helen demanded.

He shrugged, scouring out the inside of an empty locker. Over his shoulder he said, "John William Washington is my name."

"Then why do they call you 'Sandy'?" called Obie, from behind the great pilot seat.

"It's just a kind of nickname. It's short for Lysander."

And Polly cut in. "Can I see your ID?"

That was a new one. Sandy hesitated, with the scouring

stick in his hand. He didn't have any kind of papers. "I don't know what to say to that," he confessed.

Demmy helped out. "You can say you were 'mugged,' Sandy," he offered.

"What is 'mugged'?"

"You know, robbed. Like in Robin Hood."

"Yes, sure," said Sandy, beginning to catch the spirit. "I was robbed. They took my wallet and my suitcase—"

Polly interrupted sharply, "Not a suitcase! You wouldn't be carrying a suitcase, would you?"

"All right, a knapsack. They took my knapsack and all my papers."

"Phew," cried Obie, opening a locker and recoiling. "This is *awful.*"

"Awful or not," Polly said grimly, "you have to clean it up. Now, John William Washington, tell me, where are you from?"

"That's easy. I'm from Miami Beach in Florida. That's a state. I'm a college student, and I'm taking some time off to travel, and I was, ah, 'hitch-hiking.'"

"What are your parents' names?"

"My parents?" Sandy stopped to think for a moment. "Ah, my parents are named Peter and Alice. Peter is the male. Only they're both dead. They were killed in a car crash, and—and—well, I was really upset about it. So I quit school for a while. Anyway, I always wanted to go to Alaska."

Polly sneered, "What a wimp you are, Wimp. You're going to have to do better than that when you're on the Earth. Imagine not remembering your parents' names!"

"Really?" Sandy asked hotly. "And who were *your* parents?"

Polly waggled her head menacingly. "You know perfectly well that my genetic data is on file," she said cuttingly. She drew her legs in under her as though about to spring. Sandy braced himself.

He was saved by a shriek from Demmy. "Bugs! This locker is full of bugs! How'd they get in here, anyway?"

Diverted, Polly glared at him. "What difference does it make how they got here?" she demanded. "We'll have to get rid of them. Go requisition a hawkbee nest at once, Demetrius."

"And who are you to be giving me orders?" Demmy snarled, crouching down on his own strong legs for a charge.

It didn't happen. MyThara's voice stopped them. "What ith thith?" she cried. "You who are about to carry out the urgent inthtructionth of the Major Theniorth acting like new-hatched infantth? Now, tell me what ith going on?"

And when it had been explained to her she waggled her jaw. "Very well, that ith right, we need a hawkbee netht in here to thcavenge out the inthectth. Demmy, go get one. And what ith thith other thtuff?" She was pointing to a heap of foul-smelling debris.

"It's to go into the titch'hik tanks," Polly said sullenly. "It's all decayed."

"It thertainly ith! Do you want to poithon the titch'hik? That mutht go in the contaminated binth to be thterilithed. Take it there at onthe, Hippolyta."

"Why can't Sandy do it?"

"Lythander can't do it," MyThara explained, "becauthe I have inthtructed you to do it. Lythander hath a different job right now. Now get on with it." She glanced around the interior of the lander. "I thee you have all the lockerth empty," she said. "That ith good. You may each have one for your own."

"Only one?" Obie cried. "To go to *Earth*?"

"Only one," MyThara said adamantly. "The retht are for nethethary thupplieth and food—after all, you mutht take rationth for three weekth with you, you know."

"Why just three weeks?" Helen asked, licking her tongue out irritably.

"Becauthe that ith what the Major Theniorth ordered,

Helena. Now, Lythander, come with me. It'th time to try on your new garmenth!"

Come back in three weeks? But *why* did they have to come back in three weeks? As Sandy tagged rebelliously along after MyThara he thought, all right, maybe *some* of them would return to the ship in three weeks, but not necessarily all of them . . .

MyThara left him at the cohort quarters while she went to get his Earth outfit. At her orders he stripped, putting his everyday suit into the locker—

And in the middle of doing it he began to tremble.

The fact that he was going to *leave* the ship had not really worked its way into the part of his mind that felt panic before, but now it was making up for lost time.

He glanced around the cohort chamber, shuddering. He was going to leave the *ship*. But such a thing had never happened! No one ever "left" the ship—they died, true, and were minced and devoured by the titch'hik, but there was no other way that any person of all the persons he had known in all his life could ever cease to be in the ship. Outside the ship was *space*.

By the time MyThara arrived, her stubby arms laden with two baskets filled with articles of clothing, Sandy was sitting woebegone on the floor by his locker, his eyes squinted shut, his face drawn. "Now, Lythander!" she cried sharply. "What ith it? Are you ill?"

"I have to leave the ship," he told her miserably.

"Well, of courthe you do. That'th what you have been trained for all your life."

"But I'm afraid, MyThara-tok. I don't want to leave you."

She hesitated, then gently gripped his arm with one tough, hard hand. He could feel the "helper" spur digging into his flesh—reassuring rather than painful. "You will have a whole new life," she told him. "Now, pleathe, try

70

thethe on. I want to thee how beautiful my Lythander will look on Earth!"

Slowly he began to obey. MyThara insisted he dress from the skin out, so first he pulled on the white, thin, one-piece garment she called "underwear," and the "sox"—long black tubes of material, closed at one end. The shirt was a pastel pink, the trousers dark blue, the vest red, the jacket brown, and the shoes black.

"It'th beautiful," she told him.

"It's very hot," he complained.

"But that ith becauthe it'th very cold where you're going, Lythander," she said severely. "That ith why you have thethe other thingth, which you mutht altho try on." And she pulled out of the second basket a second pair of trousers, much thicker and pegged at the ankles, and heavy overshoes that went right over the soft dancing pumps, and a jacket with a hood that weighed more than all the other clothes combined. By the time they were all on Lysander was sweating.

"You look very handthome," MyThara said sadly.

"I feel like a boiled tuber," he growled.

"All right, you can take them off." She folded each garment neatly as he removed them. "Did you know that they've thtarted the perokthide plant?" she asked.

"Oh, really?" Lysander considered that fact. Landing rockets were the only Hakh'hli devices fueled with hydrogen peroxide and alcohol. So the peroxide factory sat idle for decades at a time, sometimes a century or more—there was no need for chemical rocket fuel in the long journeys between stars. Feeling better, he tried a smile. It didn't quite come off, because there was something in her tone that puzzled him. "Aren't you happy for me?" he demanded. "I'd think you'd be proud to see me go to Earth!"

"But I won't, Lythander," she lisped sorrowfully. "I won't thee you again at all. I'm to have my phythical tomorrow and, you thee, Lythander, I won't path."

And on the day when at last the interstellar ship was at

its proper point in its orbit around the Earth and the lander was poised to go, what MyThara said was true. She wasn't there. She wasn't anywhere anymore. She hadn't passed the termination examination.

There wasn't any ceremony about their departure. There wasn't even anyone to see them off, except for ChinTekki-tho, floating nervously around in the microgravity of the ship with its main engines off for the first time in decades. "There are clouds in your landing region," he announced to the cohort as they prepared to board. "That is good. It means that you will be able to land without being seen."

"What are 'clouds,' ChinTekki-tho?" Obie asked nervously, and was rewarded with a pinch from Polly.

"Clouds are good," she told him. "Don't be a wimp like Sandy!"

ChinTekki-tho was looking at Sandy, who was standing by himself, holding his parka and boots, his face damp with tears. "And what is the matter with Lysander?" he asked.

"It's MyThara. She's dead," Polly said.

"Of course she's dead; she failed her examination. But what is there in that for him to think funny?"

"He doesn't think it's funny, ChinTekki-tho," Obie explained. "He's a human being, you know. He's crying. That's what they do when they're sad."

"But what is there in a worn-out Hakh'hli being terminated to make him sad? Oh, Lysander," ChinTekki-tho said sorrowfully. "At this late time I am beginning to wonder if we have trained you properly, after all. But it's too late to worry about that. Get in, all of you. You launch in one-twelfth of a twelfth-day."

Chapter

♦ 7

The great interstellar ship is at rest now—or at least so it seems to everyone inside. Actually, of course, it is in orbit around the planet Earth, combining its orbital velocity around the Earth with the Earth's own orbit around its Sun—and with the Sun's motion within its galaxy, and the galaxy's own steady fall toward the Great Attractor; its motion relative to some stationary reference point would look like a corkscrew—if there were any stationary reference point anywhere to compare it with. But the effect inside is as though it had stopped. The engines have stopped. The thrust has stopped. The 1.4-G acceleration (or "gravity") that everyone on the ship has felt for all of their lives is gone, and Hakh'hli people and things float. So any motion is magnified. Even the tiny thrust of the magnetic grapples as they hurl the landing craft away from the great ship becomes a barely perceptible quiver. All 22,000 Hakh'hli aboard feel it, and all of them cheer; Earth is the best planet they have found in 3000 years of wandering, and now it is almost theirs.

Because there was a lot of velocity to swap around—
solar-ecliptic orbit to change to planet-polar, forward speed
to kill—the landing craft's thrusters were going all the way.
Thirty seconds after it was flung free of the big mother ship
Sandy began to vomit. He couldn't help it. He had never
experienced motion sickness before—had never, really, experienced motion, at least not in a confined space.

The six Hakh'hli, with a different arrangement of the
inner ear, didn't suffer from mal de mer. That didn't help
them. It came to the same thing in the long run, because the
violent jolting of atmospheric entry threw their bodies
around faster than their stomachs could keep up.

What made it worse was the nastiness all around Sandy's
position. "Control yourself, Wimp!" snapped Demmy.
"Wooof! Augh!" moaned Helen, and Polly, at the controls,
cried, "Confound you, Sandy, why can't you use a bag or
something?" Then she didn't have time for any more com-
ments, because the lander was in the garbage belt. The pre-
programmed approach certainly missed most of the largest
objects, but there was no possible approach that could have
been sure of missing them all. So when the radio locator
identified a smaller one on a collision course it activated the
side thrusters and they lurched away; when they could not
lurch far enough to avoid contact entirely the magnetic repellers slowed the impact down.

Even so, everyone in the lander could hear muffled
thumps and thuds as slowed and tiny but still worrisome
lumps of things hit the outside wall of the lander. Fainter,
sharper sounds were even tinier objects splattering themselves into plasma against the foil outer skin, and the plasma
thumping harmlessly against the lander skin. Polly shouted
in anger as a vagrant hawkbee flitted before her face. "Get
that thing out of my way! How am I supposed to fly this heap
with bugs flying into my eyes?"

But the hawkbee was thrown away from her face as the

lander jolted away from another object; and then the ship was in its final glide path to the only flat meadow the radio-reflection screen displayed. Even through his misery Sandy could hear Polly's agitated hissing. That should have been the easiest part of the landing. Their velocity was way down, and the automatic feedback controls were supposed to be smoothing out all the vagrant downdrafts and microbursts near the ground. Only they weren't. "For a pissant little planet," Polly snarled, "this place of yours sure has some bad weather!" The shaking of the spaceplane proved her point. Ground speed was down to sixty or seventy miles an hour, but the winds outside were gusting a lot more than that. They threw the craft around like a toy.

Polly's landing was more like a controlled crash, but the lander was built to take punishment. As they touched down the forward thrusters went on to stop them, hurling them all against their restraining nets. They stopped the roll in a couple of hundred yards, well before they were near the line of bending, flailing trees.

"We're down," Polly announced.

It didn't feel that way. Even stopped, the plane was still jiggling uneasily in the wind. Polly belched worriedly a few times as she thumbed the viewscreens on. Two of them flashed together on the bulkhead over the controls. One showed the landing site as simulated from space, the other the actual scene outside the ship. The simulated scene was glacially, whitely static. The actual one was full of horizontally driven rain and tossing evergreens.

The six-pointed star that marked their position was in the same place on both screens, winking rapidly to show that the landing was where it had been planned to be. "Why are we having a storm?" Obie called fearfully. "Did you land in the wrong place?"

"It's the right place," Polly muttered in irritated wonder. "But where's all this 'snow'?"

A couple of hours later Sandy was in his parka and mukluks, standing in the doorway of the lander. Sentimentally he touched the pocket where he had his mother's picture, but Polly was in no mood for sentiment. "Go on, Wimp!" she snapped, giving him a nudge.

He went. He managed to catch at the ladder-stick as he went out and climbed down easily enough. The fall was only ten or twelve feet, but even in this weak Earth gravity it could have done real harm if he had missed. He trudged around the back of the ship, catching a faint wind-driven whiff of alcohol from the jets. He oriented himself toward the place where the nearest road should be and began trudging through the mud and the driving rain.

It was not at all the way it was supposed to be.

Something was seriously wrong with the mission planning. This was certainly the part of Earth called "Alaska"; the navigation screens had proved it. Then why didn't it look that way? Alaska, along with all the rest of the planet, had been thoroughly studied by the Hakh'hli on their first time around. Alaska was known to be cold—at least, mostly cold during all but a brief period in the summer, and then it was only at relatively low altitudes that it could ever be called anything else. The planners had definitely assured them of "snow"; if there was such a thing (and a thousand television programs had testified there was), it might be somewhere on the Earth, but it definitely was not here.

What was here was mud, and a temperature high enough to make Sandy sweat unbearably inside his furs, and an intense, scary, blinding storm.

A storm like this could not be an everyday event, Sandy told himself. Half a dozen times, as he struggled in what he hoped was the direction of the road, he had to detour around uprooted trees—big bastards of trees, a hundred feet from root to crown, and with huge clumps of ruptured earth around their roots still being melted away by the drenching downpour. And the craters left by the uprooted trees were all fresh.

He almost didn't see the building until he was within touching distance of it. The light outside it was a crimson disk, flowing like the coals of an old fire, over the door. As he moved along the wall he bumped painfully over some metal thing with wheels—could it be a car? He knew what cars were, but did cars draw things with rows of jagged metal spikes? The pain made him blink, but he limped on.

The door opened to a push.

Inside the building three of the same dimly glowing red disks, spaced along a low ceiling, showed him a narrow aisle with stall doors opening off it. The animal reek, the faint shuffling sounds of movement, and the sounds of breathing and munching told Sandy he was not alone in the building.

Even in the gloom, Sandy recognized what sort of living things he was sharing the building with. The huge, patient eyes, the nubby little horns, the slow perpetual motion of the jaws—he had seen them in the old films often enough. They were cows.

One major worry went away. Cows, he was sure, did not eat human beings.

Soaked and exhausted, Sandy pulled off the parka and mukluks. The presence of a building implied the presence of human beings not far away. What he should do, he knew, was find them, make contact, and get on with his mission.

Sandy didn't do that. Weariness got in the way. He let himself sink into a stack of some sort of dried vegetation. He thought he should at least stay awake so that he could greet whoever "owned" these cows when he came by . . . but as he was thinking, exhaustion won out, and he was asleep.

He woke up suddenly, aware even as he woke of where he was—and that he was not alone.

He blinked his eyes open. Standing over him was a figure in cutoff shorts and long black hair. He grinned placatingly up at the person, and then something very like an electric shock ran through him, taking away the power of speech entirely, as he realized that the person was *female*. A *human* female.

He jumped up, holding his arms out with the palms open to show that he meant no harm. He proved it by putting on the friendly, well-meaning smile he had practiced so often in front of a mirror. He brushed bits of dried straw out of his hair and finally regained the use of his tongue.

The woman's lips were moving, and Sandy realized he hadn't replaced his hearing aid. He found it in the pocket of the parka, pushed it in prayerfully . . . It worked! "Hello?" the woman's voice said inquiringly.

"Hello," he said politely. "I guess you're wondering who I am. I'm Sandy—I'm John William Washington, I mean," he said. "I came in here to get out of the storm. I hope it's all right? You see, I was hitchhiking and I lost my way—"

The woman didn't seem surprised. She didn't seem to show any expression at all. She was a lot darker skinned than Sandy had expected, and her face seemed impassive. "You might as well come up to the house," she said. Turning, she led the way.

The rain had stopped. The skies had at least partly cleared—Sandy gazed entranced at white, fluffy "clouds" and blue "sky," and the green of the land all around him. They were in a valley. The Hakh'hli landing ship was nowhere in sight, but Sandy could see the mountains that surrounded them—though they did not look as they were supposed to, no doubt because he was seeing them from the wrong angle. "Come on in," the woman said, holding the door for him.

"Thank you," he said politely, and entered.

They were in the "kitchen" of a house. Sandy gazed around in fascination. The smells alone were startling. A young male was standing at a "stove," stirring a flat pan filled with something that sizzled and popped over an open flame. (An open flame!) That was the source of at least one of the odors, both provocative and repellent, but there were others Sandy could not identify.

The youth looked up at Sandy. "He's a big one, Mom," he said. "Does he want some bacon and eggs?"

"Oh, yes," said Sandy eagerly, linking the smells to the familiar words which, until then, had lacked a referent in his experience. "Yes, please. I can pay." He fumbled in his pocket for one of the little nuggets and began his rehearsed explanation. "I've been placer mining, you see. I collect sand and rocks from the stream beds. Then I wash them in running water. The lighter pieces are washed away, and I pick the gold out."

The woman looked at him curiously but didn't comment. All she said was, "Do you want some hash browns with your eggs?"

"Oh, yes, I think so," Sandy said doubtfully. He wasn't sure exactly what hash browns were, and when the human boy put a plate in front of him he was even less sure he wanted them. Or any of it. The "eggs" were round, yellow blobs surrounded by a thin film of white substance, browned at the edges; that was easy to identify. The "bacon" was the meat, and he had seen pictures of that before, too. What was left had to be the "hash browns," a doughy mess of starch, crisped and browned on top.

He picked up the fork expertly enough; all those hours of practice were paying off. But when he prodded the eggs the yolks broke and spilled oily, yellow fat over the other things on the plate.

He hesitated, aware of the woman watching him with interest. The boy had disappeared, but Sandy heard his muffled voice coming from the other room, perhaps talking to someone. Sandy took a tiny bit of the yolk-drenched "hash browns" on the end of his fork and tasted it.

It was entirely unlike anything Sandy Washington had ever tasted before. He could not say that it was revolting. He couldn't say the opposite, either, or even that it was edible; apart from the saltiness of it, there were a lot of flavors but none he recognized.

He smiled placatingly up at the woman. With every other sensation that was impinging on him, he was most aware of her *femaleness*. She wasn't pretty by any standards Sandy had learned. She wasn't even young. He had no confidence in his ability to judge human ages, but the difference between them was generational. The boy had called her "Mom," and that was a clue, because the boy, Sandy thought, had to be more or less his own age, or nearly.

The boy came back into the room. "They're on their way," he told his mother.

Sandy glanced at her, perplexed, but all she said was, "Do you want some ketchup for the hash browns?"

"Yes, please," Sandy said, putting his fork down. The woman plunked a bottle before him and waited expectantly. He picked it up uncertainly. It had a metal cap on it, but that was a known problem; he took the bottle in one hand, the cap in the other and, as gently as he could, tried pulling and twisting until it turned and came off.

There was an empty glass in from of him. Sandy poured some of the thick, red stuff into the glass, barely covering the bottom. When he heard the boy snicker he realized he had done something wrong.

Inspiration struck. "I have to go to the toilet," he said, and was glad to be escorted into a room with plumbing fixtures and a door.

Once the door was closed behind him he breathed more easily. Making his way among humanity as a secret agent was a lot more difficult than he had expected.

For that matter, so was going to the toilet. The Earthly garments were just enough different from the ones he had worn all his life on the ship that he had trouble making the necessary adjustments, and then there was the question of the plumbing itself.

It all took time, but Sandy had no objection to that. When

he had finally found a way to cause the toilet bowl to empty itself and refill, and had rearranged his clothing, he paused to regard himself in the little oval mirror over the washstand.

He pulled the hearing aid carefully out of his ear, looking it over. It didn't seem to be harmed. He wiped it as dry as he could on one of the fabric things hanging in the bathroom and reinserted it. His ear was sore, but he couldn't get along without the aid.

The silence inside the bathroom, however, was a blessing. No one was asking him questions. He didn't have to be ready to respond to a challenge, because there was nothing to respond to. He wished he could stay right there in that room until everyone went away and, somehow, he could get back to the lander, back to the ship, back to the familiar life that had been his . . .

On the other hand . . .

On the other hand, he was *home*! It was what his whole life had been aimed toward, and now it was real! Already he had been in the presence of two actual human beings—yes, certainly, there had been some little embarrassments and worries, but they had offered him food, hadn't they? And that must mean something. Yes, certainly, they looked stranger than he had expected. But they had been kind. It was hard to believe that they were of the race of spoilers who had so sadly damaged the planet that it was a devastated ruin . . .

He stopped there, struck by a thought, and went to look out the bathroom window.

His brow furrowed. From this point, the planet didn't *look* all that devastated. Actually, the long meadow behind the house was peaceful and green, and he could see that someone had let the cows from the barn out to graze in it.

It was all quite confusing.

He realized he had been in the bathroom for quite a long time. Reluctantly he patted the hearing aid to make sure it was in place in his ear and turned to the door.

There was a new noise, a mechanical one he had not heard before.

He turned around as a shadow passed over the window, and then he saw a flying machine—a "helicopter"—bob slowly to the ground just a few yards from the house. A couple of people in uniform leaped out of it.

When he came out into the kitchen again they were standing there, talking in low tones to the woman and her son. "Hello, sir," said one of them.

And the other said, "You're from the spaceship, aren't you? The one with the funny-looking frogs? We'll have to ask you to come along with us."

Chapter
◆ 8

One of the reasons the planet Venus is so hot is that its atmosphere contains vast quantities of carbon dioxide, which traps the heat from the sun. One of the reasons Mars is so cold is that its atmosphere is very thin; there isn't enough carbon dioxide to do the same thing. The Earth's air is intermediate between them, but the human race has been changing that. Every time they exhale they breathe carbon dioxide out. Every time they burn fuel to run their engines and heat their homes (which is always) they make more of it. So the Earth gets warmer and the ice melts. (There is a reason why the policewoman laughed when Sandy said his home was in Miami Beach. The only present inhabitants of Miami Beach are jellyfish, crabs, tarpon, and bonefish, because Miami Beach, like most of the low-lying coasts of the world, is underwater.) There is more. Because the atmosphere is a heat engine, the more the air warms the more energy there is to express itself as storms, air-mass movements, scouring winds ... in short, as hurricanes.

♦

Even the word "hurricane" was unfamiliar to Sandy. It was one of those words you heard on old TV weather broadcasts, but there was nothing like a hurricane on the Hakh'hli ship. But on the way to the police helicopter he saw there was a corner of the cowshed that was bent out of shape, and a tree down in the courtyard, and he remembered the other great trees he had seen uprooted in the storm. And the word "hurricane" came back out of his subconscious.

He would have liked to ask the two police officers about it, but they didn't seem to want to talk. If they had names, they didn't tell them to Sandy. They didn't look much alike, apart from the uniforms. The male one was shorter than the female, and his face was flatter and skin darker; he looked quite a lot like the animal herders. The female was paler and thin, like the picture of Sandy's mother, though neither as young-looking nor as pretty. (Nor, for that matter, as undressed.) They escorted him, politely enough, to their "helicopter" and sat him down in the right-hand front seat.

Sandy tensed when the female one buckled straps around him. Partly it was that she, a female Earth human, had *touched* him and his startled glands throbbed. Partly it was because they were binding him like a prisoner! He made himself relax when they assured him the straps were only for his safety when the helicopter took off. Anyway, Sandy had no doubt that if things turned bad he could snap those straps in a moment.

What he would do after he snapped them was another question. The male sat next to him, at the controls; but the female was in the seat right behind, and the metal thing she carried at her side was a "gun." Sandy's knowledge of guns was perfect, obtained from any number of recorded Westerns and cop shoot-em-ups. He knew that if anyone fired a gun at anyone else, the target fell over in great and often terminal pain. He also knew from the same sources that a uniformed person with a gun had the right to fire it at any "suspect" and splat his brains out.

Sandy didn't want his brains splatted out, especially by a human female—not a young one, to be sure, but very probably still capable of breeding. He turned his head as far as he could to smile at her.

She didn't smile back. She only said, "Please sit straight, sir." And then she leaned forward so that he felt her breath on the back of his neck. "Did you say your home was in Miami Beach?"

"That's right," Sandy said, sticking to the script. "I've been traveling—hitchhiking—and I guess I lost my way in the, uh, storm."

There was a skeptical snort from the woman. "Then where are your gills?" she asked.

Sandy frowned. The woman meant something by that, but what?

"Let it rest, Emmons," the male police officer ordered. "The captain will sort all this out." And he did something with feet and fingers, and the slow *flut-flut-flut* of the rotor overhead picked up speed as the helicopter lurched off the ground.

Then Sandy's big problem wasn't solving the puzzling conversation, it was trying to keep from vomiting again.

The helicopter did not shudder and leap as the landing ship had when it was bumping through the atmospheric entry. The helicopter's motion was slower and more tantalizing. But it was equally bad. Hurriedly the woman behind him pushed an air-sick bag at him. Sandy thought that, barring the tiny morsel he had swallowed at the cow farm, his stomach must be empty. But he surprised himself. He used the bag.

Then, sick or not, he had to look out the window. There were more trees down on the slopes around them, and some of the standing ones looked distinctly unhealthy—bare branches or yellowed leaves, some of them with their branches stripped away and nothing but straight, dead poles remaining. No matter. This was Earth! He thrilled to the recognition of that all-important fact. He was *home*!

The helicopter swayed as it lifted to clear a ridge. Then, as it went through a pass, Sandy could see a road below him—no doubt the very road he had failed to find in the stormy night. He could see that the storm had passed this way, for on the flanks of the mountains still more trees were down in windrows.

The flight covered the distance that had taken him six stumbling, zigzag hours in less than five minutes. Sandy was just beginning to wonder whether he would need the bag again when the pilot said, "There it is."

There it was. The Hakh'hli landing ship. It squatted peacefully on its skids on a gentle grassy slope, its pale landing lights still on though the sun was high.

The lander looked astonishingly small, squatting in its meadow. It even looked pitiful, because the trip and the storm had not been kind to it. The thin foil that took the sting out of the micrometeoroids in orbit was punctured and wrinkled. The netting the Hakh'hli had tried to string over the craft after the landing, to hide it, had been shredded by the winds. The lander looked hard used.

But what caught Sandy's eye at once was that it was no longer alone. Five other flying machines surrounded it. *Human* machines. They were helicopters more or less like the little police craft Sandy was riding in, except that most of them were a good deal bigger. And people, human people, were standing about in clusters. Some of them had television cameras pointed at the landing craft, or at each other, or most of all at the Hakh'hli.

All six of the Hakh'hli had come out of the lander. Two of them—they looked like Polly and Bottom—were talking into the television cameras. A couple of others were hunched possessively beside the ladder-stick to the door of the landing craft. And a couple were vigorously, joyfully showing off for the human spectators, leaping, with the extra strength their muscles gave them in the feeble Earth gravity, over each other in the game the Earth children he had seen on kiddy television shows called leapfrog; and froggy the Hakh'hli indeed did look.

As Sandy got out of the helicopter, Tanya came bounding toward him. The two police flinched away. Their hands strayed toward their holstered guns; but they didn't draw them, and Tanya, weeping an affable tear, cried in Hakh'hli to Sandy, "You have done badly and not at all well, Lysander. Speak cautiously to these Earth creatures until you have learned new orders!"

Startled, Sandy demanded. "What new orders? You speak confusingly and not with any clarity."

But she didn't answer in Hakh'hli. She only patted him in playful reproof, and then turned and bounded away again, crying in English, "So follow me, Sandy! We are all being 'interviewed' on 'television' by these wonderful Earth people!"

Sandy frowned in bewilderment at the two police officers. The male one shrugged. The female one said, "I guess that's what you ought to do, sir."

So he tailed after Tanya, looking around.

His spirits began to rise. In daylight the world was more beautiful and more frightening than Sandy had ever imagined. There was so *much* of it! Never in his life had he been able to look for more than a hundred feet in any direction. Now there were horizons a dozen miles away—with mountains! and rivers! and clouds! and, brighter than he had dreamed, so bright that it hurt his eyes to look at it, the Sun!

The second most startling thing was the sight of Polly, weeping goodnaturedly as she squatted on a flat, sun-warmed rock before half a dozen television cameras. She certainly was not obeying the directives of the Major Seniors. She wasn't making any secret of their presence on Earth. She was, in fact, advertising it! As Sandy approached, the people with the television cameras turned away from Polly to aim their lenses directly at him, and Obie and Helen loped toward him.

"Welcome to Earth!" called Obie—in English.

Helen, in Hakh'hli, added sorrowfully, "Oh, Wimp, you've really screwed it up this time."

Sandy blinked at her. "What are you talking about?" he asked.

"Speak Hakh'hli!" Polly commanded, leaping off the rock and waddling toward him. "Because of your folly and in-competence everything has to be changed now!"

"*My* folly?"

"Yes, and incompetence," Obie put in, looking reproach-ful. "You failed to carry out your mission properly. They knew at once you were lying and not speaking truth."

"Well," Sandy said reasonably, "all right, but I certainly didn't tell anybody about the big ship, did I?"

"Don't argue!" Polly ordered. "We have to attend to these people now and without delay! I have been in contact with the ship. The Major Seniors are very displeased with you, Lysander. However, facts are facts, eggs cannot be unlaid, and so we have new orders. We are to speak openly to these people of our purpose here."

"Speak openly?" asked Sandy, dazed.

"Oh, please behave in Hakh'hli fashion and not any more in that of a hoo'hik than you must, Lysander! Just follow my lead. Smile. Let them welcome you home. And listen atten-tively to what I say to them!"

Then she turned to the cameras and spoke in English, weeping apologetically. "Please forgive us. We were simply worried about our dear friend, Lysander. Now can we go on with the 'interview'?"

Neither Sandy nor any of the Hakh'hli had ever been "interviewed" before. But they had seen it done often enough on the old Earth television shows, and Polly was behaving like a talk-show veteran. She pulled Sandy to her side, with her hand firmly and affectionately tucked into the belt at his waist, as she spoke into the cameras. If Sandy had not been so busy staring around at the human machines, the human people, the grass and wildflowers and very rocks of the human world, he would have admired her poise. She spoke clearly and persuasively.

"Yes, we are the Hakh'hli, a race of highly technologically advanced people with a recorded history that goes back some sixteen thousand eight hundred of your years. We have come here to share our wisdom with you. Also to return the human, John William Washington. (We call him Sandy.) He is the son of two of your astronauts, whom our ship rescued when they were stranded in space, due to a war you were having, fifty-six of your years ago. We have brought him up as one of our own. The little story he told your food-animal herders was a harmless little deception. We only wanted him to be able to move freely among you, so that the first shock of his return to his native planet could be as gentle as possible, before the inevitable 'publicity' that would accompany the news of his real identity. Also, to be sure, we felt it necessary to be cautious in our first approach, so that we could find out what conditions were like in order to decide how best to make ourselves known to you. We wanted to spare you the worst shocks of encountering a race of truly superior beings." She blinked affably at the cameras for a moment, and then added, "And now, if you will excuse us, we have to go back in the ship for a while, because it is time for our midday meal. We apologize for this necessity, but because of the excessively long day of your world we can wait no longer. Are you coming, dear Lysander?"

Once the Earth humans had been made to understand that when a Hakh'hli wanted to eat his big meal he *wanted* it, they hospitably offered to feed them out of their own stocks. Of course, the Hakh'hli rejected that proposal out of hand. They were too hungry to prolong the discussion, and so the entire cohort climbed back up the ladder-stick into the landing craft and closed the door.

As soon as they were inside Sandy burst out in Hakh'hli, "What has happened? Why are plans now different and not the same?"

"Because you screwed up," Obie chortled in English.

"Speak Hakh'hli and not Earth language!" Polly thundered. "Who knows what listening devices Earth creatures have? But Oberon is correct and not in error, Lysander-Wimp. You failed and did not succeed. Those Earth creatures penetrated your ruse at once. How could you have been so foolish and not at all wise, Lysander?"

And Tanya, hurriedly loading the food cart at the far end of the chamber, chimed in, "Your incompetence has endangered entire plan, Lysander."

And Helen added, "Major Seniors are displeased and not at all happy."

And even Oberon opened his mouth for a denunciation of his own, and Sandy might have had a great deal more recrimination to endure, but Tanya was already pulling their midday meal out of the warmer. The Hakh'hli abandoned Sandy for more rewarding fare.

In the confined space of the lander there wasn't room for all six of them to attack the food at once. As always, Sandy didn't even try, but waited for the feeding frenzy to subside. Even Obie, the smallest, was pushed out of the way. He tried to squeeze past Polly, but ducked back as she reached to pinch him, bumping into Sandy.

He winced as Sandy glared at him. "I'm sorry about what I said," he offered. "Only it's all so very confusing here. They do *stare* at us so!"

Sandy snorted. "Now you know how I've been feeling for the last twenty years," he said, pleased at the role reversal— mostly pleased, anyway, although it was not altogether pleasing to find that he was no longer the unique center of attention.

Polly, mouth full, turned to glare at them. "I told you to speak Hakh'hli and not Earth language!" she said thickly, chewing. "It is in any case natural that Earth creatures should stare. It is clear in Earth history that such things happen, when primitive savages are suddenly visited by their technological and intellectual superiors; no doubt they think we are 'gods.'" And, godlike, she shoved Bottom out of the way for another go at the meal.

That made room for Obie to squeeze his way in, which he promptly did, leaving Sandy to wait outside the noisy, violent knot. Sandy didn't mind waiting. Actually, he was mildly repelled by the sight of his Hakh'hli cohort at their food. In the kitchen of the human food-animal herders things had been quite different. No one had been chewing and tearing at the meal there. Why couldn't the Hakh'hli be as—well—dignified about their eating?

There was another thought that was troubling him, and it was even more somber. How was it possible, he asked himself, that their elaborate first-contact plan had gone so wrong so rapidly? How had the Earth humans discovered the landing ship so fast?

After all, the whole plan had been devised by the Major Seniors themselves. It was their own decision that the landing ship should remain hidden while Lysander, as the human member of the party, reconnoitered with the human beings to make sure that everything was safe before the first Hakh'hli–human contact occurred. Certainly the Major Seniors couldn't have made an unworkable plan—could they?

But the fact was that the plan had gone wrong from the very beginning; which meant that the Major Seniors had failed to take all the factors into account.

Which was impossible.

The Hakh'hli were beginning to go slack and empty-eyed. As one by one they staggered to their seats Sandy moved soberly to the food cart. He made a selection of what was left and descended the ladder to eat it in the glorious Earthly sunlight.

In just the few minutes he had been inside the lander a new and bigger helicopter had arrived. It was white and powerful-looking, and the side of it bore the cryptic legend *InterSec*. Its rotors were still turning as its door opened and half a dozen new human beings jumped out.

They approached Sandy as he climbed onto the sun-warmed flat rock to eat his midday meal. The people with the television cameras, and even the police officers who were still hanging around, watching everything, seemed to defer to them. "Hello, Mr. Washington," one of them called. "I'm Hamilton Boyle."

Sandy stood up, careful not to spill the tray with his meal. He extended his hand in the approved Earth fashion. "I'm pleased to meet you, Mr. Boyle," he said, in his well-rehearsed way.

"Glad to know you—" Boyle began, and then ended with a grunt of pain. He pulled his hand back, rubbing it. "You've got some grip," he said, surprised.

"I'm sorry," Sandy said at once, annoyed with himself. "I forgot how much stronger I am than you are. It's because of the one point four gravity environment on the ship, you see. Would you—" He hesitated, trying to remember what was appropriate behavior; but surely offering food was a friendly gesture on Earth? "Would you like to try some of this?" He extended a handful of wafers.

Boyle took one and examined it carefully. "I think not, just now," he said doubtfully. "What is it, exactly?"

One of the female human beings was wrinkling her nose. Sandy wondered what the matter was. "This meat," he said, holding up the slab in his left hand, "is hoo'hik. That's a kind of meat animal. The ground-up stuff in the wafer you have is tuber. The things in it are bits of a kind of animal that lives in water—I don't know what you'd call it, but it's almost solid meat, except for the shell—no bones, and the internal organs come right out—"

"Like a shrimp, you mean?" one of the humans hazarded.

"I don't know what a 'shrimp' is," Sandy apologized. "Anyway, that's what the wafers usually are made of: dried ground tuber flour mixed with protein things. They're very good, really. Are you sure you don't want to try some?"

The human looked tempted and repelled at the same time. He sniffed the wafer carefully.

"I'd watch it if I were you," a female human said.

"They do smell kind of fishy," the man named Boyle agreed. "But you eat it, don't you, Mr. Washington?"

"I've been eating these things all my life."

The female human laughed. "Well, you look healthy enough," she said, looking him over. "Not to say, well, scary."

Sandy felt pleased. He was almost sure that was a compliment. It was quite clear that he was far stronger than any of the Earth humans—the *other* Earth humans, he corrected himself—and he was nearly certain that that was a selective breeding advantage in the eyes of human females. He wondered happily when he would have a chance to try it out. Not right now, of course. He knew well that humans did not do amphylaxis in public, as a general rule. But *soon!* "What?" he said, brought back from his tempting musings.

"I asked how you got your vitamins," one of the females repeated.

"Vitamins?"

"Chemical substances that your body needs to function, and minerals, and so on."

"Oh, I'm not your best witness on that," Sandy apologized. "You'd have to ask Bottom. The food experts arrange all that. They know exactly what we need, and they control the content of the midday meal accordingly. It has everything anyone needs for a day's nutrition. The cookies and milk don't, though; they're just a, what you would call, a 'snack.'" And then he had to explain "cookies and milk." "We usually have them six times a day," he said, "but here on Earth, with your longer day, probably we'll have them more often. I don't know what we'll do about the midday meal; I don't know if they'll want to have stun time more than once . . ."

And then, of course, he had to explain "stun time" to them. The man named Boyle sighed. He took the wafer, which he had been holding all that time, wrapped it in a handkerchief, and stuffed it in a pocket of his suit.

"Is it all right if I keep this, Mr. Washington?" he asked. "I know our food chemists would love to study it—and maybe any leftovers from the rest of the meal?"

"Sure. If there are any leftovers, I mean," Sandy said obligingly. "They'll probably be coming out in, let's see—" He consulted his watch and did a fast mental conversion from Hakh'hli time. "—in about forty-seven and a half of your minutes."

He paused as he heard a racket from the sky. The small, dark woman turned to look and then said to Boyle, "Marguery's coming in now."

"Good," said Hamilton Boyle, not taking his eyes off Sandy. He was a tall, lean man. Although Sandy had no good way of guessing human ages, he was sure that Boyle was one of the least young around the ship. He was a serious man, Sandy was sure, although he smiled frequently. "Mr. Washington," he said, "we're going to need to talk to your, ah, friends as soon as we can. That's a V-tol coming in, and we're hoping you'll all allow us to take you to a more comfortable place."

It bothered Sandy to have two questions clamoring for answers at once. He passed up the "What's a V-tol?" in favor of, "I don't know what you mean by more comfortable, Mr. Boyle. We're pretty comfortable here." He had to raise his voice as the ship appeared, dashing through the sky toward them, then almost stopping in the air as thrusters and wing flaps rotated to new positions and lowered it gently toward the ground. Its jets screamed. It was not a helicopter; it had wings almost like the spaceship lander they had come in.

The ear-piercing jet roar stopped abruptly. "I meant to a city," Boyle said persuasively. "There's nothing here for you, just farmland. We'd like to welcome you properly, in a more civilized place."

"We'll have to ask Polly," Sandy said, but he wasn't really listening. The V-tol door had opened. A tall female human was coming out of the aircraft, which had the same *InterSec* legend stenciled on its side. The human female strode toward them with determination, looking Sandy up and down.

"My," she said admiringly, "you're a big one, aren't you?"

"So are you," whispered Sandy, gazing up at her. She was not nearly as solid or thick around the waist as he, but she was a good head and half taller, as tall as any of the males; and his heart was gone. And that was how Sandy met Marguery Darp.

Chapter
✦ 9

The carbon dioxide warmup of the Earth's air was real enough to be observed through most of the middle part of the twentieth century, but it didn't really hit its stride until the twenty-first century began. That is when the global annual mean temperature began to register a seven-degree climb over the norm of the last ten or fifteen thousand years. Humans have done lots of other ingenious things to their air. They have scavenged its ozone layer with chlorofluorocarbons, burdened it with acid aerosols, even laced it with radionuclides, but it is the warmup that has produced the most interesting effects. The equator hasn't changed much, temperature-wise. The poles have. Glacial meltwater pours in Nile-sized streams off Antarctica and the Greenland ice cap. Queerly, the temperate parts of the northern hemisphere haven't done much warming. Their temperatures are either only negligibly higher—like North America—or even actually colder than before, like Europe. Europe suffers greatly from a change in ocean currents. The massive influx of fresh water, which is less dense than the rest of the sea, has stopped the long conveyor belt that brought warm surface water up from the tropics to moderate Europe's winters. Contrariwise, the Pacific, at the other end of the world-girdling conveyor, is no longer refrigerated by the sea. It hasn't meant a lot for the land areas of the Pacific, but in Europe it has meant a lot. Madrid and Monte Carlo, for instance, now have the climate once associated with Chicago.

Obie was the first of the cohort to appear at the lander door when stun time was over. Yawning and scratching, he waved down to Sandy. Then he turned around, presenting his stubby tail to the audience, gripped the center rail with hard thumbs and helper-fingers, and slid down, landing with a thump at the bottom. He turned to face them, laughing. "Oh, Sandy," he cried rapturously. "Isn't this light gravity wonderful? I feel as if I could jump a *mile*."

"Don't please," Sandy ordered, smiling apologetically at his new human friends. He introduced Oberon and Tanya, who had just come out, to the new human arrivals, stumbling over some of their names—Miriam Zuckerman, Dashia Ali, Hamilton Boyle. He didn't have any trouble remembering the name of Marguery Darp, though. He watched her carefully, trying to gauge what she was thinking from the look on her face. It didn't tell him much. She was smiling, nodding, and saying a few polite words of welcome to earth. But he still felt a little embarrassment. The humans were taking such obvious care not to say anything, well, insulting. Of course, it was inevitable that human beings should experience some culture shock. Looking at his mates through human eyes, Sandy understood that four-foot-high, kangaroo-shaped, English-speaking aliens from a spaceship were certainly going to attract attention. Especially when, like Oberon, they were always taking great, joyous leaps in the air.

"Your friend," Marguery Darp said to Sandy, pointing at Oberon, "is sure a great jumper, isn't he?"

"Well, it's a great temptation here," Sandy told her. He was heroically resisting the temptation to show off his own 1.4-G strength.

"Nevertheless," put in Tanya, standing back, "he should not make a spectacle of himself in that way." She waved commandingly to Oberon and, when he leaped back to them with an inquiring look, said in a severe tone, "You are behaving foolishly, Oberon. This Earth human female is disappointed."

Obie looked hangdog, but Marguery Darp said quickly, "Oh, no, Mr., ah, Oberon! Not at all! I think you jump splendidly. The only thing that I would suggest is—well—don't you think you should wear a hat? The ozone layer's still pretty threadbare, this far north."

Obie stared at her. "Ozone layer? Hat?"

Hamilton Boyle explained smoothly. "Lieutenant Darp is concerned about the ultraviolet radiation in the sunlight, Mr. Oberon. Since the ozone layer was weakened we've had a good deal of trouble because of it—skin cancers, crop failures, a hell of a lot of bad sunburn cases. Are you susceptible to sunburn, do you know?"

Obie looked inquiringly at Sandy, who said, "No, he doesn't know. None of us do. We've never been exposed to sunlight before."

"Then you'll all need hats," Marguery Darp said decisively. "And probably some kind of pullover to cover your, ah, arms."

"Or better still—" Boyle smiled. "—we ought to get you all indoors. What about accepting our invitation to come to a city? There's plenty of room in the V-tol."

"Go to a *city*?" Obie squealed.

"I'll have to ask Polly, of course," Tanya said. She turned and began to climb back into the lander.

Boyle called after her, "Please say that this is an official invitation from the government of the Yukon Commonwealth, who would like to welcome you all to Earth!" And to Sandy and Oberon, he added, "You'll like it, I promise. Dawson's a real city, and I guarantee we can make you comfortable there."

Marguery was nodding encouragingly. Sandy said, "Oh, I'd like that."

And Obie said gloomily, "Polly won't let us."

But when Polly at last came down from the lander—more decorously than Obie—she was all shrugs and tears of good will. "Of course we accept your invitation to visit your Dawson," she said. "Our advisor, ChinTekki-tho, asks us to thank you for inviting us. Unfortunately, we cannot all come with you."

"But the V-tol will easily hold us all," Marguery Darp said.

"It is not a matter of what the ship will hold. It is a matter of what is necessary. Some of us must remain with the landing ship as a precaution; if we left it alone some Earth person might enter it and do some hurt to himself. Also there is much work to do because of the damage the lander has received in coming to Earth. The micrometeoroid screens must be replaced, for instance; you can see how badly they have been damaged on the way in."

"But surely you're not planning to leave right away?" Boyle asked, frowning.

"It is not a matter of what we plan, either," Polly told him. "Our directives come from the Major Seniors, so we must carry them out. However, the landing craft will not leave at once. Some of us will go with you. Of course, we will have to bring provisions with us so we will have something to eat."

"There's plenty to eat in Dawson," Marguery Darp said.

Polly waggled her head. "But only of Earth food, I'm afraid. However, Lysander and I will go with you, and we will take—" She glanced around, sighed, and finished,

"Oberon; I think he can be spared most easily. The others will stay with the lander."

The flight to Dawson in Marguery Darp's V-tol plane was almost as rough as the landing from the interstellar ship; even Obie got airsick. But when they landed in the place called Dawson, Sandy got his first look at a human city. "It's so big!" he cried, staring at the tall buildings. Some of them were nearly a hundred feet high!

"Oh, it's not that big," Marguery Darp said reassuringly. "This is just Dawson. It's the capital of the Yukon Commonwealth; I doubt that there are more than twenty-five thousand people in the whole commonwealth, and most of them aren't in Dawson. They're out on the farms."

Sandy once again regretted the fact that he could ask only one question at a time. "Yukon Commonwealth?" he repeated inquiringly.

"That's what this area is called," she explained. "We don't have big countries any more—things like nations, you know? We just have commonwealths. About ten thousand of them, all over the world. I guess the biggest commonwealth in North America is York, over on the east coast, and that only has about a quarter of a million people. The place where you landed is the Inuit. This is Yukon. Just south of us there's the Athabasca Commonwealth—that's where the really big farms are. And over to the west—"

Sandy stopped her geography lesson. "Can't we go into the city?" he asked.

And Obie put in eagerly, "And get something to eat? Maybe even a real milkshake?"

"Of course we can," said Marguery, smiling. "Come on. The car's waiting for us."

The car was actually a "van"—four wheels, boxy, with seats big enough even for the two Hakh'hli to squeeze in—and it moved rapidly toward the town. All three of the visitors stared at everything they passed, Obie chattering in excitement, Polly supercilious, and Sandy wholly goggle-eyed at the wonders of a real human city. He couldn't help chuckling to himself, which made Marguery smile, and the two Hakh'hli were dripping saliva in excitement.

This part of the human world was no longer the way it had looked in the Hakh'hli records—not any of the many ways it had appeared. There were cars, of course. The Hakh'hli had seen plenty of Earth-human cars chasing each other endlessly around the "freeways" in the old films, and they knew what cars looked like. These were different. They came in three wheels or four, open ones and sealed ones, big and little. Few of the buildings in Dawson were skyscrapers. They had many stories—the "hotel" Marguery took them to had twenty-five—but most of them were underground. "There's no sunlight to speak of in the winter here anyway," she explained, "so what's to look at? Anyway, this keeps us out of the wind."

"The wind didn't seem bad," Obie offered eagerly, showing off his new connoisseurship, since they had experienced far worse winds in the storm when they landed.

"It isn't bad *today*," Marguery said. "Oh, they don't get many hurricanes this far inland—that's what they had in the Inuit Commonwealth when you landed, a hurricane. But they have what they call chinooks, and when one of them comes along they'll take the hair right off your head—well, not *your* head, of course, Oberon. Anyway, come on, let's get you settled."

"Getting settled" meant "checking in" at a "hotel." They weren't alone as they did it. They never were. People clustered around them, goggling, and they never got away from the TV cameras, except in the privacy of their rooms.

Their *individual* rooms.

That fact by itself startled them all. Whoever heard of sleeping *alone*? Oberon and Polly decided at once to share one corner of a room floor (they were not quite ready to try a "bed"), but Sandy chose to do on Earth as the Earthies did. "But then I'll just have Polly to sleep with," Obie wailed. "I'll be cold!"

Polly said irritably, "Oh, let the Earthling do what he likes. Only stay with us while I check the radio, Lysander. We have to make sure everything's all right at the ship."

Of course, everything was. Tanya responded to the first call and reported that all was well, except that some of the Earthies were eager to be allowed a look inside the landing craft. "Certainly not," Polly ordered indignantly. "Or not unless ChinTekki-tho gives permission, anyway. Have you maintained contact with the ship?"

"Of course," said Tanya. "The Major Seniors are considering that question now. Also, they wish to make a 'broadcast' to Earth themselves. I have spoken to ChinTekki-tho, and he is going to tell us how to set up a relay from the lander."

Polly swallowed. "And are the Major Seniors, well, pleased?" she asked.

"They haven't said they were not," Tanya reported.

So that was all right. Polly signed off, weeping in relief.

Then Marguery came knocking on the door. "Sandy?" she said. "I thought this would be a good time if you all would like to go shopping."

"Oh, absolutely," he said eagerly. "I've always wanted to see an Earth supermarket."

"Well," she said, shaking her head, "that's fine, sure, some other time. But right now I thought we might go to a clothing store. Your Hakh'hli friends ought to get hats, anyway, and you probably will be more comfortable if you get out of those funny-looking clothes."

Sandy's introduction to the human world as a participant in it was *wonderful*. It was also scary, and sometimes a little repulsive, but it was all, well, wonderful was still the best word. It was just one wonder after another. The biggest thing about the Earth was the *space*. There was so much of it—

and so variously filled! There were lakes and farms and buildings and people. The best, if most worrisome, thing was the smells. They took getting used to because none of them were in any way like the smells of the ship. But even the manure pile behind that first cowshed had been quaintly amusing—sort of—and the smells of the town of Dawson were far more varied. There were nasty ones, like the steamy car exhausts. There were curious ones—food cooking, human sweat—and sweet ones, like flowers and grasses. And then there were the very special smells of *women*. Marguery giggled, but she helped Sandy identify them when he asked. Perfume. Soap. Hairspray. Body odors, faint but stirring—they all added up to Human Female, and they made Sandy's belly twitch in surprising and unexpected contractions.

Human Female was never out of his thoughts, especially with this prime example by his side.

It was curious (but he had never been acculturated to think it was undesirable in any way) that he had to look up when he spoke to her. She was easily six feet tall. She was also, he learned, extraordinarily strong for a Human Female, though to Sandy she seemed willowly. She had red hair that came down her back in two, long, twisty braids; she had green eyes and a strong, almost beaked nose; and it astonished Sandy that in all his twenty-odd years he had never before realized that the ideal Human Female beauty was composed of red, braided hair, green eyes, and a nearly beaked nose.

The only thing that kept him from thinking of nothing else, in fact, was the fact that there were so many other things that were, in different ways, almost equally exciting. Shopping, for instance. When they reached the place where shopping was performed the sign over the door said:

BERNEE'S

Other signs said:

SLAX

SPORTERS

JOGGING

CASUALS

The signs were fascinating to look at for Sandy, because they lighted up in bright colors, because they moved before his eyes, and most of all because they said such tantalizingly mysterious, ineffably *human* things as the cryptic:

Double Coupon Credits on Thursdays!

In spite of the constant flashing of the signs, the three newcomers were the only ones in the store looking at the signs. Everyone else, store clerks and shoppers as well, was gaping at Obie and Polly.

Obie was clowning again. He had found a huge shoe—it was a window display, certainly not anything meant for any human being to wear—and was holding it against his own immense foot. The laughter embarrassed Sandy, but a cautious peek at Marguery Darp showed that she was laughing, too, and so apparently Obie was not giving any real offense.

Anyway, the process was fascinating. This wasn't pretend shopping, as they had practiced on the ship, but really taking "money" and exchanging it with a "salesperson" for "clothes."

"Actually," Marguery Darp explained, "you don't really need any money right now."

"I don't?"

"Oh, no. You're our guests. InterSec will pick up your hotel bills—and travel, and all that kind of thing. But if you want to pay for personal purchases yourself—"

"I'd like that," Sandy assured her. "Where do I get some 'money'?" That was the easiest part. Marguery took away a couple of his gold nuggets and came back with a sheaf, as thick as her thumb, of rectangular pieces of printed paper.

"That should last for a while," she said. "Don't you think?"

"There's plenty more gold where that came from," he assured her gallantly. He had already begun fingering some of the clothes. The stuff the Hakh'hli costumers had run up for him, he discovered at once, was nothing like the Real Thing. Trousers were not slick and poreless. Trousers came in soft fabrics that somehow nevertheless held a crease, and inside they were often lined with some fabric even softer. Moreover (ah, so *that* was how they did it!) the trousers were equipped with "zippers" in the front, so that they could be opened when necessary. Neckties weren't simple strips of cloths. They were sewn as tubes, and inside was something that stiffened them so they appeared flat. Shoes were not pressed out of a single kind of plastic; they had one kind of thing for the upper parts, a harder kind for the soles, and a hard but springy kind for the heels. Jackets had pockets on the inside. Belts weren't just ornaments; they had to go through little loops on the trousers, and then they held the trousers up. Hats didn't just keep your head warm, they protected the scalp from the sun. Socks, underwear, shirts—oh, *everything* was different, really. And a lot nicer!

The only problem was that none of these wonderful things seemed to fit Lysander Washington at all.

He could squeeze his massive torso into the largest sizes, all right, but then a sweater became almost a calf-length smock, sleeves hung down past his fingertips, and the legs of the trousers had to be rolled up nearly a foot. Marguery explained that those difficulties could be dealt with, though. They just required paying over a few hundred more of these "dollars," because the store had on its premises half a dozen humans whose only work was to cut and shape the factory-made clothing items to the particular requirements of the individual human frame. "So just pick out things you like," she said, "and we'll see about getting them fitted." She glanced worriedly toward the front of the store, where Obie and Polly were raucously telling the Earth humans the Hakh'hli names for "foot" and "head" and other, less public, anatomical areas. "I'd better see what's going on," she said. "Excuse me just a minute."

So Sandy was allowed to wander almost by himself, marvelling. So many articles of clothing! For so many different parts of the anatomy, in so many fabrics, so many textures, so many colors—and with so very many buttons, laces, zippers, cuffs, pockets, patches, fringes, ruffs, and things of every imaginable kind, structural, ornamental or, Sandy decided, just plain silly. (What could possibly be the purpose of an undergarment without a crotch? It might, he thought, conceivably be an adaptation for the pendulant male anatomy, but why was it in a section marked "Ladies' Lingerie"?)

He saw that a young woman was gaping at him. She had just come out of an alcove marked "Dressing Room," and she had tried on a bikini bathing suit; it occurred to him that he should not be in this particular place. He turned hastily away and blundered into the men's outerwear section of the huge store, which was filled with racks twenty yards long of nothing but "sports coats," or nothing but "slacks," or "suits," or "formal wear."

He wandered on, until he found himself in the section devoted to shoes. He admired the glossy, glassy finish of some of them—could almost see his own face reflected, though grossly distorted, in the polished surfaces. And the colors! Lavender inset with diamonds of pale green; peach and pale blue; rainbow scarlet, orange, yellow—why had Marguery urged him to get the dull blacks and browns? For that matter, why had the shoes she suggested for him all been flat, when here were rack after rack of perfectly beautiful ones in all colors, with heels that would easily add five inches to his height?

He smiled forgivingly to himself. No doubt she simply liked the idea of being taller than he was. No matter; he had found the shoes he liked. He marched with a pair in each hand to a desk and asked the astonished woman behind it, "Do you have these in my size, please?"

Marguery straightened that out for him. It seemed that shoes were gender-specific things, and men didn't ordinarily wear such tall heels, but apart from that everything went very easily—not only because buying clothes was considered a quite ordinary, routine kind of thing to do, but because even the sales clerks and the tailors were thrilled to be helping the stranger from an alien spaceship. Everything else waited while the whole staff ran around to do Sandy's orders. The other customers didn't mind any more than the store personnel. They crowded around when he was in the open, and some of the men peered openly through the curtains while he was in the changing room. There was no hostility in them, as far as Sandy could tell. Curiosity, yes, a lot of that; but even more, he felt, they were welcoming. *Welcoming.*

He was *home.*

And the only really worrying thing was that, with all these humans around him, especially all these human females (none of them as big and glorious as Marguery Darp, but all of them definitely female, all the same), he could not help a certain arousal.

When one of the salesgirls turned her head away, flushed and smiling, as she helped measure his trouser length, and several of the onlookers giggled among themselves, he realized that the bulge of his arousal was showing through the fabric; and what did one do about *that?*

Among the Hakh'hli, that was an occasion for rejoicing. Any female nearby would have been glad to cooperate. But he wasn't among the Hakh'hli.

All the films that ever Sandy had watched had not told him exactly how one went about getting it on with a human Earth female, however assiduously he studied them for clues. It wasn't that there weren't definite protocols. Indeed, the mating rituals were in fact the main subject of most of the films, especially the ones where the boy and the girl sang love songs to each other and then danced away to the music of an invisible orchestra. Sandy could easily have played the part of Fred Astaire as, in that first, accidental glance, he knew at once that Ginger Rogers was the only woman in the world for him—and was spurned by her with apparent loathing—and, by singing in her ear and whisking her through a waltz or tango, finally melted her frozen heart and tap-danced away with her to, presumably, a bed. But he never heard that invisible orchestra. Besides, he couldn't dance.

Then there were the ones where the boy saves the girl from the "enemy" in a "war," or from "gangsters" or "terrorists," and naturally falls into bed with her; but where was the war? Then there were the more direct ones. The boy and the girl would enter separately into a "singles bar" (whatever a singles bar was), whereupon one would sit down with a drink and the other would come up to her. Then they would address coded remarks to each other. The code was easy enough to break, but hard to duplicate. The conversations all had two levels of meaning, and Sandy was not at all sure that his language skills were up to that sort of thing. Still, it was the most direct way; because as soon as they had received each other's appropriate recognition signals it was, "Your place or mine?"

Sandy found one encouraging thing about the situation— he did have a place, a hotel room, and all his own—but where was the necessary singles bar to make the suggestion? For that matter, where was the time for such things? As soon as he had clothes to wear (the rest wouldn't be finished until tomorrow) Marguery whisked him away.

"What about Polly and Obie?" he demanded, looking back to where they were talking with other humans.

"They have their own escorts," she told him. "But the people of Earth are naturally specially interested in you, and we've arranged a television interview for you alone. It's only a block away."

She whisked him over to a different kind of building. This was almost unique in Dawson because it extended ten whole stories above the ground, and the place she took him to was on the very top floor. "This is the TV studio," she informed him. She looked him up and down. "You look very handsome," she added.

"Do I?" he asked gratefully. He caught a glimpse of himself in a mirror, admiring his new clothes—tan cotton shorts, a short-sleeved shirt open to display his chest, sandals, and knee-length white socks with a strip of red at the tops. "I suppose I do," he agreed complacently. "Now what do we do?"

"We just go right in here," said Marguery, conducting him to a large room with eight or ten human beings gathered around, with of course the television cameras (or some kind of cameras) pointed at him.

A man in a blue turtleneck advanced toward him, extending his hand. "I'm Wilfred Morgenstern," he said, wincing only slightly as Sandy remembered not to squeeze too hard in a handshake. "I'm your interviewer. Why don't you just start at the beginning and tell us your whole story?"

Sandy looked around, perplexed, but Marguery was nodding encouragingly. "Well," Sandy said, "a long time ago, when you were having your 'war' here on Earth, the Hakh'hli ship came to investigate this solar system . . ."

It was a long interview, and when it was over Marguery said sympathetically. "Would you like something to eat before I take you back to the hotel? I guess it's been a long day for you."

Sandy agreed fervently; not only long in that so much had happened, but it was one of those twenty-four-hour Earth days that stretched so much past the normal Hakh'hli span. But he pointed at the window. "It's still light out," he observed.

"We have long days here in the summer," Marguery explained. "It's quite normal to go to bed while it's still light."

He wasn't listening; he had taken a closer look out the window and he caught his breath. It was nearly sunset. The whole western sky was a mass of color, whipped-cream clouds tinted in shades of pink and mauve and orange where they were not snowy white. "It is *beautiful!*" he exclaimed.

"It's just clouds. Probably they're from the storm you saw in the Inuit Commonwealth," Marguery said practically. Then she said curiously, "Haven't you ever seen clouds before?"

"We don't have them in the Hakh'hli ship, you know. There isn't even a word for them in Hakh'hli; when the Hakh'hli talk about them they say, 'ita'hekh na'hnotta 'ha,' which means, let's see, 'liquid-phase particles suspended in gaseous phase.'"

"That's interesting," Marguery said. "I hope you'll teach me some other Hakh'hli words."

"With pleasure," he said, and then surprised himself with a yawn. He was sleepy, after all. He ventured, "Will I see you tomorrow?" he asked.

"Of course you will. I'm your personal escort, Sandy. You'll be seeing a lot of me for a long time."

He smiled gratefully. "Then let me go back to the hotel; I'll have cookies and milk with Polly and Obie."

And, he thought, there was something else he really wanted to do, for a poem was beginning to take shape in his mind.

Chapter
◆ 10

The chlorofluorocarbons don't just trap heat. They also eat ozone. Everyone has known that this is true since the middle of the twentieth century, but of course human beings didn't let that stop anything. They kept right on manufacturing them and pouring them into the air. After all, they were very profitable to make. The relevant figure-of-merit equation for human behavior has always read "$1 (now) >1 human life (later)." So the flood of ultraviolet over three-quarters of a century has taken its toll. Cloud-covered Alaskan trees have mostly survived (except where killed by acid rain). Clear-skied Scandinavian ones have not. The blistering sunlight has combined with the scourging thermal winds to damage most of the world's most fertile farmlands. Still, the arable lands that are left are now quite adequate to feed the world's population, for the simple reason that the human population is a lot lower than it used to be. The things that have helped reduce Earth's population to a manageable size include melting ice inundating the land, destruction of ozone, acid rain, dustbowl-making winds—and, oh, yes, one *other thing. The other thing isn't around any more—because it has burned itself out—but it was a remarkably efficient population-control device in its time. Its name was AIDS.*

When Marguery Darp tapped at Sandy's door the next morning he was already awake. He had been up for hours. He had spent the time exploring the novelties of his room, practicing with the curious gadgets in the bathroom, and staring at the sights visible out the window. Most of all, he had been busy with a surprise for Marguery.

He would have given it to her the moment he saw her, but he had no chance. She arrived in haste, apologized for being late, and hustled him over to the television studio for a person-to-person talk to the Hakh'hli ship itself. He decided to save the surprise. It was a pleasure he could afford to postpone, because he had plenty of other pleasures going for him. Sandy's second day on Earth was even more joyous than the first. It was less scary, because he had learned at least the rudiments of Earthly behavior; he had conquered Earthly toilets, elevators, even "shopping," and besides, at some point he could bring out the surprise he had in his pocket for the woman he loved.

When they got to the studio, his Hakh'hli cohort-mates were less joyous. They were standing in the lobby with their own escorts, Hamilton Boyle and the woman named Miriam Zuckerman. "I'm *hungry*," Obie wailed as soon as he saw Sandy. "Polly says we can't have midday meal yet, but I've been up for *hours*."

"It isn't time yet," Polly said crossly. She, too, was suffering from those long human-Earth days that never seemed to end.

Obie was not consoled. "We should've started practicing living by this dumb kind of time long ago," he complained.

"You'll get used to it," Sandy reassured him, although in fact he was a long way from being used to it himself. In his case it didn't seem to matter. He felt as though he didn't need sleep at all. When Hamilton Boyle looked at his watch and said there was time before the broadcast for them all to get some "breakfast," he assented eagerly.

At the door of the hotel, Boyle stopped them. "Hats on, everybody?" he asked, checking them. "Good. And one other thing. The ultraviolet probably isn't good for your eyes, either, so Miriam has something for you."

What the woman named Miriam Zuckerman had were shiny-faced glasses—"sunglasses," she called them—a large-sized pair for Sandy and two even larger, specially built ones for the two Hakh'hli that fitted around their heads with an elastic strap. Marguery helped Sandy on with his and paused, gazing at his ear.

"What's that?" she asked.

He said, embarrassed, "I guess you'd call it a 'hearing aid.' I'm kind of deaf, actually. It's because—well, there's a pressure difference between Earth and the ship standard atmosphere, you see, and we kept our quarters at the Earth level. So going in and out hurt my ears when I was little, and the Hakh'hli had to fix me up with this."

"Interesting," said Boyle. "Mind if we take a look at your ear later on? We have some pretty good doctors for things like that."

"We Hakh'hli have *excellent* doctors," Polly said frostily.

"Oh, no doubt. But perhaps ours have had more experience with human medicine, don't you think? Anyway, let's go to the restaurant."

"I'd rather have cookies and milk in our room," Obie said wistfully.

"It is not yet *time* for cookies and milk," Polly rebuked him. "If you are really hungry you can try some of this Earth food; it will be good to discover if you can digest it."

"Aren't you going to try some?" Hamilton Boyle asked politely. "The biologists say we have about the same kind of metabolism, you know."

Polly looked at him thoughtfully. "And how do your bi-ologists know that?" she asked.

He looked apologetic. "Well, of course, we've tested the food samples Lysander was kind enough to give us."

"Indeed!" said Polly, gazing hard at Sandy. "No matter. We will discuss that another time; but I am not prepared to experiment on myself. An astronomer like Oberon can be spared, but I am in charge of this expedition. I, at least, am not expendable."

From every side the sensory inputs assailed Sandy—un-familiar, tantalizing, mysterious—*Earthly*. He delighted in the smells of the Earth: sweat, perfume, feet, cinnamon, fresh-brewed coffee, pine trees, sewage, roses, gardenias, pepper, bakery bread, roasting meat, boiling cabbage, stepped-on excrement of dogs, fresh-cut grass, laundered clothes, hot oil, wet paving. He was thrilled by the colors of Earth: mountains that were green, brown, white-topped, rust red, mud gray. Human skin in chocolate, olive, pink, black that was almost purple-blue, pale that was almost white. It had never occurred to him that the Hakh'hli were color-deprived until he saw the cars and trucks, from white to cobalt blue and fire red and sunshine yellow; the clothing in every hue and pattern; the signs that flashed (even in day-light!) in every spectrum hue.

Most of all it was the people who thrilled him—pausing to stare, leaning out of windows to gape, calling friendly hellos as they passed. Most of all, of course, it was one par-ticular person. When they crossed a street Marguery cour-teously took Sandy's hand. Her touch made him shiver. He didn't let go of her hand even when they were safely on the other side. Marguery gave him a curious, unsmiling look. But she didn't resist, and he held her hand all the way to the revolving door of the restaurant, when she gently disengaged herself to let him go through first.

They were expected. The waitress led them at once to a table for six—four chairs and two empty spaces for Polly and

Oberon. Around them other breakfasters peered curiously from their tables as the two Hakh'hli arranged themselves, squatting comfortably enough on the floor, their heads at about the same level as the humans.

The variety of Earth food was baffling. There was a whole "breakfast" menu and a quite separate one for "lunch"; Hamilton Boyle explained that they could choose from either one. Neither Sandy nor the Hakh'hli had ever had the necessity of choosing what to eat at any meal. Sandy floundered. All the names of things were familiar—well, reasonably familiar. Though what could "Eggs Benedict" or "avocado melt" be? He had no trouble recognizing such things as hamburgers, fries, milk shakes, fudge, ice cream, and cheese sandwiches. But when the three escorts chose for themselves and the dishes arrive they offered samples, and none of the things tasted anything like the practice foods they had eaten on the ship. Certainly none of them were at all like ordinary shipfare. Hippolyta refused to touch any of them; she had brought a fistful of shipfare biscuits in her pouch and munched them doggedly.

Sandy was more daring—or more stubborn. After all, why should human fare be alien to him when he *was* human? It wasn't easy, though, until Marguery came to his aid. He let her order for him. Gratefully he found that he could manage the plain boiled potatoes she chose, and graduated from that to dry toast. But everything else he sampled only a nibble at a time, and had to force himself that far.

Oberon was more daring. He had a dozen different things spread before him on the table—a Western omelette, an avocado stuffed with crabmeat, a hamburger, a "Texas chili dog"; Sandy lost track of the names. Obie managed to eat some of the hamburger, but everything else was too startlingly strange. He wheedled a few biscuits from Polly and chewed them morosely. But he cheered up when the waitress brought them "dessert." It was called "ice cream." His first tentative spoonful made his eyes pop in surprise, but then he declared it delicious. "It's *cold*," he cried in pleased surprise. "I never heard of eating things that had been refrigerated, but it's *good*."

"If it doesn't poison you," Polly said darkly.

ChinTekki-tho's broadcast from the interstellar ship came to them through a mixture of human and Hakh'hli technology. The ship's transmission went to the communications equipment in the lander, back in the Inuit Commonwealth. There a human camera inside the lander was to pick the picture up from the lander's screens to retransmit to all the human world. When Polly heard Bottom explaining the setup she cried sharply, in Hakh'hli, "But that is wrong and not at all advisable! You were given no authority to permit humans to enter our vessel!"

"You are incorrect and not accurate," Bottom said smugly. "Authorization came from ChinTekki-tho himself."

"But that should not happen!" Polly began in indignation, and then collected herself. She turned to the humans in the studio and, weeping a friendly tear, said, "I was simply confirming the arrangements with our cohort-mates. Everything is prepared. You will be addressed by our personal leader, the Senior ChinTekki-tho."

"We're honored," Hamilton Boyle said politely. "Of course, we wondered why the Hakh'hli didn't simply transmit directly to our own Earth stations, instead of going through your landing ship."

"That was undoubtedly a decision of the Major Seniors," Polly explained. "They surely had an excellent reason. They always do."

In the screen, Bottom turned to listen to something, then turned back. "That was the twelfth-twelfth warning," he said into the camera. "ChinTekki-tho is almost ready to speak."

And then the picture on the screens in the studio switched to the lander's own receivers.

It was certainly not a good picture. In spite of the best

efforts of humans and Hakh'hli the broadcast systems were not very compatible, and annoying moire figures kept creeping across the screen in pale rainbow tints. But Sandy immediately recognized their old teacher as he beamed out at them.

"Greetings," ChinTekki-tho said in his precise Engish, weeping gladly. "It is a very great honor to be the first Senior of the Hakh'hli to speak to our friends and brothers, the human beings of Earth. As our friends in the first landing group have already informed you, we come to you in peace and friendship. Just as you humans do, we Hakh'hli have a tradition that a visitor brings gifts to his hosts,"—Sandy frowned suddenly, since he had never heard of that tradition; but Polly made a quick pinching gesture and he was silent— "and so we have first given you the gift of a member of your own race, John William Washington, known better to his Hakh'hli friends here as Lysander, restored to his native world by us in proof of our good intentions." Then ChinTekki-tho beamed and hunched himself closer to the camera. "Are you in good health, Lysander?" he inquired. "Are you pleased to be with your own people again?"

Sandy felt Polly's eyes boring into him. He said at once, respectfully. "It's wonderful, ChinTekki-tho. I'm very happy here."

He waited for a response. It took a few moments to arrive, while the Senior gazed amiably into the screen. Of course, Sandy thought; the ship was a good long distance away, and even radio signals at the speed of light took appreciable time for the round trip. Then ChinTekki-tho waggled his head. "That is good, Lysander. Now let me speak of other things. There are many other gifts we Hakh'hli wish to offer the people of Earth. I will describe only a few of them. We are aware of some of your problems. We have certain techniques for dealing with radioactive and other kinds of pollution which we will gladly put at your disposal. We also have ways of gene-splicing new kinds of vegetation to seed your devastated forests and help to redress the carbon dioxide imbalance."

ChinTekki-tho wept a charitable tear, as he allowed this to sink in for his human audience. Then he added, "There is also the question of energy. The drive engines of our ship produce enormous quantities of energy. We are willing to convert this into electricity and beam it down to the surface of your planet, wherever you direct. This is a free gift. All you need to do is put up receivers for it. Then there is the device we call an 'electromagnetic accelerator.' I believe that your own term is 'railgun.' With this as a launcher you will be able to put satellites into space again. They will go through the debris orbit so rapidly that no more than from two- to five-twelfths of them will be destroyed. This is ac- ceptably low, since the capsules themselves require no en- gines or fuel, thus making them so cheap that losses up to six-twelfths or more can easily be tolerated."

He paused for a moment again, beaming. "Finally," he said, "we have much knowledge of scientific matters which your own scientists may not have discovered as yet. And, because our ship has traveled so far and observed so much, we have firsthand knowledge of many other stellar systems. All this we will put at your disposal. For a beginning, let me now display some of the astronomical records from our archives."

And then ChinTekki-tho disappeared from the screen, and it began to show pictures—poor quality ones, unfortunately, because of the discrepancies between human and Hakh'hli broadcasting technology, but nevertheless pictures no Earthly astronomer had ever seen.

ChinTekki-tho's voice described what they were seeing as the views unfolded. "This is the star you call Alpha Centauri from no more than one thousand radii away. These display the planetoids of the star Epsilon Eridani—as you see there are many of them, but all small and without significant at- mospheres. Our colleague Oberon can tell you more of all these things. Now we are seeing the pictures of your own Sun and planets and the Earth itself as our ship approached."

The astronomical pictures winked away and ChinTekki-tho reappeared. "This is only a beginning, my friends of Earth," he said. "My dear student, Oberon, is a certified astronomical specialist." In the studio Obie happily gazed around at the audience, waggling his head in confirmation. "He has with him a library of data in the memory stores of the lander and ten thousand times as much at his command on the big ship itself. He will supply you with as much astronomical data as you can wish. And our other experts also will instruct your specialists in their own areas; and all this we give you as our guest present." He paused for a moment, beaming into the camera. "And now," he said, "I will leave you for the moment. But we will speak again—many times—in this new age of shared knowledge and friendship that has opened up for us all."

The image disappeared. Marguery sighed and uncrossed her legs. "You know," she said conversationally, "it's still hard to believe."

"Believe it," Sandy said smugly. "The Hakh'hli have all sorts of things they can give you—us, I mean," he added quickly.

Hamilton Boyle was looking at him quizzically. "I'm sure of that," he said. "I wonder what they're going to want in return?"

When the broadcast was over the two Hakh'hli hurried back to the hotel room for their midday meal. "What about you?" Marguery asked Sandy. "Are you hungry? Would you like to have a drink first?"

He hesitated, not because he was in any doubt about what he wanted to do—he wanted to be alone with Marguery Darp, the sooner the better—but because he wasn't sure of the best way to arrange it. "Do you mean a milk shake?" he ventured.

"I was thinking more of a different kind of drink," she said, grinning, and took him to the rooftop cafe.

When Sandy discovered that a "different kind of drink" involved alcohol he was startled. "But alcohol's a poison, isn't it?"

"Well, I suppose it is," Marguery agreed. "But it's a special kind of a poison. It helps relax people, you know? And it's supposed to help your appetite, too, to have a drink before a meal. Look. We'll get you a spritzer—that's just white wine and soda water—not very much wine, all right?"

The magic word for Sandy was "wine." "Oh, yes," he said enthusiastically. A glass of wine or two would be just about right to set the scene for his surprise, for he knew that in human affairs wine was inextricably linked with romance. But when the glass came and he tasted it, he looked up at Marguery in pained surprise. "It tastes spoiled," he said.

"It isn't spoiled. It's *fermented*. That's how wine is made," she told him.

"Aren't fermented and spoiled the same thing?" He didn't press the point. He was determined to do all the things that human males did in pursuit of human females. The second sip tasted as bad as the first, but then he began to become aware that a sort of inner warmth flowed from the drink. He decided he could get used to it.

He reached for the surprise in his pocket, preparing to smile, but Marguery was getting up. "Let's go out on the balcony," she said. "There's a nice view."

That was true. He looked around at the town of Dawson and the countryside so near beyond it. Everything seemed propitious for his surprise. As she sat down he remained standing. "Marguery," he began, "I have something to— ouch!"

He swatted at his neck. When he pulled his hand away

there was a drop of blood on it. "What was *that*?" he demanded.

She inspected his hand. "A mosquito, I guess," she said, sympathetically. "That was just bad luck; there aren't usually any up this high. But we've had a lot of them these past years. The birds used to eat them, but the birds got pretty well decimated in the bad years, just like us. What was it you were going to say?"

He sat down, rubbing his neck. "Just that I have something to give you," he said, scowling. He had planned a more graceful presentation, but his neck really itched.

Marguery took the piece of paper he handed her and glanced at it curiously. It was the poem he had written for her that morning:

O my
very
Dear sweet Marguery!
How I desire to love
All the parts of you
The sweet limbs yes
The big breasts yes
The lips & eyes yes
The other parts yes
And all the rest yes
Love   yes!
Love   yes!
Love   yes!
Love   you!
Yes!   You!

"My God," she said, looking up at him.

He asked eagerly, "Do you like it?"

She didn't answer right away. She read it over again carefully, then gave him a sidelong look. "Is that supposed to be a picture of me?"

"Well, no, Marguery," he said, embarrassed. "It's not a *picture*. That's not how Hakh'hli poems go. It's just supposed to sort of *suggest* you."

"You made me look like a man."

"Oh, but no! Not at all! You don't look like a man in the least, dear Marguery. If I've offended you in any way—"

She put a finger across his lips, laughing. "Sandy, you haven't offended me. That's really nice, in fact. I don't think anybody ever wrote a poem for me before. Only—"

He waited humbly for what was to come. "Yes?"

She bit her lip. "Well, the thing is—I guess I probably should have mentioned it before. I'm married, you see."

He stared up at her in horror. "Oh, Marguery!" he whispered.

She seemed to be displeased. "Well, you don't have to take it *that* hard."

"Oh, but I do! I had no idea that you were a 'married' person. Can you possibly forgive me?"

"Oh, hell, Sandy! Of course I forgive you. There's no law against hitting on somebody, even if they're married. Especially if you don't know they are. It's really kind of flattering. In fact, I appreciate it."

"Thank you," he said gratefully. "I promise I won't do it again. After all, there are plenty of other Female Hu—of other attractive women around for me to, uh, 'hit on.'"

She didn't look pleased at that. In fact, she was scowling. "Look, Sandy, slow down a minute, will you?" she commanded. "You're a nice guy. I like you. There's no reason to jump into something, like."

He said simply, "I don't understand what you mean."

"I mean there's no hurry. We've got plenty of time."

He was puzzled. "But you said you were married?"

"Well, I am," she said shortly. She picked up her drink and took a thoughtful swallow, while Lysander gazed at her in bafflement. "Only," she added, "I'm not really *working* at being married. I haven't even seen Dave for three or four months."

"Dave? Is that your 'husband'?"

She thought that over. "In a manner of speaking. It's pretty much in the past tense, though. Look," she said, putting down her glass. "Dave and I got married in college, seven years ago. He was a football player—could've done basketball if he wanted to, because he's seven feet two. I don't know if you've noticed, but I'm a pretty big woman, and there aren't that many men that go for my type. You'd think the big ones would, but you look at the couples and you'll see those seven-footers are always with chicks no more than five feet three."

"Why is that?" Sandy asked, interested.

"Why? Men! That's why, because they're men. Or anyway," she added fairly. "I don't know what the reason is, but that's the way it goes. So when Dave asked me to marry him I didn't know how long it would be before I got another chance. Anyway, I liked him. And we got along fine, too, while I was still trying to get into astronaut training—maybe he figured that was safe enough, because there weren't any manned launches—until I signed up with InterSec. Then I think he felt threatened. He didn't mind me being big, but he really didn't like the idea of being married to a cop."

"A *cop*? You mean, like Kojak?"

She looked puzzled. "What's a Kojak? I mean a police officer. That's what InterSec is, you know; it's the overall security agency for all the commonwealths. Its full name is InterCommonwealth Security. So Dave and I hacked along for a couple of years . . . only the last year or so it hasn't really worked. He's asked me if I want a divorce."

"Oh!" Sandy cried joyously. "I know about divorcées!"

She gave him a hostile look. "You know *what* about divorcées?" she demanded. "No, don't answer that. Anyway, I like your poem, and I think I probably like you, too. Only let me think about it a little bit, okay?"

"Oh, right." Sandy nodded enthusiastically, because that was how they did; the girl never said yes right away, at least not in the kind of movies he liked best, with a lot of tap-dancing. But still—

The other thing he knew was that there was a necessary next step.

The wine was helping out his decisions. He leaned closer to her in a preparatory way. She look worried, then comprehending. "Sandy," she began. "People are watching us inside the bar—"

But when he put an arm around her she didn't resist.

As a kiss it wasn't much, apart from the startling discovery Sandy made. He hadn't expected her mouth to be open, after all! But as a definite first step toward doing *It*, the sensations were dizzying. He was breathing hard when she broke away, laughing. "Ouch, Sandy," she said, rubbing her neck. "You don't know your own strength, do you?"

"Oh," he said abjectly. "I'm so very sorry—"

"Oh, cut that out! I liked it, only next time don't squeeze so hard. You've heard the expression about being built like a brick, uh, outhouse? Only in your case it isn't brick, it's granite slabs."

He hadn't even heard the last part of that. "Next time?" he repeated, eyes wide with hope.

She sighed and patted his arm. "I did say next time, didn't I? Okay, but just remember that next time isn't this time. Give it a rest. I'm not going anywhere. I'll be right around you; that's my job, after all."

He sighed and straightened up. "All right," he said, and took another swig of his drink. The warm feeling was becoming even more pronounced, and it seemed to have spread agreeably to his groin. He was smiling to himself when he saw that Marguery was watching him out of the corner of her eye. "What?" he asked, surprised. He wondered if he had missed an obvious cue.

She hesitated for a moment. Then she asked, "What's it like?"

He looked at her in puzzlement. "What's what like?"

"Being in space. Tell me what it's like. Please. I've always wanted to know."

He sat up straight, peering at her. She was in dead earnest. She wasn't being flirtatious or even friendly; she was staring at him as though he had some kind of secret that her life depended on, waiting for him to speak.

But he didn't know what to say. "Oh," he said, waving a vague hand, "you know."

"I *don't* know," she said harshly. "I *want* to know."

He looked at her in surprise. "Sorry," he said. "Only there isn't much to tell about what it's like. When you're in the big ship it doesn't feel like you're in space. It doesn't feel like you're anywhere in particular, just there. The engines are going at the regular G-thrust all the time, and you don't feel anything except when there's a course change, like when we went around the Sun—"

"Around the *Sun*?" she whispered, her eyes wide with fascination. So he had to tell her every bit about it—what they saw in the screens, what they felt as the ship heated up, what it was like when the main engines at last were turned off in Earth orbit, and most of all how it felt as they came down in the lander. "And you flew that thing?" she asked, her eyes bright.

"Oh, no," he admitted. "They wouldn't let me do the actual piloting. That was Polly's job. I know how, though." And then he had to tell her about the hours in the flight simulator.

Before he finished she had whispered to the waiter, and two new drinks were in front of them—not wine for him this time, but a carbonated soft drink that made him sneeze. "Gesundheit," she said dreamily. "You know, I trained in one of those things, too."

He blinked at her. "A Hakh'hli flight simulator? But you weren't on the ship!"

"No, of course I wasn't on your ship. How could I be? But we had flight simulators of our own. There are still volunteers to go into space, you know."

"But they can't, can they? That ring of debris—"

"Right," she said bitterly. "We can't get through the garbage ring. Unmanned satellites, yes. Sometimes. We send them up every once in a while, and about one out of five of them survives for a year without damage. Well, without being totally destroyed, anyway. That's not bad, for unmanned satellites. We can always make more of them. But it isn't good enough odds to send up people. People are a lot more fragile. So when I signed up for astronaut training Dave and I had a big fight. He called me a kamikaze—well, actually it was, 'You kamikaze bitch!'"

"Kami—? Oh! You mean, like the Japanese suicide pilots from your World War Two?"

"That's right. It meant he thought volunteering to go into space was like committing suicide. The way it turned out, he was pretty near right. The first two ships they launched did, in fact, kill their crews. Four astronauts. Two in each ship. People I'd trained with. So they called off the program, and then the rest of us never got up there at all."

"But you'd still like to?"

She blazed at him. "You're goddamn well *told* we'd like to. Not just me! There are millions of kids out there who'd give their right eyes to do what you've done—and hundreds of millions of grownups who'd kill you in a hot minute to take your place."

"Really?" he asked, alarmed. "But that wouldn't work, Marguery. The Hakh'hli wouldn't be fooled. They'd know right away—"

He stopped, because she was laughing at him. "I'm sorry, Sandy," she said. "I didn't mean that literally. But I didn't exactly not mean it, either, only I don't mean you should worry about somebody actually trying it. No one will."

"I didn't really think anyone would," he assured her, almost truthfully.

"But don't think the human race isn't interested in space! In fact, there's going to be an astronomical convention in York next week. They're probably going to ask all three of you to come to it, so they can see the pictures and listen to you talk—and, I guess, most of all just to be in the same room with somebody who's been there."

Sandy took a thoughtful sip of his drink. The fizziness in his nose stopped just short of being actually painful; he decided he liked it. "Marguery?" he asked. "How did you get into such a mess?"

"Mess?"

"The mess in the world. The debris in space. And letting things warm up so the ocean levels went up, depleting the ozone layer, acid rain. All those things. How did you human beings let it all get so bad?"

"Us human beings? And what are you?" she demanded harshly. "Chopped chicken liver?" And then, as he opened his mouth for a puzzled question, she shook her head. "Never mind. I know what you mean." She reflected for a minute. "Well, I guess the only answer is that the old people didn't know they were doing wrong. Or anyway the ones that did know it was wrong didn't count, and the ones that counted didn't care."

"They didn't know *war* was wrong?"

"Oh, well," she said doubtfully. "I guess they knew that, all right, only they got themselves into a place where it just happened. There was a place called the Near East—"

"Near to what?"

"That's just what it was called, Sandy, the 'Near East.' Anyway, they had a little war, only they got to using what they called 'tactical nukes.' And then people outside that part of the world got involved, and then the big countries began

using the big nuclear missiles. On each other. Well, the orbital defenses took care of most of them, but it was really a
mess, you know."

"I wish I did know," Sandy said wistfully. "We stopped
getting your broadcasts along about then, you know."

"Really? Well, all right, I guess I can fill you in. It's a
long time ago, but I think I know most of it, anyway. About
five percent of the nukes got through. A submarine-launched
one took out Washington, D.C.—that was where the government was then—and a bunch landed in New Mexico and
Arizona and so on, but, really, it wasn't a big nuclear war.
I think altogether only fifteen warheads hit their targets.
Only that was really all it took, you see. And after that—"

She paused, staring into her drink. Then she said, "Well,
things got pretty bad. There were a lot of people sick from
radiation, and then it was hard to get food to the cities, and
nothing could come at all from the Near East, where it all
started, and a lot of fuel came from there . . . and then there
was the AIDS. That was bad stuff, Sandy. It was bad around
the old United States, but in lots of places it was just, well,
there wasn't anybody left after a while. Before they got the
vaccines they'd just send people with it to Africa to die, because everybody there was going to be dying, anyway. Not
just from AIDS; from malaria, and typhus, and just plain
starvation." She looked sad. "They had ten times as many
people back then. Now Africa's empty. There's only about
half a billion alive in the whole world. A single country like
China or India had a lot more than that all by themselves
before the war."

"Are you telling me that five billion *people* died?" Sandy
gasped.

"Sandy," she said reasonably, "they'd probably all be
dead by now, anyway. And—" She hesitated, then burst out,
"And they deserved it, damn them! All of them! The thing I
can't forgive them for is that they shot us out of space,
forever!"

Chapter
♦ 11

The thing that keeps the human race trapped on the sur-
face of the Earth is its own previous activities in space. Just
as has happened often before in human history, the human race
has been defeated by its own success. As soon as the first rockets
reached Low Earth Orbit they began shedding pieces of them-
selves. By the 1980s more than seven thousand objects were
routinely tracked—pieces the size of a baseball and up, from a
wrench dropped by a space-walking astronaut to abandoned
fuel tanks the size of a box car. In those days it required a full
day's computing before any Shuttle flight to plot an orbit that
would not result in a catastrophic collision with some spinning
piece of space junk. But at least the big pieces could be located.
The ones too tiny to be tracked were the real killers. At least half
a dozen working satellites were by then known to have been
damaged or destroyed. Any scrap of metal—any crumb, even a
chip of paint—at the velocities of Low Earth Orbit could punc-
ture and even destroy another satellite. But that was only the
beginning. Then along came Star Wars. Some people thought

the Strategic Defense Initiative wouldn't work. Unfortunately, it almost did. After the war, all those thousands and thousands of pop-up lasers and killed satellites and "smart rocks" and exploded missile parts filled the Low Earth Orbit volume with an impenetrable spinning mine field of junk. So space travel came to a shuddering stop, just when it had become almost easy. There were places where the mine field was thinner than other places—the least dangerous were above the planet's poles—but even in the thinnest places only armored satellites could hope to get through, at great cost in launch mass because of their great weight and the fact that they had to be launched without help from the Earth's spin. Even those stayed operational only as long as it took for some colliding scraps of metal, plastic, or paint to pit their mirrors and fry their instrumentation. Of manned flights after that, there were none at all. Not successful ones, anyway. Not for more than half a century, and none likely until the junk orbits decay, a matter of hundreds of years.

The Major Seniors saw how obviously hungry the human race was for space, anything that had to do with space. That was good news for the Major Seniors; they decided to authorize the trip to York Commonwealth.

Polly got the news relayed from the lander by Tanya, and she greeted it, as she greeted most news, with an irritated twitch of the forearm. "But the Major Seniors have not instructed which of us to go and not remain behind," she complained.

"For this reason," Tanya said smugly, "it appears you must decide. Their order cannot now be questioned. Ship's orbit has taken it below Earth horizon and not in range of our transmissions."

Polly switched off the radio and looked at Obie and Sandy grimly. "Then that is how it will be," she declared. "Let me see. Obie, you are our astronomical expert, therefore you must go."

"Oh, pellets!" Obie grumbled. "Do you mean that I am to go alone and not with company?"

"Of course not. You would behave irresponsibly and not with adult Hakh'hli prudence. I myself will accompany you."

"No, I want a *friend*," he said in English. "I want Sandy to come with me."

Polly glared at him, pinching her thumbs together warningly in air. Obie quivered but belligerently stood his ground. After a moment's thought Polly gave a shrugging twitch of her forearms and declared grandly, "I decide that that is how it is to be; we will all three voyage to this York. Lysander, instruct your Earth female that this is so."

"Gladly!" he cried, and hurried out ahead of the others to meet Marguery Darp.

The news seemed to make her happy. In fact, they were all happy. Sandy was pleased because Marguery Darp was pleased. Polly was self-righteously pleased to be doing what the Major Seniors wished of her. And Obie—well, Obie had decided to be ecstatic. At the curbside, he showed it with a whole new repertory of cries and cavorting. "New York, New York," he shouted, leaping to the top of the hotel marquee and down again. "Oh, Sandy! We will have so much fun on the Great White Way! We will give our regards to Broadway, and remember everyone to Herald Square—but what," he asked, coming breathlessly down beside Marguery Darp, "is a 'Herald Square'?"

"I think it was an old street corner in New York City," she said. "I guess it's underwater now." And then, to Sandy, she said, "I'm really pleased. Hudson City's a great town. I have a place there myself, and it'll be fun showing you around."

"Thank you," Sandy said promptly. "I too think it will be fun, only—" He hesitated, swallowing. "Only, will it be necessary to travel again in that very rapid aircraft of yours?"

She patted his arm. "Not at all. We don't use those vertical-takeoff planes for long distances; they use too much fuel, even if it's only hydrogen. No. We'll go by blimp. It's a little over a twenty-four-hour trip, and I promise you'll love it. It's almost like a cruise."

"A *cruise*? Like 'Love Boat'?"

She frowned. "I don't know what 'Love Boat' is, and you're not starting that again, are you? Because we've got a busy day today. If you're all going off to York, there are about a hundred people here in Dawson who are dying to ask you questions."

Obie made a face. Sandy didn't, because he did not want to be undignified in Marguery Darp's presence, but all the same he complained, "They're *always* asking us questions. Don't we get any time off?"

"This evening," she said firmly. "After all your interviews. We'll have a kind of a bon voyage party, up on the rooftop. All right? But now let's get busy."

Busy they certainly were. For the morning's interrogation they were all three confronted by half a dozen polite, insistent questioners. And the questions they asked! Why did the Hakh'hli freeze their eggs instead of letting them hatch? What were the names of the Earth films shown to the entire ship's company? What was the Hakh'hli word for "magnetic repeller"? What would happen if, say, something like a little asteroid struck the interstellar ship in its drive compartment? Even Polly shivered when she was asked that last one. "It would be *terrible*," she said, presenting her tail to be licked in sympathy (but none of the humans understood the gesture, and Obie and Sandy were too far away). "It would *wreck* the ship."

It was a sour note to end the morning's questioning. Polly muttered darkly that she didn't see how she could even eat after that, but of course she and Obie did. Sandy was not so lucky. Marguery Darp had disappeared on some errand, and all he had was a sandwich before the afternoon session began.

This time he was questioned alone, by three separate waves of interrogators. Most of them he had never seen before, and though they unfailingly told him their names and, wincing, accepted a handshake of greeting, he could not tell them apart. The first batch wanted to hear his personal story, starting with the Hakh'hli discovery of his parents' spaceship. They took a full hour to cover every detail of his childhood, his education, and his relationships with the other members of his cohort—with ChinTekki-tho and MyThara, too. It was almost the first time Sandy had given his dear, lost nursemaid a thought since the lander pulled away from the interstellar ship, and he almost wept with sorrow and guilt. The second batch was more specific. In his training, they said, he had spoken of games and contests. Were any of those, well, military? (Oh, no, he assured them; the wrestlers used to fight to the death, but even they didn't do that any more.) And no one used 'weapons'? (Of course not! Why would a Hakh'hli use a 'weapon' against another Hakh'hli?) Not even 'police'? (But of course not again! The Hakh'hli didn't have 'police'—what would they be needed for? The Major Seniors did not permit 'crime,' and no Hakh'hli would go against the wishes of the Major Seniors.)

After the first two shifts of questioners, the third was almost like a casual chat. One count in that shift's favor was that Marguery Darp was a member. She sat down in front of him and said simply, "We want to know everything there is to know about the Hakh'hli, Sandy. So please just start at the beginning—whatever you think the beginning is—and tell us whatever you think we ought to know."

That was easy enough. The more Sandy saw of Marguery Darp the easier he found her to talk to. He simply sat there, telling her everything he could think of about Hakh'hli and titch'hik and the way the magnetic repellers made the lander lurch as they came in and the fact that his mother, or anyway some part of his mother, was still alive, or in a manner of speaking alive, in the genetics files on the interstellar ship; and she listened. She listened very well. She didn't speak, except now and then to give an encouraging grunt or a "Then what happened?" but her broad, strong, interested face spoke for her.

It was almost an annoyance when there was a knock on the door. Hamilton Boyle leaned in to report that the two Hakh'hli were finished with the afternoon's interrogation; they were having their "cookies and milk," and did Sandy want to go with them? Marguery answered for him. "Oh, I don't think so, Ham. We'll go upstairs and get a drink until they're ready to join us—if Sandy doesn't mind."

Well, of course he didn't mind. In fact, it was close to perfect. "What would you like?" Marguery asked as they found a table, warm in the afternoon sun. "I'm going to have a cup of coffee. Care to try one?"

"Certainly," he said, bracing himself for another ordeal by ingestion but pleased for a chance to try to redeem himself for that unisex poem. As the waitress brought the two cups and the silver pot, he reached for his pocket, but as he opened his mouth to speak Polly and Oberon appeared in the doorway. He scowled at them. "I didn't expect you so soon," he said accusingly.

"We wouldn't be here if the Earth people were behaving properly," Polly said disagreeably, advancing out into the sunshine of the patio. She had every appearance of being in a pinching mood.

"What's the matter?" Sandy asked.

She bore down on Marguery Darp. She said, "I've been talking to our cohort-mates. Do you know that some of your Earth people have been taking 'souvenirs'?"

Marguery looked astonished. "What do you mean, souvenirs?"

"They've stolen pieces of the lander shield. Tanya says big chunks of it have been cut away while they were in stun time."

"I'm sorry about that," Marguery said contritely. "Did you mention it to Hamilton Boyle?"

"I haven't *seen* Hamilton Boyle since I discovered the crime. You must deal with it. It is an offense to the Hakh'hli to steal parts of our lander. I want it stopped."

Obie put in, "I told her it didn't matter, Sandy. It was only the old shield anyway; it was all going to be replaced." He ducked as Polly turned toward him, but added defensively, "Well, it's the truth."

Marguery Darp said firmly, "No, Obie, she's right. That was a bad thing to do, and I'll see that it doesn't happen any more. I apologize, Polly."

Polly flounced. "And that's not all of it. Your Boyle person has been grilling me all afternoon about how the lander works, what kind of fuel we use, whether we can take off again without refueling—it is very tiring, to be asked so many questions! And that other person has been doing the same to Oberon, and Titania and Bottom and Helena and Demetrius have all been interrogated. We come in friendship! We should not be cross-examined like Perry Mason!"

"Who's Perry Mason?" Marguery asked; and then said, "I'm sorry. It's just that we're all so very curious about you, uh, you very advanced people from space."

Sandy decided to get into the conversation. "It's all right, Marguery. We understand that. If you have any other questions, ask them."

Marguery hesitated, nibbling at her lower lip and smiling a little. "You're sure you're not too tired?"

"Of course not!"

"Well—" She thought for a moment, then smiled apologetically. "There is one little thing that I've been wondering about. It's silly, really, but—your names."

She stopped there. Waiting for the question, Sandy said encouragingly. "Yes? What about them?"

"Well, this is really unofficial. Just my own curiosity, but they don't *sound* like Hakh'hli names or anything, do they? Where did you get them?"

"Oh, our *names*," Sandy said, flushing. "Well, they're just a kind of a joke, you know."

And Obie jumped in, relaxed now that Polly had stopped making pinching motions with her thumbs. "Yes, a kind of a joke," he said happily. "They come from a play. An Earth play; we all did it, years ago. We performed it for the whole ship! They were fascinated! It was a great hit; of course, they didn't understand the language—it was the first we did in English. Sandy? Can we show her? Polly?"

"Show me what?" Marguery Darp asked, sounding a little apprehensive.

"We can't. We don't have Theseus here," Sandy objected.

Obie wriggled in protest. "We don't need him. I know his lines! And I'm sure Polly knows her own part still, and maybe you could do Egeus—here, let's do it!"

Obie leaped, laughing, to the top of a parapet and began to declaim:

"Now, fair Hippolyta, our nuptial hour
Draws on apace. Four anxious days bring in
Another moon, but oh, methinks, how slow
This old moon wanes, like to a step-dame or a
dowager,
Long withering out a young man's revenues.

"Now you, Polly," he coaxed.

Polly looked sullen, but played along. "All right," she sighed.

"Four days will quickly steep themselves in night.
Four nights will quickly dream away the time.
And then the moon, like to a silver bow
New-bent in heaven, shall behold
The night of our solemnities."

As Sandy opened his mouth, trying to remember the next lines for Egeus, Marguery said, startled, "But that's *Shakespeare!*"

"Right, right!" Obie cried happily, leaping down beside her. "It's called *A Midsummer Night's Dream.* Oh, it was wonderful, the way we did it. Shall we go on?"

But all Sandy could remember of Egeus's part was "Full of vexation come I, with complaint against my child, my daughter Hermia," and then he stalled.

"Aw, *try,*" Obie coaxed. Sandy shook his head. "Well, we could get the others on the radio," he offered wistfully, but Marguery shook her head, marveling.

"You don't have to," she said. "I see the point. Really, that's wonderful. Is that how you all learned English?"

"One of the ways. That was the best, only ChinTekki-tho got angry at MyThara for getting us to do it. He said we were learning the wrong dialect."

"We really weren't," Sandy said, loyal to MyThara still. "We all knew the difference."

"But we did keep those names," Obie said. "Which is lucky for you, Marguery Darp, because you wouldn't want to have to learn our Hakh'hli ones. Don't you want to do just a little more, Polly?"

Polly waggled her forearm negatively. "I'm going back to tell Tanya you said that the vandalism would be stopped," she told Sandy frostily, "so she can advise ChinTekki-tho. Are you coming with me, Obie?"

"No, no! I'm going to stay here and talk to Marguery about New York New York—Times Square, Harlem, Wall Street—" Weeping, he leaped away, singing to himself.

Marguery stared after him. "What did he mean about your real names?" she asked Sandy.

He shifted position, trying to follow Obie as he leaped happily around the almost-empty sun deck. "Well, the Hakh'hli names tell a lot about the person," he began, and explained about the way the name reflected lineage and status in the Hakh'hli society; and how the numbers that followed the names reflected the egg batches in storage, which led inevitably to the Hakh'hli habit of freezing eggs as soon as they were laid, so as not to overburden the ship's carrying capacity.

"And Polly says that if you human beings had done that," Obie called from three tables away, "you wouldn't have got yourselves into all this trouble."

"Thank her for her good advice," Marguery said, which caused Sandy to give her a sharp look. The words and the tone had not matched.

"That's irony, right?" he asked.

She started to answer, then sneezed instead. Sandy, startled, asked, "Are you all right?"

"Just say gesundheit, all right? I'm fine. What were you asking me?"

"I said—"

"No, now I remember what you said," she interrupted. "Yes, Sandy, that was irony. There's something about your friend Polly that gets my nose out of joint."

He stared at her. "Your nose out of—?"

"Oh, for heaven's sake! I just mean she irritates me. I'm sorry about that."

"Why would you be sorry? She irritates me, too. She irritates all of us; she's always been the bossiest one in the cohort."

"Oh, really?" Marguery seemed to relax. "Well," she said, "I'm glad to hear that. I wouldn't like to think that all the Hakh'hli were as snotty as she is."

"'Snotty'?"

"Mean, uh, well, unlikeable. As a matter of fact," she added, looking to the far end of the terrace, where Obie was practicing high jumps, "I do like Obie. He's a little, ah, *youthful*, isn't he? But he's cute."

"He's my best friend," Sandy said. He thought about asking exactly what "cute" meant in that context and decided

off to the left there, just above that cloud? It's our blimp! It'll stay here over night, and then we'll get on it tomorrow for the trip to York."

Sandy craned his neck to see, delighted. From behind him he heard Obie call, "Here I come!"

And he jumped—his eyes on the blimp, and not on the parapet he was aiming for.

That was a mistake. He misjudged his trajectory—just slightly—too much. He did hit the railing, but he didn't stop there. Marguery screamed; Sandy shouted and jumped up to reach for the Hakh'hli, but it was too late. Obie, legs scratching in terror as he tried to stop himself, hit the parapet. He bounced and kept right on going, over the edge. They could hear him squealing all the way down to the ground.

Chapter · 12

A person falling off the top of a twelve-story building hits the ground at a speed a little faster than seventy miles an hour, and that is easily enough to kill him. A Hakh'hli falling the same distance strikes the ground at the same velocity. True, a Hakh'hli is used to a gravitational force forty percent higher than the Earth's. A Hakh'hli can survive decelerations that would cripple or kill any Earthman, but even for a Hakh'hli there is a limit. In relative terms Obie's fall was only as though he had fallen, say, seven or eight stories. But a fall of seven or eight stories is enough to kill either human or Hakh'hli, anyway, and the impact was quite enough to do the job.

"But he was my *friend*," Sandy wailed. He could not get out of his mind the picture of Oberon splatted on the sidewalk of Dawson, the eyes wide and empty and the body simply burst open. Twelves of human beings had crowded around to stare, fascination and revulsion mixed. They had no right to gape at Obie, so exposed.

"Of course he was your friend," Marguery Darp soothed. "Sandy? I know you don't want to think of such things now, but—well, are there any special Hakh'hli funeral arrangements that should be made?"

"Funeral arrangements?"

"For the disposal of the body," she said. "They've, uh, picked it up in an ambulance, but what do we do now?"

He stared at her. It did not seem the time to remind her what the Hakh'hli used for "funeral" arrangements, especially as there was no possible way to manage them in this place. "It doesn't matter," he said. "Ask Polly."

"But Polly's not here," Marguery pointed out. "She's in her room, talking to somebody—the people on the big ship, I suppose. And when we asked her she said she didn't care."

"Well, she doesn't," Sandy muttered. "I don't suppose any of them do. What do you do here for that kind of thing?"

"It depends. Whatever the family wants. Burial sometimes. Cremation, usually."

"Burial?" He winced at the thought; Obie's corpse thrust into the Earth, to rot and decay? He shuddered. "Whatever you think best. Cremation's all right—but, oh, Marguery, this is *terrible!*"

When at last Polly came grumpily out of her room she showed little enough interest in what had been done with Obie's body. It was the future that concerned her. "This is *terrible*," she said, in Sandy's exact words but a context all her own. "HoCheth'ik ti'Koli-kak was our only—what? Oh, Oberon, then. Oberon was our assigned astronomical specialist. ChinTekki-tho says the Major Seniors do not wish to send another one down."

Marguery asked tentatively, "Does that mean you don't want to go to York for the conference?"

Polly sniffed and writhed her torso in disgust. "Not at all! The Major Seniors direct that I take Oberon's place; after all, I am well informed in the area of astronomy, too. So I suppose we might as well go on with it. And anyway," she added, looking almost amiable for a moment, "I do think it would be interesting to ride in a 'blimp.' Don't you, Sandy?"

But Sandy was too deep in misery to agree.

Chapter
⋄ 13

If a world traveler of the twentieth century were brought back he would wonder greatly at the map of the Earth. The coastlines are all different. All the land San Francisco and Chicago had stolen from the lake and the bay the waters have won back as they rose. Libya's Qattara Depression is a brackish lake, half rainwater and half overspill from the Mediterranean Sea. Bermuda is a memory. The polders of the Netherlands are part of the North Sea again, and a sluggish oozing of the lower Mississippi River has drowned out New Orleans—the main channel of the river has long since broken through the dams put up by the Corps of Engineers and forced its way through the Atchafalaya. Hawaii has lost the tourist traps of Waikiki, though there is plenty of the islands left—they began as volcanic mountains, after all. All along the east coast of North America the low, sandy barrier islands are only shoals now. Sharks nose hungrily through the gambling casinos of Atlantic City, and coral grows on the golf courses of Georgia's sea islands. New York Bay is three times its former size, pocked with islands, and the Statue of Liberty stands with her feet wet up to the ankles. When the ice around the North Pole began to melt it made no difference. It was floating anyway, and so it added nothing to the oceanic water levels. The glaciers were a different matter. But even they were as nothing, nothing at all, compared to what happened when Antarctica lost the Ross Ice Shelf. So the edges of the continents are awash; and in their centers the searing, drying winds have left new dust bowls.

Aboard the blimp, Polly perched on a settee that groaned underneath her weight. She was peering out through the slanted windows at the ground and commenting acidly on what she saw. "Your Earth people," she commented dispassionately to Sandy, "certainly are wasteful. Look at all this space down here, and hardly anyone using it."

Sandy didn't answer. He wasn't thinking about the faults of Earth humans. He was thinking of his dead friend. Halfway across what had once been the province of Manitoba, he had not yet gotten used to Obie's loss.

Yet . . . he was on a "blimp," and the blimp was taking him to new experiences in the world of mankind.

It was certainly an interesting experience. It wasn't in the least like any of the other forms of transportation he had already experienced. The blimp was helium filled and carried three hundred people with staterooms, music rooms, lavatories, and a dining room. One didn't sit strapped in a seat on the blimp, one moved around. And yet it wasn't like the interstellar vessel, either, because it moved underfoot; it throbbed with the noise of its engines and bobbled in the winds that struck it, and most of all it had windows you could look out of to see the ground.

As the blimp found an altitude without much turbulence, Sandy began to get used to the physical sensations, and his mood lightened. When Marguery Darp knocked on the door and invited him to join her for a drink, he accepted, glad enough to get away from Polly; even more glad to have Marguery for company.

They sat side by side on a light, soft settee, gazing out. The trip, Marguery said, would take a day and a half, and the dark of the first night was coming early, because they were heading toward it. Below them the darkening plains rolled past, and Marguery took Sandy's hand.

"I'm really sorry about what happened to your friend, Oberon," she said.

He squeezed her hand—gently, as she began to wince. "I know you are. He was my best friend, you know."

"Yes." She was silent for a moment, regarding him. Then she said, "Do you want to talk about him?"

"Oh, can I?" And, yes, he discovered, that was exactly what he wanted, very much. He wanted it even more than he wanted to work on the new poem he was meditating— even more than any of the other things he wanted to do with Marguery Darp. And so she listened, quietly sympathetic, while he told her about their childhood on the Hakh'hli ship, and the scrapes they'd gotten into together, and the way Oberon would be his buffer and bodyguard in the roughest of the Hakh'hli games, and how they'd share their "cookies and milk," sometimes, just off by themselves—and about the funny scene when Oberon came into season with the Major Seniors, and how proud he was to have fertilized the Fourth Major Senior's eggs. "And I *miss* him," he said, squeezing her hand again.

She didn't wince this time. She squeezed back. Then she said, "There's something that surprises me. I mean, the other Hakh'hli don't seem really broken up about it, do they?"

"Well, death isn't a big thing with the Hakh'hli," he explained. "See, there was my old teacher—well, maybe you'd call her a nursemaid. Her name was MyThara, and she was pretty nearly a mother to me." And he told Marguery about the way MyThara had gone uncomplainingly to the titch'hik when the medical examination showed she was wearing out.

Marguery shuddered. Sandy said quickly, "That's the way they are. MyThara felt she was doing the right thing, you know? She was making room for another egg to hatch. Nobody ever really objects when it's time to die, that I ever heard of. And nobody mourns."

"But you do, Sandy," she pointed out.

"But I'm not a Hakh'hli," he said with pride.

The door opened and Polly stalked into the lounge toward them. "Sandy," she complained, "it is sleeping time. I wish you would come to bed with me. I'm, what is the word, lonesome!"

"But I don't want to come to bed with you," Sandy said reasonably. "I want to be with Marguery."

Polly licked her tongue out unhappily. "Will she come to bed with us?"

"Certainly not," Sandy said, flushing. "Polly, you are on Earth now, and you must learn Earth ways. Earth people sleep alone, except during amphylaxis."

"But I don't *like* it," she wailed. "I miss Obie, too!"

That decided him. He knew that what Polly missed, of course, was only warmth and company in the sleeping tangle. Nevertheless, there was nothing she could have said that would have melted Sandy's heart more. "I think I should keep her company, just for a while," he told Marguery Darp. "I'll be back, I think. Probably."

But the fact of the matter was that he, too, was tired. These long twenty-four-hour Earth days were taking their toll on him, too. In Polly's stateroom, his arms around her and her arms around him, he found himself relaxing.

He really wanted to go back to Marguery Darp, too. When Polly's gentle, hiccoughing snores told him she was asleep he tried gently disengaging himself. He didn't succeed. Polly moaned and reached out, pulling him back . . .

And the next thing he knew he was waking up next to her, and he knew that a good many hours had passed.

As he moved, Polly snorted a huge sigh and rolled over. He detached himself and scuttled out from under just in time to avoid being crushed. Moving as quietly as he could, he stood up, looking around. The stateroom window was still black. He had no idea of the time. He thought for a moment of lying down next to Polly again, soaking in the warmth of her great, muscular torso; but there was, he thought, the possibility that Marguery Darp was still in the blimp's lounge, waiting for him to return.

It was a silly thought, and of course it was wrong. No one moved in the narrow passageways of the blimp. The lights were all turned down. The lounge was empty.

Sandy sat down on a window seat, gazing out. The sky was dark, but filled with bright stars. The gentle motion of the blimp wasn't worrying any more; it was almost comforting. Perhaps he was getting his "sea legs," Sandy thought, and then leaned forward, perplexed. For a moment he thought he saw another constellation of stars, actually below him, a bright cluster of red and white and green lights.

It wasn't stars. It could only be another blimp, sliding silently along a thousand feet below them, crossing their track from somewhere to somewhere else.

"Sir?"

He turned around guiltily. A sleepy-eyed crew member was peering at him from the doorway. "Would you care for some coffee, sir?" she asked.

"Oh, yes, please," he said at once. "With a lot of cream and sugar."

"Right away, sir," she said, and hesitated. "I can turn the television on for you, if you like. Or there's music on the ship system—there are headphones at your seat."

"Maybe later," he said politely. He wasn't quite ready to watch Earthly television. He wasn't even quite ready to talk to Marguery Darp, he decided, even if she had been available, because there was a lot that he needed to think about. The first, and worst, thing, of course, was Obie. He felt the tingle at the back of his nose that warned him that tears were nearby as he thought about Obie. He didn't try to restrain them. He was, he realized, probably the only person in the universe who would even consider crying over Obie. Certainly no one on this planet would. Just as certainly, no one on the Hakh'hli ship would mourn, though a few members of the ship's crew might be interested enough to check the name and lineage of HoCheth'ik ti'Koli-kak 5329 against their own, out of curiosity, to see what sort of kin they might have been.

But Obie was *dead*.

And Obie was not the first. One after another, the people dearest to Sandy went and died on him—his mother, before he was born; MyThara, going voluntarily to feed the titch-'hik; and now Oberon, foolishly showing off and paying for his folly. But he wasn't the only one who had paid! Sandy had to pay, too! He wasn't merely grieving for Oberon, he realized; he was definitely angry at him.

When the coffee came, Sandy swallowed the first sweet, thick cup fast enough to make his throat burn, then poured another. The sugar relieved the nagging hunger he hadn't realized he was feeling. It also, for some trivial reason he could not quite identify, elevated his mood—not a lot, maybe, but to a point where the tears were no longer threatening. Partly, he thought, it might have been the fact that "coffee" contained "caffeine" and "caffeine" was called a "stimulant." Partly it was a kind of interior pride that he was adjusting so well to Earthly foods and drinks. The next time Marguery suggested a "drink," he decided, he would be a little more adventurous than diluted wine. He had seen Hamilton Boyle drinking what was called a "Scotch on the rocks," and if Boyle could enjoy it, Sandy could, too.

He thought, remembering what the crew member had said, that there were other Earthly pleasures for him to practice enjoying. He found the headphones for his seat, managed to get them more or less comfortably in place without

squeezing his hearing aid too painfully and, after a little ex-
perimentation, found a channel of music that seemed to fit
his mood. He lay back, listening. His mind began to blank
out. Just by turning his head he could gaze at the bright stars
above, and the infrequent lights of some small town sliding
by on the ground below, while Tschaikovsky's Pathetique
Symphony lulled him back to sleep.

He woke up to the faint murmur of his own voice.

He sat up quickly, pulling away the earphones that had
twisted around his neck. He saw Hamilton Boyle standing
by the lounge's big television screen, and on the screen Sandy
saw that he himself was describing to an unseen interviewer
the Questions Game he and his cohort had spent twenty years
playing.

"Oh, sorry," Boyle said. "Did I wake you?"

It was a silly question. The facts spoke for themselves,
but Sandy said politely, "That's all right."

"I was just trying to get some news on the television,"
Boyle apologized. "Lieutenant Darp will be coming along in
a minute. We thought you'd like some breakfast."

"Oh, yes," Sandy said eagerly. The window beside him
was bright with sunlight. Fleecy clouds were below them,
and the warmth of the sun felt good on his skin. He stood
up and stretched. "I think I would like to see some 'news'
too," he observed.

Boyle grinned. He was a handsome man, Sandy thought.
It was hard to believe that he was sixty-two years old, but
that was what Marguery had told him. He had thick, pale
hair, close cropped, and his face was not lined. It was a little
sharp featured, Sandy thought critically, and the man smiled
a lot more than there seemed to be any reason for. But he
appeared to be willing to be friendly. "You're most of the
news yourself today, you know," he said. "The only other
thing that's interesting is a reentry—one of the big old satellites is about to deorbit, and there's some chance it will

153

come down where it can do some damage. But we won't know about that for sure for a couple of days yet."

"Does that happen often?" Sandy asked, interested.

"Often enough," Boyle said shortly, snapping the set off. He didn't seem to want to pursue the matter, so Sandy changed the subject.

"I didn't know you had cameras in the room yesterday. When I was talking about my life on the ship, I mean."

Boyle looked at him speculatively. "You don't mind, do you? Everyone's so interested in you."

"Especially you cops," Sandy pointed out.

Boyle took a moment to respond, but then he said, easily enough, "Yes, I'm a policeman, more or less. It's my job to protect society."

"Like Kojak?"

Boyle's eyes widened. Then he grinned. "I keep forgetting how many old television shows you've seen. But, yes, like Kojak. Like any good cop. I need information, and the best place to get it is from someone on the inside."

"The inside of what?" Sandy asked. Boyle shrugged. "I don't know much about cops," Sandy went on. "Do you still get your information by the—what is it?—the 'third degree'?"

"I've never done that!" Boyle said sharply. Then he added, "I've never had to. I admit some cops have, sometimes, but that's natural enough, isn't it? Don't the Hakh'hli ever do anything like that?"

"Never," Sandy said positively. "I've never heard of anything like deliberately inflicting pain, for any reason at all."

"Not even threatening someone?"

"With pain? No! Do you mean threatening them with death? But that wouldn't work, either," he explained. "Hakh'hli don't fear death the way you do—we do."

"Yes, that's what you told Lieutenant Darp," Boyle agreed. "Therefore—well, suppose one Hakh'hli went crazy.

Antisocial. There wouldn't be any good way of, say, forcing him to tell anything he didn't want to?"

"I don't think so. Not by threatening him or torturing him, anyway."

Boyle seemed to lose interest in the subject. "I wonder what's holding our breakfast up," he said, and then smiled. "So you didn't know we had cameras on you?"

Sandy shrugged. "For that matter," he added, "until we landed, we didn't really know if you had TV or not at all anymore. Years ago, the first time the Hakh'hli were in this part of the galaxy, they got all kinds of broadcasts. Radio, television, all sorts of things. This time there was hardly anything; we thought you'd stopped broadcasting for some reason."

Boyle looked pensive. "Well, in a way we did. With all that stuff floating around, satellites aren't too useful for communications any more. So it's almost all microwave or optical cable. Even local stations have directional antennae, so they don't waste much energy transmitting to the sky."

"It's not because you're being secretive?" Sandy hazarded.

Boyle looked really surprised. "Of course, not! What makes you think that? We didn't even know the Hakh'hli were out there, did we?" He shook his head. "No, it's just that we made such a mess up there. It's not just the physical obstruction; some of those old satellites are still radiating all kinds of stuff. The effects of the Star War will be with us for a long time—but still, I have to admit it was a beautiful light show while it lasted."

Sandy pricked up his ears. "You *saw* the war?"

"Well, of course I saw it. I was twelve years old. I didn't see much personally, I mean with my own eyes—there wasn't much to see, from Cleveland, Ohio, especially because it was daylight. The Star War started at two o'clock in the afternoon, Cleveland time, and it was all over by sundown. But they had it all on television, and it was pretty spectacular fireworks out in space, believe me." He hesitated, looking at Sandy. "Didn't your parents ever tell you anything about it?"

"How could they?" Sandy asked bitterly. "They died before I knew them. I never saw them, really—except for the picture of my mother."

"Oh? Can I see it?" Boyle studied the little rectangle Sandy pulled out of his pocket. He didn't speak for a moment, and then chose his words with care. "She was certainly a beautiful woman," he said. "Would you mind if I made a copy of her picture?"

"What for?" Sandy asked, surprised.

"I think the public would love to know what she looks like," he said, putting the picture in his pocket. "Did you ever see their ship?"

"My parents' ship? Not exactly. That is, just pictures there, too."

Boyle nodded quickly, as though he'd just had an idea. "I'll tell you what, Sandy. Suppose we showed you all the pictures we could find of spaceships of that time. Do you think you could pick their ship out?"

"I could try, I suppose."

"And that's all anyone could ask of you," Boyle said heartily. "Ah, here's Lieutenant Darp and our breakfast!"

One of the crew members was following Marguery into the lounge, pushing a wheeled cart. As Marguery greeted them the crew member pulled dishes covered in silver domes out of a heating compartment under the table and set places for three.

Although Sandy's first interest was in the smells of what they were being offered, he didn't fail to notice how Marguery looked. She looked beautiful. Her hair was gleaming in its long, scarlet braids, and she wore a completely different outfit than she had the night before—a skirt the color of her hair, that reached barely to her knees, a white, fringed leather jacket, bright blue socks that went halfway up her calf and ended in a plaid of red, blue, and white. Frowning, Sandy noticed that Boyle's clothes, too, were not the same as the night before, and wondered if he was not making a mistake by continuing to wear the same outfit day after day.

But then it was time to eat the "breakfast," and that took all of Sandy's concentration. The "pancakes" were fine, especially with gobs of the thick, sweet "maple syrup." So was the little dish of cut-up pieces of "fruit." He nibbled at them very tentatively at first, but the contrasting flavors and textures of "oranges" and "grapefruit" and "melon" were irresistible. And then Polly showed up; and the day's questioning began, and it wasn't until Polly retired for her private midday meal and stun time that Sandy had a chance to take Hamilton Boyle aside and ask him if, really, there was any reason to change clothes so often.

He was still blushing as, hastily retiring to his own cabin, he stood in the tiny shower cubicle, with the hot water pouring down on him.

No one among the Hakh'hli had ever pointed out to him that he might smell bad. It was not a Hakh'hli concern. None of the Hakh'hli ever bothered to disguise their natural odors themselves, for that matter; but still, he told himself remorsefully, he should have noticed by himself that the pleasant odors that came from the human beings almost all came out of a bottle.

When he was out of the shower and dried, he experimented with the flask of men's cologne that Boyle had loaned him. It certainly smelled pleasant enough. He filled a palm with it and began slapping it onto his body.

His yell of angry surprise woke Polly from the last of her stun time and brought her waddling in to see what was the matter. When he told her indignantly that the stuff *stung*, she was unsympathetic. "Perhaps you are putting it in the wrong places," she suggested. "At any rate, it is a human foolishness and, as you are human, you might as well get used to it. Put on some clothing so we can go out and be interrogated some more."

"They aren't *interrogating* us," he corrected. "They are simply asking us questions, because they are naturally so interested in us."

"Not just in us," she said darkly. "What have they been asking you?"

He shrugged, pulling on a new pair of pants and studying himself anxiously in the little mirror. "All sorts of things. Nothing in particular."

"But in particular they have been asking me about some very serious things," she said, her tone grim. "About the history of the ship. About whether the Hakh'hli have ever before encountered intelligent beings, and what they did about them. About the technology of our ship's engines, which are powered by what they call 'strange matter'—though how they know that I do not know. Especially about we Hakh'hli ourselves—why we allow ourselves to die when it is our turn, how many eggs are kept in storage, for how long, for what purpose . . . there is nothing they do not want to know."

"And there is nothing we should not tell them," Sandy said virtuously, combing his hair to see if he could make it look like Hamilton Boyle's. "That is our purpose here. To exchange information."

"To *exchange*, yes," she agreed, "but what information are they giving us in return?"

"I'm sure they'll tell us anything we want to know," he said stoutly.

She gave him a bitter look. "You are quite a human being after all," she announced. "Please remember to act like one next time we sleep together."

He turned to gaze at her, surprised by her tone. "Have I offended you, Hippolyta?" he asked.

"You have behaved quite badly in your sleep," she announced crossly. "You should swallow your own spit! Were you dreaming last night? What were you dreaming of? Twice last night you woke me and I had to push you away, for you seemed to be trying amphylaxis with me. That is foolish, as well as disgusting, Lysander! Save such things for your human female, Marguery Darp."

"Don't I wish," Sandy said wistfully.

There weren't as many questions as usual that afternoon, but Sandy found the session wearing. What Polly said had spoiled things for him, a little. He didn't like the idea of being interrogated. He began taking careful note of the number of questions he was asked, and what they were about.

That part was easy. The answer was "everything," from the Hakh'hli name for their sun, and for airships, and for the lander, to why ChinTekki-tho, though a Senior, was not a *Major* Senior. Hamilton Boyle had the same curiosity Marguery had shown about the films that had been shown to the entire ship's company; Marguery wanted to know, all over again, how the landing craft's magnetic repellers at least slowed down the bits of debris in orbit. Sandy sulked. Even though Marguery complimented him very kindly on how well he looked in his fresh clothes (and, when he asked, yes, on how well he smelled now, too), he was not enjoying the time spent with her and was glad when Boyle announced that they would stop the conversation for a while, because Bottom was on television, speaking from the lander site.

The lander was no longer as Lysander had left it. The Hakh'hli housekeeping crew had been busy; most of the tattered micrometeorite screen was gone, and they had already begun laying on the shiny new one that would be needed for takeoff. And a whole little town had sprung up around it— three big oblong structures on wheels (Marguery explained that they were called "trailers") formed an arc around the little rocket. Half a dozen fabric things ("tents") housed some of the human beings who worked in the trailers; half a dozen helicopters sat around, some of them with their rotors steadily turning. It was drizzling in the Inuit Commonwealth, and the Hakh'hli were staying inside. Sandy caught a glimpse of Demmy watching from the doorway, and then the scene switched to pick up the picture of Bottom, squatting inside one of the tents, explaining exactly what the "railgun launcher" was to be like, and where it could be built; and all Polly and Sandy had to do that afternoon was watch and explain some of the details Bottom was leaving out.

By the end of the long day Sandy was exhausted again, but he had discovered that coffee would keep him awake. "I don't know if you should hit it that hard," Marguery said, concerned. "It's all new to your system, isn't it?"

"It'll be all right," Sandy assured her. No risk to his system was going to keep him from spending private time with her. But he finished with a huge yawn.

Marguery looked concerned. "Haven't you been getting enough sleep?"

"I can't sleep as long as you do," he said defensively.

"Well, if you'd like to pack it in for the night—"

"Oh, no! No. I like spending time just with you, Marguery."

She gave him a kind of Earth-female smile that was totally unreadable to Sandy. "You aren't about to produce another poem, are you?"

He shook his head, but thoughtfully. Were the poems doing what he hoped for them, after all? But he said, "It's just that I'm more comfortable with you. Not that Hamilton Boyle isn't all right, but—I don't know. I don't think he trusts me, exactly."

"Well, he's a cop," Marguery said, and then, before Sandy could say it, added, "So am I, of course. But he's been one all his life. It's kind of instinctive with him now, I guess."

"Would he third-degree me, Marguery?"

"Third-degree? *Torture?* Of course not! Or anyway," she added unwillingly, "not unless he really had to. Why do you ask a question like that?" Sandy shrugged. "Are you keeping secrets from us?"

Sandy considered the question. "I don't think so," he reported. "I mean, I've told you everything you asked."

She sneezed, then looked at him thoughtfully. "And is there anything we ought to know that we haven't known enough to ask you about?"

"Not that I know of." Then he looked harder at her. "Do you think there is?"

Marguery said slowly, "There is one thing that I've been wondering about, actually."

"And what's that? Just ask, Marguery. I'll tell you if I know."

She gazed at him for a moment, and then, oddly, asked, "How old are you?"

The question took him by surprise, but he answered promptly. "In Earth years, I'm about twenty-two."

"Yes, that's what you've told us. And you said you were rescued, unborn, from an Earth spaceship?"

"Yes, that's correct," he said, wondering what she was up to.

"But that was right after the war, and that happened fifty years ago."

"Oh, yes," Sandy said, grinning with pleasure. It was good to be able to explain something simple to her, when so many of the questions were harder to deal with. "That," he lectured, "is because for so much of the time the ship was traveling at a major fraction of the speed of light, you see. This causes a time-dilation effect, as your Albert—as Albert Einstein predicted in his theory of relativity. So time passed more slowly for me, on the ship."

"I see," she said, nodding. "So it's actually been about fifty years, Earth time, since you were born. And that was twenty-five years out to Alpha Centauri, and twenty-five years back, right? Only it only seemed like about ten years each way because of time dilation."

"Exactly," he said, beaming with gratification at her quick understanding.

She asked, very seriously, "What was it like at Alpha Centauri?"

He blinked. "I beg your pardon?"

She repeated, "What was it like at Alpha Centauri? I mean, that was only ten years ago as far as you were concerned, right? So you were about ten years old, in your own subjective terms."

He frowned. "I don't see your point."

"Well, Sandy," she said unhappily, "when I was ten years old I was pretty immature, but I wasn't stupid. I wouldn't have been totally oblivious to an occasion like that. I'd remember *something* about Alpha Centauri, even if it was only how excited the grownups were. Don't you?"

He scowled more deeply. "I've seen pictures of it," he offered.

"Yes," she agreed. "So have we. The Hakh'hli have shown us tapes. But I wasn't there. Were you?"

"Of course I was. I *had* to have been," he said reasonably, though he was still scowling.

She sighed. "I don't think you were," she said. "I think they lied to you."

He stared at her, thunderstruck and slightly offended. "Why would they do that?" he demanded. She was, after all, talking against the oldest friends he had.

"That's what I'd like to know," she said seriously. "What reason could they possibly have? For instance, suppose when they captured your parents—"

"They *rescued* them," he snapped.

"When they took them aboard the Hakh'hli ship, then. Suppose your father wasn't dead. Suppose your mother wasn't even pregnant. Suppose you weren't born until early in the return trip, and then something happened to your parents, and they brought you up—"

"Something did happen to my parents. Then the Hakh'hli did bring me up."

"But you don't remember anything about Alpha Centauri. So it couldn't have happened the way they told you, Sandy," she pointed out.

He was definitely edgy now. He snapped, "What's your point?"

"Only that they lied to you, Sandy."

"But that's silly! There wasn't any reason for them to lie, was there? Why would they do that?"

And she sighed. "I wish I knew."

Chapter
◆ 14

Good seaports make great cities, but seaports have one inescapable flaw. They are inevitably located at sea level. With the swelling of the oceans New York City has gotten wet. Of the five boroughs the Bronx has suffered the least; the heights around Inwood and Riverdale still stand proud. Brooklyn, Queens, and Staten Island are mostly shallow shoals, apart from the stretches left over from the long glacial ridge, the scrubbings of the last Ice Age, that made their few hills. The island of Manhattan is somewhere in between. Where it rose in hills, even minor ones like Murray Hill, it is still dry. But the Wall Street area is a new Venice. Blue water fills the streets between its skyscrapers. The great bridges rise from water and return to water. Across what used to be the Hudson River—now just a brackish extension of the Lower Bay—the Palisades still tower above the sea, and that is where Hudson City has grown. It has two qualities that make it an important metropolis. One is the salvage industry it supports, for there are treasures still to be rescued from those flooded buildings of downtown New York.

The other is sentiment. No former New Yorker could possibly accept a world in which there wasn't any New York City, even if it had to be in New Jersey.

The blimp landed at Hudson City while Sandy was still asleep. He missed the first sight of what once had been, or once had thought it was, the central city of the human race. He was still bleary eyed as they drove through Hudson to their hotel. Even though he was both sleepy and abstracted, he could not help noticing that Hudson City was orders of magnitude huger and busier than Dawson had been, but the puzzlement in his mind drowned out the curiosity about this huge, human place.

Their quarters weren't two separate rooms this time. Instead they had a "suite" of three linked rooms, a bedroom apiece and a larger sitting room between. As soon as they were alone Sandy followed Polly into her bedroom to confront her with what Marguery Darp had said.

Predictably, her response was belligerent. "Lie to you?" she cried. "What sort of statement is that? Of course our Major Seniors did not *lie* to you. Is your mind disordered and not functioning clearly because you are so obsessed with prospect of amphylaxis with that Earth female?"

Sandy made a fist and slammed it against the nearest wall. The wall shook, and Polly giggled in alarm. "Stop talking about me and the Earth female!" he shouted. "Answer the question! What she said was true. I don't remember the ship visiting that other star. Do you?"

Polly hesitated. "Perhaps not very well," she admitted. "But what does that prove? Earth people don't know anything about time dilation, do they? When we get back to the ship you can ask the Major Seniors to clarify your understanding."

He glared at her. "Who says I'm going back to the ship?"

"Well," she conceded, "perhaps you are not. I do not know if that has been decided."

"Perhaps I *definitely* am not. In any case, who asks the Major Seniors anything?" he growled in English.

"Well, then you can ask ChinTekki-tho by radio. I must call him this morning; when I am finished and not at any earlier time you can speak to him yourself. And speak Hakh'hli to me and not that Earth language," she finished.

He blinked at her. "What is purpose of that?" he asked, but obeying.

Polly looked sulkily righteous. "You simply have not been using your senses, Lysander. Earth people are observing us at all times. Look in your room. Look here—" She pointed at a lighting fixture in the ceiling. "Do you see that lens? It is a camera. Cameras are in all rooms. I have seen them all along and not now for first time."

Sandy stared at the tiny, barely visible disk of glass. "Do not look at it so!" Polly ordered. "Do not let them see we have discovered their secrets."

He looked away. "In all rooms?" he repeated.

"Certainly in all rooms and not just this room" she said severely. "As you should have observed for yourself. Earth people watch us at every moment, even sleeping. Now you must go away and not return for a twelfth-day—" She paused, consulted her watch, and corrected herself. "For some eighty-five Earth minutes, so that I may speak with ChinTekki-tho in private and not be overheard."

"Why in private? Why do I have to leave?" Sandy demanded.

"You must leave because you are directed to and not for any other reason," she said firmly. "Now go. Do not keep the Earth female waiting."

When Sandy got to the hotel lobby the first thing he saw was Marguery Darp, looking fresh and desirable. Just the sight of her came close to mending Sandy's mood, but when he told her that Polly was staying in her room with the radio her expression, too, clouded over. "But Ham Boyle wants to take her to meet some space experts. They need to talk about the conference," she said. Sandy shrugged. "Well," she went on, "I suppose that can wait. Everybody's got Perth on their minds, anyway. Maybe you'd just like me to show you around the city for a while?"

"I am tired of being *shown* things," he said bitterly.

She looked at him speculatively. "I guess you got up on the wrong side of the bed this morning," she offered.

He said, "I understand that figure of speech. You mean to say that I am in a bad mood. That may be true. It may be that the reason for that is that I am suffering from what is called 'culture shock.' There is every reason for that, after all."

She put her hand on his arm. "Of course there is, Sandy. Well, what would you like? There were some people that wanted to meet you, but I suppose that can wait." She thought for a moment. "Do you want to go for a walk?"

"Walk where?"

"Anywhere you like. Just around the town, maybe. I've got your hat and sunglasses in the car."

He pursed his lips. "Without being questioned by these people who want to meet me?" he stipulated, and Marguery laughed.

"Sandy, hon," she said, "it'll just be the two of us. I won't promise I won't ask you any questions, but whether you answer or not, you know—that's entirely up to you."

"It is?" he asked, astonished at the thought. "Well, I suppose we could at least try it." And it was only then that he thought to ask, "What's 'Perth'?"

Perth, Marguery reminded him as they strolled through the streets of Hudson City, was a city in Australia, and the reason people had it on their minds was that one 150-ton monster piece of space junk was in the process of deorbiting itself. Unfortunately, its orbit took it right over the city of Perth, in Australia; and since the moment of impact could not be predicted very precisely, the people of Australia were jittery. Which made everyone else jittery.

"I suppose," he said, as they stopped at a little park that overlooked the swollen river and bay, "that I too am 'jittery.'"

Marguery said comfortably, "You'll get over it. That's what's nice about this place. Looking at large bodies of water is soothing to the nerves."

"It is?" He considered the thought and decided that it was true that he was feeling more relaxed. He pointed at the skyline across the water. "Is that New York City over there?"

"It's what's left of it," she said. "You can see that parts of it are flooded. They tried diking all around the city when the sea level started to rise, but that only worked for a while. Then the storm surges just came right over the dikes. We can visit it if you like."

"Now?" he asked, surprised.

"Whenever you want to," she promised.

He thought about Polly's call to ChinTekki-tho. "Not right this minute," he said, looking at his watch, reassured to find that they had been gone only half an hour. He leaned out over the parapet and gazed down. Boats were moving silently up and down it, far below them, and just under them was a strip of sand. People in skimpy costumes were sitting or lying by the water, or actually splashing around in the water itself. "What are those people doing down there?"

She looked over the railing. "Just swimming," she said. "Would you like to try it?"

"Me?" He gave her a doubtful look, then turned to gaze down at the people by the water. "I don't know if I can," he confessed. "I've never done that."

"There's nothing easier," Marguery assured him. "I don't suppose you have a bathing suit, but we can pick one up for you easily enough."

"Not right this minute," he said again, temporizing. He looked around at the peaceful scene below and the vista of the old city. "Maybe after lunch," he finished. "There's something I need to do at the hotel. Let's start back."

"All right," Marguery said; but as they turned away a young woman in glasses, sun hat, and shorts approached them, holding a notebook and a pen out to Sandy.

"Excuse me," she said, "but you're the man from the spaceship, aren't you. Can I have your autograph?"

When Sandy got back to the hotel room he was far too late to talk to ChinTekki-tho. The radio in Polly's room was silent, and the table was littered with scraps of her midday meal. Polly herself was snoring stertorously in stun time.

"Oh, turds," Sandy said aloud. But then he looked more closely at the scraps Polly had left on the meal cart. They smelled attractively familiar, after a few days of trying the exotic Earth foods. He chose a few fragments, piled them onto a silver dish that had, until then, held a vase of flowers, and took them back to his own room.

When he had finished he gazed out of the window for a while. Then, sighing, he sat down once more and began to sketch out another poem.

This one, he decided, would be a real *human* poem. Well, not *rhymed*—he wasn't sure enough of himself for that—but anyway *like* a human poem, meaning not twisted into the shape of a significant object. By the time Polly came grumpily yawning into his room to complain that he had missed his appointment to talk to ChinTekki-tho, Sandy was smiling again.

Polly was not. "You were late and not on time," she said accusingly in Hakh'hli.

Unrepentant, Sandy counterattacked. "Did you ask him about why we didn't remember visiting Alpha Centauri?"

"Why should I have? You could have been here to ask him yourself."

"But did you?"

Polly said in triumph, "Of course I asked him. And he

gave me an answer. He said, 'Such things will be discussed when Major Seniors decide it is time to discuss them and not before.'"

The "people who wanted to talk to Sandy" were gathered in the hotel's ballroom when he came down in response to Marguery's telephone call. "There are so *many* of them" he said, displeased, peering in at the nearly a hundred human beings who were sitting there, talking among themselves.

"It's just what we call a press conference," Marguery said. "The people just want to get to know you, that's all. After all, you're a celebrity."

"I am?" he asked, pleased.

"Of course you are. Can't you tell? Why else would people be asking you for your autograph?"

So he let himself be led into the room without protest. He stood at a lectern on a platform at the front. Lights went on. Cameras began winking red-eyed at him. Marguery Darp said a few words of introduction, and the questions began. What did he think of Hudson City? Had he enjoyed his afternoon at the "beach"? What was the Hakh'hli, Hippolyta, going to tell the Earth's astronomers? Were any more Hakh'hli going to land from the ship? and when? and how many of them, exactly?

The answer to most of the questions was, really, "I don't know," but Sandy did his best, aware of Marguery Darp sitting quietly behind him on the platform. But some of the questions made Sandy swallow hard. "Where do you want to live?" for instance. He turned to look at Marguery for help, but she didn't offer any. "I mean," the reporter persisted, "will you stay here in Hudson City? Or, actually, are you going to stay on Earth, or will you go back with the Hakh'hli ship when they leave?" A hard question. Sandy had not until that moment considered the probability that indeed the Hakh'hli ship would leave some day for another star. Thinking about it made him furrow his brow. And then, came the question that was hardest of all, because it was the one he had least expected. "If you stay on Earth, what will you do?"

Sandy blinked into the lights. "Do?" he repeated uncertainly.

"I mean, what kind of job will you have?" the woman persisted.

Sandy thought hard for a moment. It had never occurred to him to think of it. Really, what could he do, that would constitute an Earthly "job"? He ventured, "I can pilot a Hakh'hli landing craft."

There was a faint chuckle all around. "But we don't have any Hakh'hli landing craft," the reporter pointed out. Then, at last, Marguery came to his rescue.

"Mr. Washington has any number of skills," she told the reporters, "but you have to give him time to decide how he wants to use them. Anyway, I think we've imposed on his good nature long enough for this session . . . and besides, I've promised to take him swimming this afternoon!"

In Marguery's little car, Sandy tried to tell her why that question was so hard. "I'm not used to having to decide things like that, Marguery. The Hakh'hli don't pick where they're going to live or what jobs they're going to do. The Major Seniors decide that for them."

She patted his hand reassuringly. "We do things differently here," she told him. Then she pulled the car into a parking space and turned to look at him before opening the door. "You are going to stay with us, aren't you?" she asked.

"Oh, yes, that's definitely what I want to do," Sandy said.

"And what about the Hakh'hli?" she pressed. "Are they going to go on with their voyage?"

He scratched his cheek. "I suppose they will," he said.

"You don't sound very sure," she pointed out.

He shook his head. "As far as I remember, I don't think that question ever came up. But what else would they do?"

Marguery nodded soberly. "That's the question, isn't it?

Anyway, here's the beach." She leaned back to reach a package in the rear seat of the car. "I picked up a bathing suit for you in the hotel shop; hope it fits."

"Thank you," he said absently, beginning to unbutton his shirt.

"But you don't undress here," she said quickly. "There are changing rooms for that. I'll meet you when you come out."

That presented another mystery to solve, but a simple enough one this time. He copied what he saw other men doing, aware that they were looking curiously at him, as well. He didn't think about it. His mind was filled with all the questions Marguery had raised and kept on raising.

There were plenty of questions. What was in very short supply was answers.

For twenty years everything had seemed clear to him: He would come back to Earth, as a gift from the Hakh'hli to the human race, and that would be that. He had never considered the possibility of an "after"—either for himself, or for the Hakh'hli ship.

When Sandy left the row of cubicles marked "Men" he was properly garbed in a pair of bathing trunks that did, just about, go around his considerable girth. Then the unanswerable questions vanished, because there was Marguery, waiting for him at the section marked "Women."

He swallowed hard. Marguery Darp in ordinary clothes had stirred his passions. Marguery Darp in a bikini took his breath away. She had a loose, thin, nearly transparent robe over her shoulders, but it hid no more than the bathing suit did. "But you're *beautiful*," he told her.

She laughed out loud. "Well," she said, "you're certainly good for a person's vanity, Sandy Washington." Then she frowned. "I forgot to get you a sun robe, so we'd better not stay out too long. Come on. Let's get our feet wet!"

And they did, and the experience of entering the water drove all other thoughts out of Sandy's mind.

He was aware that people were staring at him, but they were smiling encouragingly, taking pictures. He grinned happily at the other bathers. It was fun! To be almost immersed in a liquid that supported, or very nearly supported, his weight! It was like flying—except that when they waded out to waist depth, Marguery holding his hand, and he tried lifting his feet off the bottom under her tutelage, he sank.

He got his feet under him and came up, gasping and snorting and laughing. "I'm sorry," he said. "I'm afraid I can't swim at all. I think the average density of my body's a lot more than water."

She pursed her lips. "You're pretty solid, at that. Well, that's not a big problem. We'll get you a life preserver or something, if you want to try. And I'll be right with you, all right?"

"Maybe another time," he said cautiously. "Is it all right if we just, what do you call it, 'wade' for a while?"

"Whatever you want."

He splashed about, thoughtfully. "The water isn't very cold," he said.

She laughed. "It isn't always like this. You should have been here last winter. The whole bay was frozen over!"

Lysander gazed around, perplexed. "You mean 'ice'? Frozen water? But why?"

"Just because it was winter, of course," she said, and then had to explain what a "winter" was. "The old people never had freezes like this around here," she said with a certain amount of pride.

"But you said it was warmer now, not colder," Lysander said humbly. "How could warming up make the air colder?"

"That cold air around here last winter wasn't any colder than usual," she explained. "It was just in a different *place* than usual." She frowned up at the hot sun overhead. "But

back on the Hakh'hli ship. But if Marguery were with him—especially if she were wearing, as she certainly would be, that wonderful bikini bathing suit . . .

He smiled up at her. "I'd love it," he said.

She looked at him with an expression he couldn't read. "I hope you will," she said, and left it at that.

Chapter

· 15

At this time, half a century after Star Wars, there are 90,000 trackable objects in Low Earth Orbit. Most of them are too small to survive reentry when, at last, they fall to the surface of the Earth. So they aren't likely to do anyone on the surface much harm. They range from the size of a monkey wrench to the size of a beachball, and when they deorbit they are almost sure to burn up from the friction of the air. All they will contribute to anything on the surface is to add an undetectable additional patter to the steady infall of meteoric dust that has drifted onto the Earth for four and a half billion years. Seventy-two thousand of the Earth-orbiting objects are in that size range . . . but there are eighteen thousand others. These can't be ignored by the people below. They range in size from kitchen refrigerator to railroad locomotive; some are even bigger. And when one of these chunks of metal decays out of its orbit it will surely strike the ground—at least in fragments—at speeds of several miles a second, with an impact that can level buildings. Nor is that the worst. Unfortunately, some of these big ones still have internal power sources. The sources are generally nuclear, and when they strike it is not merely the kinetic energy of the fall that can kill.

The phone rang as Sandy was on his way to Polly's room to see if she was up yet. It was Marguery Darp. "Sandy? I'm in the lobby, but I thought I ought to tell you that the meeting has been postponed for an hour because of the deorbiting. Yes, it's supposed to happen on this orbit. You can go over with me to watch it at Lamont-Doherty, or I'll come back and get you later. Whichever you want."

"I'll be down in a few minutes," he told her, and knocked on Polly's door.

She was up, all right. She was squatting before the desk in her room, making notes. When he told her about the delay she gave a resentful twitch. "What fuss these Earth humans make about possible damage and loss of life to one city. They have thousands of cities! No, go if you wish, I will remain here."

"All right," Sandy said. "Polly? Do you remember when the ship was at Alpha Centauri?"

She grimaced in annoyance. "You have asked me that, Lysander. Why do you ask it again?"

"I don't remember it at all. Do you?"

She looked up at him. Then she did what he expected her to do. She continued making notes at her table for a moment. Then she gave a superior twitch. "This is no proper occasion to ask silly questions about ancient Hakh'hli history, Lysander. I am too busy and have not time for such things, since I must prepare my address. There will be some surprises in it; I will give them solution to their little problem."

"What solution do you mean?"

"You will hear when I give it," she said, weeping a small self-satisfied tear. She returned to her notes—all of them upside-down to Sandy as he stood—with one double-thumbed hand over the top of them so that he couldn't read what she was writing. As though there were any reason to keep them from him! How annoying she could be!

"You're not a Senior," he told her. "Don't treat me like a child. What problem are you talking about?"

"I am talking about this deorbiting question, which Earth human beings cannot deal with themselves," she said frostily. "I am talking, as well, about many other things of importance. For these things I have had complete instructions from ChinTekki-tho, in private."

"In private again!"

She emitted a faint, disdainful belch. "Yes. In private, since this is a matter for Hakh'hli and not Earth persons."

That took Sandy by surprise. "Cohort-mate! Am I not Hakh'hli?"

"Of course you are not Hakh'hli, Lysander," she said, patiently reasonable. "You are Lysander John William Washington, and if you are not Earth human you are nothing at all, are you? Now leave me, Lysander. I have much to do." She slapped her stubby tail against the carpeted floor for emphasis. Then, as he was almost at the door, she stopped him by adding, "However, your statement is almost correct and not entirely wrong, Lysander."

She was looking at him with malignant pleasure, and he had no idea what she was talking about. "What statement is that?" he asked.

"The statement that I am not myself Senior. I would add only one word to make that statement accurate. The word is, *yet*."

Sandy was quiet on the way to the meeting hall. He was tired of talking. Every conversation he had seemed to turn up questions he couldn't answer, and that those who could answer annoyingly wouldn't. Imagine Polly treating him like a child! Imagine her thinking she might some day be a Senior!—when it was she whose behavior was so childish!

He got out when Marguery parked the car, looking up at

the building they were about to enter. It was perched on the edge of the Palisades, tall and glass-walled, and the sign over its entrance gave its name:

LAMONT-DOHERTY SCIENCE CENTER

"Who were these Lamont and Doherty people?" he asked.

"It's just a name. This used to be a geology center, until they began moving other things into it out of New York City." She looked around, getting her bearings. They were almost alone in a large terrazzo-floored hall. The few others around were hurrying toward a flight of stairs. "They'll be watching the deorbit in the auditorium. This way—"

But as they climbed the stairs they heard a sudden outburst of laughter and cheers from the room they were going to. Marguery tugged him ahead. Over the stage was a great screen. It was a television picture, apparently taken from the deck of a ship—it seemed to sway disconcertingly, and sometimes Sandy could get glimpses of what looked like masts and antennae. But the picture wasn't of the ship. It was of the sky. It was filled with lancing lines of fire stabbing down, like a meteor shower.

Marguery caught the arm of a stranger standing next to her. "What's happening?" she demanded.

"It's down. It missed," he said, grinning. "It started reentry near Madagascar, and it was pretty well broken up twenty minutes ago. That's the last of it. It's just about all down now, and it's still way out in the Indian Ocean. Perth won't be touched."

"Thank God," she said sincerely. She turned and looked at Sandy almost with surprise, as though she had forgotten he was there. "Oh," she said. "Well, the show's over. Want to get a cup of coffee?"

"If you like," he said. And then, curiously, he asked, "Marguery? Did you have friends in Perth?"

"Friends? No. Not that I know of, anyway. I've never even been in Australia."

"But you looked worried," he pointed out.

She stared at him. "Jesus, Sandy, you say some funny things," she told him. "Of course I was worried. They're human beings in Australia, too, aren't they? And anyway, who knows where the next one might come down? It could be right on top of us!"

He thought of Polly's promise of mysterious surprises and wondered if he should mention them to Marguery. But he didn't really know what they were going to be. Instead, he said seriously. "The statistical chances of any particular person being hit are quite small, Marguery."

"Chances! Sandy, what do you know about it? You haven't lived your whole life under a slow-motion blitz. It makes you nervous. Come on, let's get the coffee." And then as he followed her back into the hallway she softened. "I'm sorry if I bit your head off, Sandy."

"Bit my head off?" And, while he was asking, he added, "And what's a 'blitz'?"

She laughed. "I keep forgetting you're new around here, Sandy," she said. She explained while they were waiting in line to get to the coffee table and then she said, "Look, we've still got some time now. Do you see what's down there?"

She was pointing to the end of the hallway. All he saw was a door marked *Sky Survey Monitors*. "What is it?" he asked. "It's what it says it is. It's where they keep tabs at this installation on everything in near-Earth orbit—including the Hakh'hli ship. Would you like to take a look at it?"

There were people working in the room, but Marguery talked to one of them in a low voice. The woman nodded and pointed to a work station. Marguery sat down, frowned over the keyboard for a moment, and then began to tap out codes.

"I guess an InterSec cop can do pretty much anything she wants," Sandy observed from behind her.

"She can if she has you with her," Marguery said, studying the screen. "Especially if she used to be in the astronaut corps herself. Here, take a look."

On the screen a picture began to form—a bright, small object like a soup can, far away.

"We're watching in the infrared," Marguery told him. "These are the same kind of telescopes that were tracking the reentry. You'll see a streak across the picture now and then. Pay no attention to them, they're just space junk in Low Earth Orbit, like the piece that just fell in the ocean. Here, I'll zoom in a little closer."

Sandy stared. It was the Hakh'hli ship, all right! It seemed to glow with its own light. It was stark and clear, and he had never seen it thus. Every detail showed. As it slowly turned to even the heating from the sun, even the little welt on its surface that had been the cradle of his own landing craft was clearly visible.

"I didn't know you could *see* the ship from Earth," he said numbly.

"Well, hell of course we can see you," she said, cross. "Do you think we're ignorant savages? We've been watching you for nearly two months."

"Two *months?*"

She made an impatient gesture. "Just because we can't *go* into space doesn't mean we don't keep *looking*. They found the gamma-ray emission weeks ago in a routine sweep. The source was obviously moving pretty fast, so naturally they followed up on it. The gammas came from your drive, I believe."

She touched a few more keys, and the image grew larger still. "Your ship was still out of the plane of the ecliptic, more than a billion miles out. We couldn't get decent optics at first. Then, after you came around the Sun, we followed you on radar."

"Radar?"

"Radio beams," she explained. "We bounce them off things and pick up the reflections."

"Ah," he said, gratified that one point at least was coming clear to him. He nodded. "ChinTekki-tho said there were transmissions from Earth, but the Hakh'hli didn't exactly know what they were. They didn't seem to carry information."

"Not on the way out, they don't," Marguery agreed, "but we could see you very clearly from the reflection. Then we could get you optically, too, at least in the infrared—your ship soaked up so much solar heat at perihelion that it sticks out like a light bulb. Sandy? Do you see those lumps on the side of the ship? What are they for?"

He peered at the screen. "Those five in a row, there? They're other landers. The ship has half-twelve of them, al-together—you can see that landing craft is gone. That was ours." Then he glared at her. "You watched us coming?"

"Of course we did. Wouldn't you?" she asked patiently. "We kept a pretty close eye on you. We were listening on all frequencies, too, to see if you would send a signal to let us know who you were. You didn't, though."

"Well," Sandy apologized, "the Major Seniors weren't sure of what kind of people you were, you know."

She shrugged. "We weren't sure of you, either. As soon as you launched the lander we tracked its landing orbit. You didn't have to wander around in the rain, Sandy. If you had just stayed put, we would have come to you as soon as the storm was over."

"But why didn't you tell us?"

"Well, I'm telling you now." Then, unwillingly, she added, "The fact is that I wasn't supposed to, before. It's just been cleared."

"I see," Sandy said bitterly. "You are now permitted to share some truths with me. But not all, I suppose?" She scowled at him, not answering. "So besides being my jailer,

183

now you are permitted to give out certain little crumbs of information, to see what I'll make of them?"

"I'm not your *jailer*, Sandy!"

"Then what do you call it?"

"The term," she said primly, "is 'escort.'"

"But you're a policeman. Woman, I mean."

"InterSec is not *police*. Not exactly police, anyway. Oh, hell," she flared, "what do you expect? It was just a precaution. Naturally we have to make sure of what we're getting into, so we—" She stopped. She glanced at the ceiling, then said stubbornly, "So we keep an eye on you. Just as you did on us." She changed the subject. "Do you want some more coffee?"

"Is that what my 'escort' takes me to do next?" he asked bitterly. "Then what am I required to do after that to satisfy your natural concern?"

She gave him a look he couldn't translate. "That's up to you," she said.

"Oh, but surely you have instructions," he persisted.

She stared into space for a moment. Then she sighed and looked at her watch. "It's almost time for Polly to speak," she said.

"Then, of course, we have to go there, don't we? To carry out your instructions for me?"

She didn't answer that. He turned to leave, but she put a hand on his arm. She glanced at the other people in the room before she spoke. "Sandy," she said, almost whispering. "You told me you might like to visit the old New York City. We can do that this afternoon, if you want to."

The tone of her voice was odd, but Sandy was not mollified. "Of course," he snarled. "I will want to do exactly what you say. What choice do I have, after all?"

Polly was late. Nearly everyone in the audience was already seated when she made her entrance, *splatsplatting* down the center aisle in the long, galumphing Hakh'hli strides, with Hamilton Boyle grimly keeping up beside her. He lost her when they got to the first row. Boyle pointed politely to the stairs that led up to the side of the stage, but Polly was having none of that. As Boyle turned toward the steps Polly gave him a disdainful look. Then she launched herself in an easy jump onto the platform. By the time he got to her she was already squatting before the podium, studying her notes.

There was a faint titter from the audience.

It was a typically Polly sort of thing to do—no, Sandy corrected himself, a typically Hakh'hli thing. Polly looked up, acknowledging the chuckle with a pleased tear. From Sandy's seat in the first row, with human beings all around, he looked at her through Earthly eyes, and he had no doubt that to them she looked comical.

While Hamilton Boyle introduced her, Polly preened herself. She looked up, twitching in annoyance, as Boyle pressed a button and a screen descended behind them, and when he finished by saying, "So our distinguished guest will show us some of the astronomical records her people have acquired in their long voyage," she turned on him.

"Must I?" she demanded.

Boyle looked astonished. "But I thought you wanted to. That's what you were invited here for," he reminded her.

She twitched irritably. "Oh, very well. Let's get that part over with, then. Is this the picture control?" Impatiently she allowed Boyle to show her how to use it, then snatched it away from him. "All right, have the lights turned out," she ordered, craning her neck to see the screen. Before the room was fully dark she began clicking rapidly. "These are some of your nearby stars," she said, as the pictures flicked by, half a second apart. "This first series is what you call Gamma Cephei and its two planets—not very interesting; they are what you call 'brown dwarf' objects, of no use to anyone. We were leaving the Gamma Cephei system en route to what you call Alpha Centauri when we detected your radio signals and passed here, some fifty of your years ago. Now, this is Alpha Centauri. It does not have any sizeable well-formed planets, only a great many objects which most resemble comets or asteroids. Here they are. Now we come to your own system—why are you interrupting me, Boyle?"

The InterSec man had put a hand on her forearm. He said politely, "Don't you think you could go a little slower?"

"What for? All these pictures now are in your files, and I have more important things to get to. This is your Sun, and here are some of your planets—" Sandy blinked. The pictures were coming faster than he could take them in, and he could hear people grumbling around him. Polly paid no attention. "Earth, Venus, Mercury, Jupiter, Saturn, Neptune, Mars. The interesting part to you, I suppose, is that these are mostly polar views—taken from north of the ecliptic as we came in from Gamma Cephei, south of it on our trip to Alpha Centauri. There are many other pictures, of course, which will be made available to you later. That is enough on that subject. Lights!" she called peremptorily, and gazed complacently out at the muttering audience as the overheads went on again.

"Now," she said, "let me get to the more important part of what I have to say today." She broke off, peering at a man near Sandy, who had his hand up. "Do you want something?" she asked.

"I just want to know if we'll have a chance to ask questions," the astronomer called.

"I suppose so, but not until I have finished. Please pay full attention now, all of you. I have been instructed by my superior, ChinTekki-tho, to inform you that you should begin construction of a magnetic-impulse thruster—what you call a 'railgun'—at once. We have identified two suitable sites. One is on the island you call Bora Bora, the other is the peak you call Mount Kilimanjaro in Africa. Our specialists are now completing detailed plans for construction, which will be transmitted to you shortly, and we are prepared to land two teams of specialists, one for each thruster, to supervise the construction and then the operation of the machines. The most important use of the thrusters will be to launch needed raw materials to replenish the stores of our interstellar ship, but ChinTekki-tho has decided that, as a special favor, several of the first launches will be to put self-propelled objects into Low Earth Orbit. These will be used to collide with, and thus decelerate, some of the objects that are likely to deorbit in the near future, so that they can be caused to descend in whatever parts of their orbit you think least dangerous to any of your installations or people. Thus," she finished triumphantly, "we have solved one of your great problems for you. Now you may ask questions if you wish to—but, please," she added, glancing at her watch, "not for very long, as it is nearly time for my midday meal."

To Sandy's surprise, there weren't any immediate questions. The audience was silent. It surprised Polly, too; she was twitching resentfully as she waited. Then at last she pointed to a man midway back. "Ask," she ordered.

"I was simply wondering why you didn't photograph Uranus and Pluto?" he called.

Polly snorted in displeasure. "Why don't you ask about the more important things I have said? We simply did not happen to observe Uranus and Pluto."

"But if you missed them," the astronomer persisted, "how do you know there weren't some you missed at the other stars?"

"We did not 'miss' any planets," she corrected him coldly. "We did not concern ourselves with possible objects that would be of no use to us, because they were too far from their sun. Of course, there are many more pictures. We Hakh'hli have visited some sixty-five stellar systems in this journey, and of course we have records of many other visitations by other ships."

Another astronomer called, "Are you still getting them?"

"You mean reports from other ships?" Polly hesitated, then replied unwillingly, "Not at present."

"How about the planets of your own original system?"

"We have no pictures to show of our own planets. Our ancestors knew it quite well. They had no need of photographs to remind them."

"Can you at least identify your own star from our catalogues? You said it's only eight hundred and fifty light-years away; if it's as bright as the Sun, it should be at least a fourteenth or fifteenth magnitude object, and we've got all of them on our atlases."

Polly hesitated. "It can be identified," she said.

"By you?"

Unwillingly, she said, "Not necessarily by me, at present."

"You mean you're lost, don't you?"

"We are not *lost*! It is simply that we have not yet reestablished contact with the home star, because of the great distance involved—as even you should know, to communicate over a distance of eight hundred light-years takes sixteen hundred of your years for a message to be sent and an answer received. When we have accomplished our mission we will notify the home planets."

"What is your mission, exactly?"

She paused, then flared up. "Our mission is to explore and learn! Have you no better questions to ask than this?"

"Have you no better pictures than this?" an astronomer demanded. "These are just optical-band photographs! Don't you have infrared, ultraviolet, X-ray, gamma ray observations to go with them?"

"It is not our custom," Polly said sharply. She was obviously beginning to get angry. "Are not any of you going to ask questions about the magnetic launchers?"

There was a pause, then Hamilton Boyle leaned forward

to the microphone. "I have one," he said. "These plans you're going to give us. Have you ever built a launcher from them?"

"I myself? Of course not."

"Or anyone on your ship?"

"Not recently, no," she conceded.

"So how do you know they'll work?"

She glared at him, divided between astonishment and anger. "They are *Hakh'hli* plans," she explained. "They have been approved by the Major Seniors! Of course they'll work. Aren't there any *sensible* questions?"

When it appeared there were not, Polly stormed off to her midday meal, refusing Hamilton Boyle's offer to accompany her. As the meeting broke up, Boyle caught up with Marguery and Sandy. "Got any plans for lunch?" he asked amiably.

Marguery answered for both them. "We're going to explore New York," she said. "I think we'll just get some sandwiches and eat them on the way."

Boyle nodded, gazing shrewdly at Sandy. "Your friend wasn't happy with us, I'm afraid," he offered.

Sandy decided not to mention that Polly was seldom happy. "I think she was surprised that no one seemed to want to talk about the railgun offer."

"Oh?" Boyle said, raising his eyebrows. "Was that what it was, an offer? It sounded like marching orders to me."

"That's just her way, probably," Sandy said.

Boyle nodded. "Do you think it's a good idea?" he asked.

Sandy looked at him in surprise. "Of course it's a good idea. The Major Seniors wouldn't approve it if it wasn't. You can put thousands of capsules into orbit, very cheaply. And what about kicking some of that garbage out of orbit in safe areas? Don't you want to save your cities from the kind of thing that almost happened to Perth?"

Boyle sighed. "Yes," he said meditatively. "That certainly sounds very good, shoving the trash around so that it will miss cities. It's the other side of that coin I'm thinking about."

"I don't understand," Sandy said.

Boyle shrugged. "Well, if you can make an object deorbit to miss a city," he said, "don't you think it would be just as easy to make it hit one?"

Chapter
◆ 16

The four lasting legacies of the twentieth century are radionuclides, atmospheric gases, toxic chemicals, and plastics— and plastics is the greatest of these. Ten billion transitory hamburgers are long since digested, excreted, and gone; but they have left ten billion immortal Styrofoam boxes behind. Plastics are generally light enough to float in water. So when nylon fishing nets are lost overboard by trawlers they drift eternally through the seas and kill fish as long as they hold together, which is forever. Coca-Cola jugs and shampoo bottles wind up in the oceans and bob onto all the beaches of the world. The Rockies may tumble, Gibraltar may crumble, but a plastic six-pack container will never die. Like diamonds, plastics are forever. For some members of the animal kingdom, this is good news. Jellyfish, for instance, benefit from the situation. The animals that feed on jellyfish are likely to eat a drifting sandwich bag by mistake and die of it, so the jellyfish survive uneaten and prosper. But it is bad news for seals, diving birds, turtles, fish . . . and people.

♦

On the trip across the wide Hudson River to old New York Marguery was curiously silent and detached. Sandy hardly noticed. He was thinking hard himself—not, for a wonder, about whether he would get seasick again, although the river was rough at first, the river current flowing south to collide with the tide sweeping in to the north, but about what Hamilton Boyle had said.

"Would you like another sandwich?" Marguery asked, delving into the box she had brought.

Sandy saw that he still had almost all of the first one in his hand. "Not right now. Marguery? Do you think the Hakh'hli would do anything like that?"

"Blast our cities? I don't know, Sandy. Do you?"

"No! It's totally against all their principles, I'm almost certain."

She nodded, but all she said was, "Finish your sandwich."

Once they were out of the currents of the Hudson it was more like the pleasure trip it was supposed to be. The little inertial-drive motor purred reassuringly as they glided to a landing on what Marguery said was West 34th Street.

There wasn't a "shore" to land on. The old shore was underwater. Buildings were on every side, and with them breaking the force of waves and current the water was placid. Often it was even so clear that, peering over the side, Sandy could see the bottom—streets, with abandoned cars and trucks and huge things Marguery told him were city buses.

They beached the little boat between two tall buildings, and the two of them pulled it up past the high tide mark. The sidewalk was littered with brightly colored scraps of plastic brought up by waves. When Marguery explained casually that they were left-over garbage from the old days, Sandy looked back at the water with distaste. "Do you actually 'swim' in garbage?" he asked.

"Oh, the biological stuff is gone long ago," she assured

him. "There's nothing in the water that'll make you sick. Not here, anyway. If you went a little farther south there are real problems—when the old nuclear power plants went underwater all sorts of nasty stuff soaked out—but that's there. Now, do you want to go up to the top of that building?"

Sandy squinted at what she was pointing at, shrugging out of the funny orange "life preserver" Marguery had made him wear. "What is it?"

"It's the Empire State Building," she said shortly. "From the top of it you can see all around. Well?"

He stepped back as a gentle wave from the river came close to his shoes. "Oh, sure," he said sourly. "We're having fun, right."

It was almost true. If it hadn't been for his injured feelings it would have been wholly true, because certainly what they were doing and seeing was exactly the sort of thing he had dreamed of all his young life. He was right in the heart of the Big Apple! It wasn't at all the way he had expected it to be, to be sure, but there it was, all around him. Overhead were blue sky and towering white clouds; all around them were the windows and facades of the buildings that had made Manhattan the first skyscraper city.

They were not alone. Back on the river, just a block away, other little boats, inertial driven like their own or puffing steam from their purring little hydrogen motors, were skittering about, filled with people on errands he could not guess. There was a great barge moored stem and stern between two buildings at the river's edge, and cranes were lowering masses of objects into it: spaghetti strands of cable, office machines, lighting fixtures.

"They're mining," Marguery said briefly. "These buildings are full of useful things, and it's all going to go to waste here if the water gets any higher. Which it probably will . . . The amount of copper those old people used! So we just take what we want while we can."

"It looks dangerous," Sandy offered, watching two men in a building far over his head leaning out to guide a descending bundle of what seemed to be metal rods.

"Well, it is, a little," Marguery said. "A lot of those buildings are rotten at their foundations—the water has eaten them away. Every once in a while one falls. But you don't have to worry about the Empire State. It was built for the ages!"

Staring up at it, with his head thrown back until his neck hurt, Sandy wasn't as much concerned about the building's falling down as he was about getting up to the top of it. He didn't think it was much of a worry for himself; the muscles that had grown up on the Hakh'hli ship were ready enough to lift him a mere thousand feet or so. He wondered if Marguery could make it. When they entered there were water stains in the lobby. When he pointed them out Marguery nodded somberly. "When there's bad weather you can get storm surges all the way in here," she told him. "They're getting worse, too; I guess we haven't finished with the warmup. Come on!"

It turned out they didn't have to climb all the way to the top of the Empire State Building. From the lobby they had four flights of stairs to go, passing stories filled with stacked materials and a whole floor of buzzing, whining electrical generators, hydrogen fueled and providing power to the floors above. There wasn't any external electrical power in most of the city, Marguery explained, because the underground mains were now also underwater. But because of the generators they were able to ride in a comfortable elevator to the observation platform eight-odd stories up.

No one else was there, and even if they had had to climb, the view would have been worth it. In spite of himself, Sandy found that he was entranced. He was gazing down at the whole human world! There was Hudson City to the west and north, across the wide span of river and bay; there was the almost-unbroken sweep of ocean to the south and east, punctuated with the few islands that had been heaped up in Brooklyn and Queens by the glacial drift ages earlier; there were the surviving lesser towers of old New York City, and the greater pair at what had once been the tip of the island. And there—he could see it plainly—sticking up from the middle of the great sweep of the bay was the body and upraised lamp of that most famous of heroic sculptures, the Statue of Liberty.

He said happily, "It's great up here!"

Marguery didn't answer. She was looking at a fixture in the ceiling, and when she looked back at him her gaze was clouded.

"Marguery?" he ventured.

She shook herself and glanced around. They were still alone on the old observation deck, though they could hear the hammering of a salvage crew only a floor or two below. She glanced at the fixture in the ceiling and then she seemed to make her mind up—about something, though Sandy could not tell what. She turned to him with an unexpectedly warm smile.

"Yes," she said. "It's really nice to be alone, isn't it?"

Surprise made him scowl at her. The woman almost seemed to be giving him some sort of sexual signal! He cursed internally at the baffling rites of the human libido. What was he supposed to do? Should he throw his arms around her and do *that* right here, on the sun-drenched observation platform of the skyscraper, with every chance that someone would step out of that elevator at any moment?

It almost seemed that he was. She had moved a step closer to him, still smiling. She had even bent her head toward him, so that her lips were no more than an inch or two above his own.

Angrily Sandy lifted his face to her and reached out for her. To his great astonishment, though she allowed his arms to circle her and even put her own around his neck, she turned her face away. She nuzzled his ear. When he tried to twist his face to hers she held tight.

He realized she was whispering to him.

It was only her breath that told him that; she was whispering into the wrong ear. He pulled back and said, "That's the wrong one. The hearing aid is on the other side."

She scowled, then quickly put the smile back on her face. She moved her lips closer to the good ear, and whispered again.

"Sandy. Don't say anything. This is important. I'm going to ask you if you want to do something. Just say yes, and then we'll do it. And *don't argue*."

He pulled away, perplexed, and was even more perplexed to see that she was smiling at him in a way even more overtly inviting than before.

"Ah, Sandy," she sighed, caressing the back of his neck, "this place isn't quite perfect, is it? Listen, hon. I know a neat place downtown—you'll have to swim to get there, but we can work that out. What do you say? Would you like to find a more private spot, so you and I can get together?"

And she winked at him.

Sandy exhaled a deep sigh. Whatever was going on, it was sure to be interesting. "You bet," he said, and then added, "Hon."

Chapter
◆ 17

New York City's central island of Manhattan does not have many hills. It used to have them, long ago. The English colonists and the Dutch before them, the Indians who were there first of all—they all spoke of hills, valleys, ridges, wide streams, and ponds big enough to sail on. Only vestiges have remained of any of these. When New Yorkers began the task of covering their island with concrete, they didn't want any grades steeper than a horse could pull a wagonload of bricks—or, later, than an eighteen-wheeler tractor could pull twenty tons of steel girders. So they lopped off the tops of all the hills, and they filled all the ravines, and they piped all the streams into sewers underground. They did not count on what might happen to that flattened island when the carbon-dioxide warmup began. When it happened, their descendants tried diking the island to keep the rising waters out. But storms overrun dikes when the storms are big enough . . . and the storms of the Age of Warmup are definitely big enough.

◆

"I should have brought your bathing suit," Marguery sighed when Sandy came out from behind the shelter on the building roof in only his bright green underwear. She inspected him absently. Her mood was still curiously detached, almost somber—considering, Sandy thought resentfully, that she had all but promised that they were going to do *it*. She concluded, "I guess you look all right. Nobody's here to see, anyway. Here, put these on."

He took the inflated rubber thing she handed him and managed to squeeze his head through the hole, tying the tabs at his waist as ordered. They were on the roof of a low building—the water level was only feet below. He could not help being distracted as he saw Marguery peel off her slacks. She had her bikini bathing suit on underneath her other clothes and looked quite ready for anything.

Sandy was a long way from ready—for anything. All this equipment was bafflingly new. There was not just the air-filled rubber thing to get on, there was a backpack tank to strap into place, and a mask to try to learn to breathe through, and weights to hang on his belt for what Marguery called "neutral buoyancy." Sandy scowled. "Can't we just let a little of the air out?" he asked.

"I don't want to drown you. No," she said shortly. "Let's get in the water. We really shouldn't stay exposed to the sun this far south."

She sat on the edge of the roof and eased herself over, floating easily in the water just below him. "Well?" she called, waiting.

Sandy took a deep breath and followed her example.

He didn't do it as rapidly as she. He took a firm grip on the parapet and lowered himself, inch by inch, into the water. As soon as his legs were in he gasped in astonishment; it was *cold*. Well, not really cold, he conceded; it wasn't really unpleasant, except at the first unprecedented shock. But it was water rather than air that his legs were in, far quicker than any gases at soaking heat out of his body.

If Marguery Darp could stand it, he could. Grimly Sandy lowered the rest of his body into the unfamiliar medium. It took an effort of will to make his fingers release the edge of the wall.

Then he was floating.

It was a queer sensation. It was a dozen different queer sensations, none of them ever experienced before. When he moved his arms through the water his body moved in the other direction—just like the main drive engines on the interstellar ship; action and reaction held here, too! The first chill disappeared as his skin got used to the surrounding liquid. It felt, actually, rather nice. When he ducked his face under the water experimentally, some got into his mouth; it was salty, but not at all unpleasant.

He called to Marguery, floating watchfully a yard away, "I think I like it!"

"Let's get your weights adjusted," she said.

That didn't take long. Marguery had made a good guess, and only two small ones needed to be added to counteract the buoyancy of his floats, so that his whole body, flesh, floats, tanks, weights, and all, added up to just about the density of the water he was in.

Then there was the necessity of learning to breathe out through his nose and in through the rubber tube held in his mouth. Sandy choked and strangled half a dozen times before he finally got the hang of the breathing procedures.

Then he peered down into the water. It was less clear here than it had been in midtown, or perhaps simply deeper. "What's down there?" he asked.

"You'll see. Nothing to worry about. There's not much that can hurt you around here, outside of the occasional shark."

"*Shark?*" Sandy gasped.

"They won't bother us," she promised. "You just keep an eye on the little fish; as long as you see them, there aren't any sharks around."

Sandy wanted to believe her. He tried to believe her, but he couldn't help ducking his head underwater to see if some great, gray, mean thing was down there.

She stopped him. "Don't go all the way under yet." She meditated for a moment, then said, "I guess you're as ready as you're going to be. Is that hearing-aid thing of yours waterproof?"

Sandy considered. "I don't think so."

"Then give it to me," she ordered. "Will you be able to hear me at all with it out?"

Glumly, he said, "No."

"Then, when I give you the sign, spit on your faceplate like this—" She demonstrated. "—and follow me down." She carefully stowed the little button in a pocket in her scuba gear, sealed the pocket, and gave Sandy a meager smile. She said something. He knew she was saying something because he could see her lips move, but he didn't hear a sound.

"What?" he bellowed.

She frowned, shrugged, and pointed to the face mask. When he followed her example and spat in it before pulling it on, she looked as though she were sighing, but only waved to him and fell backward into the water beside him.

And they were on their way down, into the dimness of the Wall Street underwater canyon.

He clung to one of Marguery's heels, letting himself be towed as he stared at marvels. He almost forgot to breathe properly and found himself coughing and gagging before he got the procedure right. But it was worth it!

At street level there were abandoned cars, tossed at crazy angles by the tides. It was twilight there, the sunlight dwindling, but Sandy could pick out objects: a fire hydrant, a bent bicycle frame, a garishly painted cart on which the words "PRETZELS • FRESH JUICE • TOFU" were still visible.

Marguery tapped his shoulder, pointing to a great doorway. Once a revolving door had been the way of entrance, but its wings were folded back. She swam inside, towing Sandy.

They were swimming through what seemed to have been one of those places that the humans called a "bank." Inside, things became both easier and more difficult. Easier because there were railings and counters to cling to, so that Sandy's amateurish efforts at swimming weren't needed. Harder because there was no sunlight at all inside the great room, only diffuse, pale light from outside.

Marguery didn't seem to mind. She did something to an object on a band around her head, and a beam of light sprang out. Then she swam ahead, beckoning Sandy to follow, right through the doors of a vault. Sandy's eyes began to compensate, and he could see that inside were cabinets, their doors broken and hanging loose, all empty. At the far end of the vault was a spidery spiral staircase. Marguery pulled herself up it, Sandy following; and at the top of the staircase—

Marguery wasn't swimming any more. She was walking up the staircase. The water level stopped just before the ceiling of the vault, and the staircase opened into a dark chamber that was not flooded.

When Sandy poked his head out of the water to follow her he saw that she had flipped her breathing mask off. Wondering, he followed her example and found that he was in a room with couches and chairs—all moldering, with a not wholly unpleasant smell of damp.

Marguery was moving around, touching things, the beam of her headlamp picking out walls, ceiling, fixtures—a pole light went on, and they were in a chamber with its own bubble of air trapped under the surface of the flood. She was speaking to him over her shoulder, as he saw when the light came on, but he couldn't hear anything. "I . . . can't . . . hear . . . you," he said.

She paused and opened the pouch on her belt. She unwrapped the little hearing-aid button, rubbed it dry on a cloth over the table, and handed it to him. As soon as he had screwed it into his ear she said, "Do you like this place?"

He looked around. "What is it?"

"It was where the old people kept their valuables. It's what they call safe-deposit boxes." She waved at the walls lined with little doors, most of them open. "They kept money here, and jewels, and their wills, and their divorce papers, or anything they wanted to make sure wouldn't get lost. Then they'd come in here and go into one of those little rooms and clip their coupons, or whatever."

"What is 'clip their coupons'?"

She laughed. "Well, that's a long story. They all had 'stock' and 'bonds'—the rich people did, the kind that used a place like this—and so if they had money it made more money for them, only every once in a while they had to cut off a piece of one of the 'bond' certificates and mail it in and then they would get the money." While she was talking she was taking towels off a rack, tossing one to Sandy, and drying her hair with another. The towel was musty, but dryer than his body. He found himself shivering. Marguery noticed. "Ah, wait a minute," she said. She touched another switch, and a ring of orange-red light began to glow in a round metal reflector on the floor. "It's always wet in here," she said, "but I like it anyway. The electric heater will dry us out a little. Every once in a while I have to recharge the batteries, but they're good for a few hours yet."

"Why do you need 'batteries'?"

"There isn't any other electrical power down here, of course. There isn't any communication with the outside world at all."

Sandy sat down on the leather couch, testing it to make sure it would support his weight. It creaked, but it was a sturdy piece of furniture. He looked around curiously. "What do you use this place for?"

She hesitated. "Well," she said slowly, "mostly it's just a place I use to get away to." She looked at him for a moment.

tauri?" He looked both baffled and resentful, but finally said, "To Polly, yes. She said to talk to ChinTekki-tho, but I didn't do that."

"Ah." Marguery looked pleased. "Why didn't you?"

The good after-making-love feeling was dissipating, and Sandy began to feel belligerent. "Do I have to have a reason why not? I just didn't, that's all."

She nodded, gratified. "I was hoping you wouldn't, Sandy."

He said logically, "If you didn't want me to tell them, why didn't you say so?"

"I wanted to see if you'd do it by yourself. Because—" She hesitated, shifting position uncomfortably, and then finished reluctantly, "Because there's something else I wanted to talk to you about."

He looked at her with concern. All he knew about love-making suggested that she should have been relaxed and happy now, but she seemed both ill at ease and uncomfortable. "Are you all right?" he demanded.

"Of course I'm all right! Why wouldn't I be all right? It's just—" She grinned at him. "Maybe it's just that you're a little stronger than I'm used to, you know what I'm saying?"

Sandy accepted that to be a compliment and allowed himself to preen a bit. But the good feeling didn't last. He said, aggrieved, "You didn't really have to spy, you know. You could have just asked."

"We did ask, Sandy. We're still asking. *I'm* asking. But what if there was something the Hakh'hli didn't want to answer?"

Sandy shrugged. She said, her tone wheedling, almost as though she were asking to be forgiven, "So we simply took normal precautions. We've bugged your rooms, wherever you were. We've taped everything you've said. We've listened in on the landing craft's transmissions to the ship—"

Sandy looked at her, amazed. "I didn't know you could do that."

"As a matter of fact, we almost couldn't. That's some tight beam the Hakh'hli've got. We can't pick it up more than a mile from the lander, but we've got our own ground stations right there. And just to make sure we have a high-altitude aircraft orbiting overhead to hear what the lander is sending back."

"But it's in Hakh'hli!"

"It's in Hakh'hli, right," she agreed grimly. "That makes it tough. We've picked up some words from you, and we've got a whole bunch of linguistics people analyzing and correlating. We can't read it all. Just enough to be worrying." She peered at him. "We *have* to, don't you understand? Wouldn't the Hakh'hli have done the same thing?"

Sandy remembered the hundreds of Hakh'hli who did nothing else—who, for half a century, had done nothing but to pore over every scrap of data from Earth's broadcasts, trying to penetrate every hidden part of human activities. "Well, maybe so," he said reluctantly. "It doesn't matter. You're not going to find out anything bad."

"We're not?" Marguery said sadly.

He stopped short, struck by her tone. "What are you trying to say?" he demanded.

She said unhappily, "Start with your mother. That picture Ham Boyle borrowed from you."

"What about it?"

"Well—" She hesitated. "Do you remember your mother at all?"

"No. I told you that. She died when I was born."

"But you did have that picture of her. Well, Ham put it on television to see if anyone would recognize it. A lot of people did. But that picture isn't of an astronaut, Sandy. It's of a movie actress from the last century; her name was Marilyn Monroe."

"That's *impossible!*" Sandy shouted.

"It's true, Sandy. And there's more. You said she and your

208

father were American astronauts, and they were stuck out in space because of the war."

"I said that, yes. It's true!"

She sighed. "Sandy," she said, "it didn't happen that way. InterSec has checked the records really carefully. Every space flight was recorded, even during the war. We know for a fact that there weren't any manned American rockets in space at the time of the war."

"But," Sandy said reasonably, "there must have been. That's where the Hakh'hli found my parents."

She shook her head. "The records show that there was one spacecraft that was out at the time," she said. "Just one. It was a Mars orbiter. They had sent a probe down to the surface of the planet, and they were waiting for it to come back with samples. But it wasn't American. It was Russian."

He gaped at her. "Russian? Oh, no. That has to be wrong. The Hakh'hli told me my parents were *American*. The Major Seniors wouldn't make a mistake like that. I mean, by the time the big ship got here the Hakh'hli had been monitoring broadcasts for fifty years. They'd know the difference."

"That's true," Marguery agreed.

"So my parents couldn't've been Russian!"

"Well," she said sadly, "I would tend to agree with you about that. That was the only Russian spacecraft out, and it had only two people in it. I don't see how they could have been your parents, though, because InterSec has double-checked the records and the cosmonauts were both men."

Chapter
⋅ 18

The countries of Earth, which are now broken up into commonwealths too tiny to be called "countries" anymore, try as much as they can to eliminate governmental power. Especially international power. They know they can't get along without any at all, though. They do need some sort of network to deal with criminals—thieves, murderers, people who damage the peace and security of others in any way—who are quite capable of flitting from one commonwealth to another. (As everyone is, since there are no such things as "passports" or "visas.") There aren't as many criminals as there used to be, even considered as a percentage of the much diminished world population. But they are there, and they need to be dealt with. That's what InterSec is designed to do. What it is not designed to do is keep track of alien visitors from space . . . but who else is there to do it?

"InterSec's records are wrong!" Sandy shouted. "That's impossible."

Marguery didn't answer. She looked very tired. She only shook her head.

"But if they're right—what am I?" he howled.

Marguery took the question at face value and answered it. "You're a man," she said positively. "It also happens that you're a man I like very much—couldn't you tell that?"

"But—"

"But we don't know how you got to be a man, exactly," she agreed. "Right. That doesn't change anything, does it?" She paused to cough. "I really don't feel so well," she said reflectively.

He wasn't even listening. "I can't believe what you said about my mother," he told her somberly.

Marguery shrugged and made an effort to be responsive. "I'm really tired," she said apologetically. "It's been a pretty tough few days—spending all your waking hours with you, then as soon as you're tucked in I have to go for briefing and debriefing. Find out everything else that's been going on, so I'll know what to ask you about." She shook her head, and then added, "Maybe that's why I'm acting this way. I can't believe what I've been doing. I'm not in the habit of making love with the suspects I'm surveilling."

"*Suspects!*"

"Well," she said reasonably, "people that I'm assigned to keep an eye on. I didn't mean for the love-making part to happen, Sandy. Ham's going to be really ticked off."

"That's none of his business!" Sandy barked.

"Sandy, hon. *Everything* is InterSec's business." She shook her head, looking exhausted and worn.

Sandy's heart melted. "Oh, Marguery," he wailed, and reached out blindly toward her. They held each other for a moment, while Sandy shuddered and shook . . . until the tactile quality of the smooth, soft female flesh he was touching began to suggest possibilities to him, and he altered his grip.

Marguery fended him off, smiling wanly. "Not this time,

hon. You're almost too much, you know? You've got me sore."

She released him suddenly to sneeze. "Actually, Sandy," she said in the tone of someone making a not agreeable discovery, "I don't feel particularly well for some reason."

Sandy saw with concern that her lips were swollen. He scowled, perplexed. He had not expected anything like this. He knew that postcoital Hakh'hli were uniformly euphoric. Why weren't Earth humans? Could they be this different? And if they were so different, if this sort of thing were normal, why in the world did they *do* it?

She had gotten back into her bathing suit and was wrapping both the damp towels around her, sitting as close to the electric heater as she could. All the same, she was shivering. She tried to smile at Sandy. She said, "It would probably be a good idea for us to get out of here. But this is the only chance we've had to talk in private. And there's more."

His heart sank. "What more?" he asked. What more could there possibly be?

"Oh, I don't mean anything else about you, hon," she said, trying to reassure. "There are some things that the Hakh'hli haven't told us, and we don't know what to make of them. The bugs, for instance."

"I don't know anything about bugs," he said positively.

She explained. "The people at the lander have caught three new insects—well, technically they're not insects, they say. Bugs, anyway. They're all the same, and the entomologists say they're not related to any Earthly species at all. And one of them was seen coming out of the lander when one of the Hakh'hli was standing in the doorway."

"What do they look like?"

She made a restless gesture. "Big as my thumb," she said. "They fly."

"Oh," said Sandy, enlightened and reassured. "I bet I know what they are. They're just hawkbees. They're harmless. Except to other bugs, I mean. A few got trapped in the lander with us, but you don't have to worry about them. There wasn't any queen with them, and so all we had were sterile males."

She didn't answer at first. He looked at her with concern. She was breathing hard, and her eyes were closed. Suddenly, without opening her eyes, she giggled. "Sterile males, hey? Remind you of anything?"

He frowned at her. "What are you talking about?" he demanded harshly. But she wasn't listening to him. She was talking. At least, it seemed she thought she was talking, because her lips were moving and there were faint sounds. But even with his hearing aid almost touching her mouth Sandy could make out no coherent words.

Sandy knew what the word "delirious" meant. It was what people were in hospital beds, while the policeman was begging them to name their murderer; but he had had no previous experience of it at first hand.

It seemed probable that she should be gotten to medical attention as quickly as possible. But how?

There was no telephone in the room. There was no doorway that opened to the surface. There was no hope that Marguery could lead them back through the underwater passages to safety—even if they still had two air tanks.

Which they didn't.

When he touched her again, Marguery's skin was hot, and she was breathing very raggedly. Worse than that, one of her eyes was no longer closed; it was halfway open, but the pupil had rolled up under the lid so that she looked . . . she looked . . . the only word Sandy could find to fit the case was "dead." And if she hadn't been breathing so raggedly he might have believed that to be true.

She had to be gotten out of there!

There wasn't any question about it. What she needed was medical help, and Sandy couldn't supply it himself.

With only one air tank, what could he do? Not to mention the fact that he couldn't swim.

It was impossible; but it was also absolutely necessary, and so, grimly, Sandy fitted the mask over the unconscious, groaning woman and clumsily attached the one filled air tank. He closed his eyes, visualizing the path they had traced on entering. Down the spiral staircase. Across the bank floor. Out into the open water, then up to the surface.

It had, he thought, taken no more than five or ten minutes for them to enter in the first place. That was with Marguery in command, and Marguery knew what she was doing; so call it fifteen for him to make it out. Well, then. He could hold his breath for, probably, three minutes—call it two and a half to be safe. That meant he needed to empty his lungs and fill them again half a dozen times.

Was that possible?

The only way to find out was to try. Holding his breath, he slipped his hand under the mask on Marguery's unconscious face and pulled the mask away. His great hand covered her mouth and nose easily as he exhaled all the air his lungs would surrender. His other hand put the mask over his own face long enough to refill his lungs, and then he replaced the mask.

Then he squatted on his heels in dismay. He was not at all sure that he would be able to keep water from entering Marguery's lungs, but that wasn't the worst thing. Still worse was the fact that the process took far too much time. He couldn't go on breathing only once every two minutes for very long. There was another consideration, too: He didn't have enough hands to go around. He needed one to keep the water out of Marguery's nose and mouth, one to hold the mask to his own, and a third one to hold onto whatever rail or article of furniture was mooring them at the moment, and still a fourth hand to hold Marguery.

The whole thing was impossible. It wouldn't work. They needed two tanks—

Abruptly Sandy roared with surprised satisfaction, making the unconscious woman stir and moan. They *had* two tanks! The only problem was that one of them was empty.

By the time he had figured out how to bleed some of the contents of the full tank into the other Marguery's moaning had stopped. She seemed to be asleep. She simply did not rouse from that sleep, even when he shook her.

Sandy hooked her into her gear, slipped his own mask on, and began the long climb down into the water and under it, pulling himself hand over hand along the rail of the spiral staircase, retracing their steps. Finally, once they were down, he could see the glow of sunlight outside.

Three minutes later he was at the surface, bawling frantically for help to the people who were staring at him from a passing work boat.

Chapter
◆ 19

Because the Earth human body is constantly exposed to attack by organic things of all kinds from its environment, most of which would do it harm if they could, it has a complicated and very effective system of defenses. Antibodies form. Glands flood the system with prophylactic agents. The body mobilizes to defeat the attacker. The system works very well—that is why life has survived on Earth for four billion years—but sometimes the very mobilization of defense systems by itself causes fever, itching, sneezing, the formation of pimples or blisters or blotches—even syncope; even, sometimes, death. Then the syndrome is called "an allergic reaction," and it can be more serious than the original attack.

When one of the air-evac medics took time to explain that to Sandy, he understood—more or less. What he understood best was that it was serious. It kept the medics busy. By the time the helicopter had made the ten-minute flight to Hudson City and was swooping down on the roof marked with a squared-off red cross, Marguery was shrouded in blankets, with a tube in her nose and another tube taped to a needle that entered a vein in her arm and her face mostly hidden under a mask.

She wasn't talking, even incoherently. She was unconscious. After those first quick words of explanation, the medics weren't talking, either, or at least not to Lysander Washington. No one paid any attention to him at all, at least not until they had pushed the wheeled stretcher Marguery was on into one elevator and hurried Lysander himself into another, with instructions to sit in the emergency waiting room—and the only attention he got then was from the other people sitting around, some with crutches, some with babies in their arms, some half asleep, some nervously pacing back and forth as they waited to hear the prognosis on their friends or relatives within.

The seats were flimsy aluminum-tubing things with canvas backs. Sandy did not want to trust his weight to them. He was more inclined to join the pacers, anyway, because the whole thing was a terrible mystery to him, and he couldn't help feeling that in some way—what way it could possibly be he couldn't imagine—the whole thing was his fault.

And no one would tell him anything.

A little girl in shorts and tennis shoes was staring at him, diverted from the situation comedy on the waiting-room TV screen. She had a carton of popcorn from a vending machine in her hand, but she wasn't eating the popcorn because her thumb was in her mouth. She pulled it out long enough to ask, "Mister, are you the spaceman?"

He scowled at her. He was not in a talkative mood. "No," he lied. Why should he be truthful when all about him deceived? "I'm, uh, just a normal Earth human waiting for my wife to have a baby."

"I don't think that's so," the child said critically, "because we go to the other side of the hospital when we come here for babies. My brother's getting a marble out of his nose; he's dumb. Do you want some popcorn?''

He shook his head and got up to visit the drinking fountain. He peered down the forbidden corridors of the hospital, pale green and white, with carts that bore unplugged machines and stacks of linen, and people in pale green smocks hurrying back and forth. Ignoring the girl, he went to the reception desk again. "Can you tell me anything about Marguery Darp?" he begged.

"The doctor will be with you when she can," the receptionist said, eyeing him curiously. "There's a film room down the hall if you'd like to watch some other kind of television while you wait."

"Do they have decent chairs?" he asked ungraciously.

The receptionist studied his build. "They have couches, anyway. I think they're pretty strong," she offered.

"Then maybe I will," Sandy growled, but what he decided to do first was to visit the men's room. He was brooding. This world was entirely too full of unexpected crises! He was tired of being taken by surprise. It wasn't the way he had been brought up; on the big interstellar ship you at least always knew where you stood, and if there was ever any doubt about what to do next the Major Seniors would tell you.

He did not want to face the curiosity of the people in the lounge again. When he found the film room the couch did, at least, look sturdy enough to bear him. But as soon as he sat and gazed at the screen, he was taken aback to see a familiar face. It was his old cohort-mate, Bottom! He was on a platform, just as Polly had been, and he, too was lecturing an invisible audience. Not on astronomy, of course. His topic was biological control of radioactive and toxic wastes, and he was showing microscope pictures of tiny organisms that, he said, would concentrate all the undesirables into their own bodies, simply by feeding on them, and then

do not understand Earth humans. Do you know that hardly any of them have spoken to me about thruster project? It is as though they do not appreciate what great gift Hakh'hli are making to them."

"Well," Lysander said helpfully, "maybe they don't see it as a gift, exactly. After all, you told them there would have to be Hakh'hli supervisors and not merely Earth humans in charge."

"But of course there must be Hakh'hli supervisors! Who knows what Earth humans might do otherwise? They are violent and not wholly civilized, Lysander! Remember all you have learned! They are capable of converting all technology into weapons."

"How could they make railgun a weapon?" he asked reasonably.

"That would be easy and not difficult at all! They might shoot one massive capsule up very fast and ram our ship! Can you imagine what would happen in that case? And our ship could not maneuver to get away, since main engines are completely off at present." She woofed angrily. "It could be even worse! They could send nuclear bombs, such as those they are always dropping on each other."

"They haven't dropped any of those for years."

"For years!" she mimicked. "For years, only! And does not that perhaps make it time for them to use such weapons again?" She glanced over Sandy's shoulder and made a face. "We will talk of this again if you like," she said, "but not now. Here is my watchdog coming, and I do not wish to speak to him."

She hobbled angrily away. To Lysander's surprise, Hamilton Boyle seemed more interested in him than in his charge, Polly. He nodded to her as he passed, and advanced on Lysander.

"Marguery's going to be all right," Boyle said, patting Lysander's shoulder reassuringly. "It looked bad. In fact it *was* bad; there's no doubt that you saved her life by getting her out of there. But it's just some kind of allergic reaction. They've given her histamine blockers, and she's conscious now. I just left her."

"I'm going to see her," Sandy decided, turning toward the emergency room door. Boyle put a hand on his arm.

"Not just now," he said. "She's, uh, she doesn't look her best right now. She'd rather wait until she's prettier for you to see her."

Sandy gazed up at him, making a sound that was somewhere between, "Oh, hell," and "Oh, wow!"—as much delighted that Marguery wanted to look her best for him as he was dejected that he couldn't go in. "What is an allergic reaction?" he asked; and when Boyle explained, he asked curiously, "But what was she allergic to?"

Boyle tamped his pipe, considering. "It could be a lot of things," he said at last. "Mold spores, for instance. That vault's been wet for years; it's probably full of them. How about yourself?"

"What about myself?"

"Are you having any allergic symptoms? Things like sneezing, itching, dizziness, hoarseness—anything like that? Look, as long as you're here, why don't we get the medics to check you out?"

"I don't see any reason to be checked out," Lysander said.

"But Marguery would want you to," Boyle assured him. "It only takes a minute to get a sample, and it doesn't hurt."

It took a lot longer than a minute, counting the time for dropping his pants and stretching out, face down, while a gum-chewing young woman in one of the pale green uniforms poked for a soft spot in the fleshy part of his hip; and the part about it not hurting wasn't true, either. The pokes with the woman's finger were only annoying—well, "disturbing" was a better word, because Sandy was very conscious of the fact that she was female and he was exposed, and he had not been touched by any other human female but Marguery in such an intimate way. But when the woman had found a spot she liked the next thing was a click and a prod and a sudden sharp stabbing feeling, as though a rattlesnake had bitten him on the butt.

Sandy rolled instinctively away, shouting in astonishment, resentment, and hurt. When he looked around he saw the woman holding up a spring-loaded needle as long as the first joint of his thumb. "Please hold still," she ordered, annoyed. "It's only a cell sample, after all . . . There. You can go now."

Full of vexation, Lysander went back into the waiting room. He did not smile when he saw Hamilton Boyle standing there, puffing his pipe right under a large "No Smoking" sign. "That wasn't too bad, was it?" Boyle asked genially.

"It was bad enough," Lysander growled, rubbing his buttock. "Now can I see Marguery?"

Boyle shook his head regretfully. "I'm afraid not. She's asleep, and they don't want her disturbed."

Lysander blinked at him, suddenly worried. "But they said she was doing well!"

"And so she is, my boy! It's just that she's had a close call, and so they want to keep her until they get some test results. She ought to be fine tomorrow morning. You can see her then, I'm sure—maybe even take her home."

"Take her home?" Lysander felt a sudden glow. "That'll be fine." He thought for a minute, then had an inspiration. "Flowers! It is an Earth custom to send flowers to people in hospitals, isn't it? Where does one get flowers?"

But Boyle was shaking his head, amused but tolerant. "It's late, Sandy," he pointed out. "The florists are all closed. You can bring some in the morning if you want to, but right now I think I ought to drive you home. My car's in the lot."

When they got to the car Boyle drove efficiently and fast, but when they reached the hotel he paused before getting out. "There's one thing I'm kind of curious about, Sandy," he said. "Did you see your friend Bottom's speech on television?"

"Not really. I didn't pay much attention."

Boyle nodded. "Most of what he said was old stuff, if you don't mind my saying so—we've done a pretty good job of working out detox systems for the soil and water ourselves. Had to, you know. There was just one little thing. Bottom said the Hakh'hli were going to start field trials themselves."

"Yes? Why shouldn't they?"

Boyle pursed his lips. "Perhaps there's no reason. Only he said they wanted to do it in conjunction with the railgun project they want us to build for them. In Africa."

Lysander shrugged. "Why not? It couldn't do much harm there, could it?"

"But it couldn't do much good, either, Sandy. Africa's about the least affected continent as far as acid rain and heavy metals and so on are concerned. The Hakh'hli seem to be very interested in it, though. I wondered if you might know why?"

Lysander shook his head. "You'd have to ask ChinTekki-tho that," he said. But as a matter of fact he had a pretty good idea what the answer would be, and an even better one that Hamilton Boyle would not get that answer from ChinTekki-tho.

Chapter
◆ 20

It may be that the disease called "AIDS" originated in Africa—the source was never entirely clear. It is certain that it ended there, and it ended the human population of Africa with it. By the time the Star War began ten thousand men and women were dying every day, worldwide. A year later it was a hundred thousand a day. The vaccine came along in time to save the remaining millions in most of the world. But in Africa there simply was not enough of anything to deal with the problem. While America was frantically diking and poldering its coastlines against the rising seas, while Europe was trying to save its crops from scouring winds and sudden freezes and ultraviolet burn, no one had energy to spare for helping the "emerging" countries of the Third World. They were thrown on their own resources, and they didn't have enough resources for the job. Now Africa's surviving populations of elephants, gorillas, rhinos, and tsetse flies are reclaiming their old ranges. They don't have to compete with human poachers or farmers any-

more, because the human beings are dead. AIDS didn't kill the Africans. Neglect did.

For the first time since his landing on Earth, Lysander slept the whole night through. It was broad daylight when he woke, and he would undoubtedly have slept longer if Polly hadn't wakened him. She wasn't gentle. She shook him and shouted peremptorily in his ear. "Get up, Lysander! ChinTekki-tho wishes to speak to you, at once and not after any delay. Come quickly!"

Unhurriedly, Lysander opened his eyes and looked at her. "I will come," he said, "since I have questions to ask ChinTekki-tho. Tell him I will be there in some few minutes."

"Tell him? Ask questions? Lysander, it is you who must answer questions and not that Senior! He is displeased with you."

Lysander stretched and yawned. "That makes two of us," he said in English. "Go now."

"For this," she promised, "you will swallow your own spit!" Fuming, she hurried back to the radio in her room.

Lysander didn't hurry. He methodically pulled on his clothes, then paused in the bathroom to relieve himself and wash his face before he followed. By the time he was in Polly's room he had made up his mind what he wanted to say. Polly was crouched over the radio, muttering into it. She looked up malignantly as Lysander came in, and hissed in astonishment when he ordered, "Leave us. I want to speak to ChinTekki-tho in private."

"That is foolish and improper for you to say!" she cried. "Why should I leave you?"

"Because if you do not," he told her, "I will not speak to ChinTekki-tho." He waited patiently until she left, licking her tongue out in baffled annoyance; then he turned to the radio.

He spoke in English and left off the honorific in the name.

"ChinTekki," he said, "why was I not told that there was to be a landing in Africa?"

It took a second for the response to come, but then ChinTekki-tho's tone was icy. "Speak of such things in Hakh'hli and not in the Earth language!" he commanded. "Why do you ask such questions in such tone?"

"Because I have been kept from information and not informed fully," Lysander said. "Must I learn of Hakh'hli plans from Earth humans and not from Hakh'hli?"

The pause was longer than the round-trip required. Then ChinTekki-tho said slowly, "It was not your habit to speak to me in this fashion, Lysander. Why have you changed?"

"Perhaps I've grown up a little," Lysander said.

"Perhaps you have grown more Earthly," the Hakh'hli said thoughtfully. "It is said that you caused injury to one Earth-female through amphylaxis, Lysander. Why did you do that?"

Lysander flushed. "I caused her no permanent harm. Is it not privilege of Earth-human male to perform amphylaxis with Earth-human female? Am I not Earth-human male?"

"It appears," ChinTekki-tho sighed, "that you are, indeed. Certainly you are no longer true Hakh'hli, for Hakh'hli would not speak in such tone to this Senior."

"Perhaps," Lysander snapped, "Hakh'hli would not have such cause. I was not informed of any plan to visit Africa."

"But why should we not do this?" ChinTekki-tho asked reasonably. "What value has Africa to Earth humans?"

"It's *theirs*!"

Lysander could hear the reproachful hiss. "Africa is not in use," ChinTekko-tho said stubbornly. "We ask little of Earth humans and not very much at all. We ask an island so that railgun can be built to benefit both Hakh'hli and Earth humans, and Earth humans respond that cannot be because inhabitants object. Will they now tell us we cannot have empty Africa because elephants will object?"

227

Lysander frowned. "I do not understand," he said. "What is value of Africa to Hakh'hli?"

ChinTekki-tho said sternly, "That is for Major Seniors to decide and not to be decided by one young person not fully mature." There was silence for a moment, then the voice from the radio resumed, its tone heavy. "I had hoped to speak more profitably to you, Lysander. I perceive that cannot happen. So there will be no more discussion with you. I will speak privately with Hippolyta now. You, Lysander, think carefully of what you do—for remember, it was Hakh'hli, not Earth humans, who gave you life!"

When Lysander reached the hospital Marguery Darp was not in her room. A nurse showed him to a solarium lounge, where Marguery was talking on the telephone. She was dressed and apparently ready to leave, but when she put down the phone she patted a space on the couch beside her. She looked at him inquiringly. "Is something the matter, Sandy?" she asked.

He laughed at her. "Which something do you want to hear about?" he asked.

"You pick," she said, and listened carefully as he told her about his unsatisfactory conversation with ChinTekki-tho. She looked different today, he thought—not ill, at all; not hostile; not even remote, but somehow more serious than she had seemed before. When he finished she commented, "It looks as though they've got more plans for Africa than they've told us. Did he say anything about what they're building out there?"

Lysander was startled. "Building? No. Are they building something?"

"It looks like it," she said. She hesitated for a moment, then asked, "Lysander? You know we've been taping the Hakh'hli transmissions. Would you be willing to translate some of them?"

He frowned over that. "The reason they're in Hakh'hli is that they don't want humans to hear them," he pointed out.

"Naturally. But if they aren't up to anything, why shouldn't we know what they're saying?"

Another hard question to think about. While he was thinking, Marguery added softly, "As a favor to me, maybe?" Then she saw the sudden expression of pain on his face. "What's the matter?"

He said gruffly, "I'm confused. Are we falling in love, or what?"

She answered him in perfect seriousness. "The only way to tell that is to wait and see how it comes out, I think."

"Yes, but—but it's all so mixed up! Are we friends? Or sweethearts? Are we going to get married? Or is all this just because you were assigned to keep me interested so you can spy on me?"

She flared at him, "That *was* my assignment, yes. In the beginning. What's wrong with that? Weren't you assigned to spy on *us*?"

He scowled. "Well—sort of, I suppose."

"So we're even on that, aren't we? Sandy, dear," she said, putting her hand on his, "we've got two different things going here. One is you and me, and that'll just have to work itself out however it comes. The other's a little more urgent. That's the human race and the Hakh'hli, and you have to decide what side you're on. Now."

He looked at her angrily. "Why do I have to take sides?"

"Because there are two sides," she said firmly, "and there's no room in the middle. Will you translate?"

He thought it over for a long moment. Then he decided. "If there's nothing bad in what the Hakh'hli are saying to each other, then I'm not doing them any harm by translating, am I? And if there is—all right," he said, standing up, "I'll do it. Let's take you home."

She stood up too. "That's my boy," she said, applauding. "Only we're not going home right now."

229

"But I thought that was what I came here to do."

"Dear Sandy," she said, half-affectionate, half-somber, "you can take me home later. Maybe even often. But right now we've got somewhere else to go."

The "somewhere else" was a windowless, gray granite building that bore a legend incised on its stone facade:

INTERSEC
YORK COMMONWEALTH
DIVISION OF CRIMINAL JUSTICE

It was neither surprising to Lysander nor reassuring. They paused at a garage ramp, where Marguery opened the car window and displayed a medallion to a guard. Then they were passed into an underground garage.

Hamilton Boyle was waiting for them at the elevator. "Through there," he ordered Sandy, pointing at a flat-topped archway. Marguery didn't say anything; she just motioned to Sandy to go first. As he passed through it he saw a uniformed woman studying a screen beside the arch and realized he had just been inspected for weapons.

"What's this all about?" he demanded.

"You'll see. We have to go up to the third floor," Boyle said.

At least Marguery took Sandy's hand in the elevator. Boyle noticed, but didn't comment. When the elevator door opened at the floor a tall, elderly woman with a gun strapped to her belt was standing before a control panel. She nodded to Boyle and pushed a button. To their right a metal-barred gate slid noiselessly back, and Boyle motioned Sandy to pass through.

An armed guard! A prison door! Sandy had seen such things only on television, but he knew what they meant.

He released Marguery's hand and confronted Hamilton Boyle. "Are you arresting me?" he demanded.

Boyle gave him an unfriendly look. "Why would I do that? We're on the same side—I hope."

"Then what?"

"I want to show you something," Boyle said grimly, motioning for them to enter a room. In the center of the room, almost filling it, was a conference table, with half a dozen chairs around it. On one wall was a large television screen. "Sit down," Boyle commanded, and took his place at a console.

As the room lights went dim Lysander looked at Marguery and got a faint, unreassuring smile back. Then the screen lit up.

They were looking at the Hakh'hli ship again. It glowed as clearly as before. But it was not the same as before.

Perplexed, Lysander frowned at the picture. Something had been added to the ship. A structure was beginning to take shape. Extravehicular-labor Hakh'hli were visible, using small tugs to move concave metal shell sections of—something or other—into position.

"There it is, Lysander," Boyle said. "They started doing it yesterday. Do you have any idea what it is?"

Lysander shook his head.

"You've never seen it before?" Boyle pressed.

"No. Well, I couldn't have, could I? I mean, that looks pretty flimsy. It isn't something they could have built onto the ship while it was in drive; it would have needed all kinds of bracing and support, or it would have just broken away."

"Maybe they didn't need it before," Boyle commented.

Marguery stirred. "There's a chance that it's nothing to worry about," she said. "Remember, the Hakh'hli were talking about beaming microwave energy down to us. This could just be the antenna for that."

In the semidarkness, Boyle turned to stare at her. "Do you believe that?"

She shrugged, and looked to Lysander.

"I don't actually think so," Sandy said. "Power trans-

231

mission isn't my specialty, but I learned a little about it. I think they use a different kind of antenna."

"Then what?" Boyle demanded. "It's awfully big, Lysander. Bigger than anything I've seen. Bigger than the old dish at Arecibo, even." He paused. Then he asked brutally, "Is it a weapon?"

"A weapon?" Lysander cried, startled. "Of course not! The Hakh'hli don't even have any weapons, that I ever heard of. One of the worst things they used to say about Earth people was that they—we—used weapons all the time; I just can't believe that they would use any themselves." He shook his head vigorously. "No, maybe Marguery's guess was right—a microwave beam, only a different design than anything I saw—"

"But Lysander," she sighed, reaching for his hand again, "even that could be a weapon, couldn't it? Can you imagine what a beam like that could do if it struck Hudson City or Brasilia or Denver?"

"And why do we have to guess," Boyle demanded, "when we've got tapes of everything they've been saying to each other, if you'd only translate them?"

Lysander looked from one to the other of them, then back at the picture. "Do you know," he said conversationally, "those extravehicular Hakh'hli are bred to be bigger and stronger than anyone else? So they can do that kind of work? Only they don't live as long. When I was little I kind of wished I could be one of them."

Neither of them responded. They just continued to gaze at him.

"You said you'd do it," Marguery reminded him.

Lysander sighed. "Turn it off," he said. "All right. I'll translate your tapes."

It wasn't that easy. At least, it certainly wasn't fast. It appeared that one or another of the Hakh'hli on Earth had been in communication with someone on the ship nearly all the time the ship was above the horizon at the Inuit Commonwealth. Even subtracting the conversations Lysander had already heard and those in English, there were nearly twelve hours of tapes to listen to. Some were sound only. Some were full picture displays.

None of them carried much useful information.

After the first half hour Lysander turned from the screen. "Stop it for a moment," he ordered. "Did you hear the part I just translated?"

"Of course," Boyle said. "Wait a minute." He pushed some keys, a speaker whirred and then emitted Lysander's voice:

"ChinTekki says they will proceed with the third alternative. Bottom says they have completed the rescreening of the lander and are ready to take off on short notice. ChinTekki says it may be necessary to refuel, so that they can fly in atmosphere to Site Double-Twelve. Bottom says they will ask the Earth humans for fuel."

"They did ask," Boyle corroborated. "We told them we'd need samples of their alcohol and hydrogen peroxide so we could duplicate them. But what's this 'third alternative'?"

"That's just it," Lysander said gloomily. "I never heard of a third alternative. I never heard of a Site Double-Twelve, either."

Boyle thought for a moment, then stood up. "I've got some errands to run. Keep going. Maybe there'll be something more helpful later on."

Lysander did keep on—and on and on, through the long day. Either Boyle or Marguery Darp was with him all the time. They brought him sandwiches, which he ate while watching the screen and translating into the recording device with his mouth full. It didn't matter. There wasn't much to say.

Late in the afternoon it occurred to him to ask whether he shouldn't call Polly to let her know he was safe. "That's

233

all right," Marguery told him. "Ham's already told her that you're with me."

"Yes, but she'll wonder what we're doing all this time," he objected.

"Sandy," she said, managing a real smile, "she thinks she *knows* what we're going. Let's get on with this."

That brightened his mood for a moment. There wasn't much else that was cheering. When the last tape was played he sat back, rubbing his eyes. He said somberly, "I don't know what the Hakh'hli are doing. I don't want to think they are doing anything sinister. But there is a great deal going on that they have never told me about."

Marguery touched his shoulder comfortingly. "It's all right, Lysander," she said.

"I don't think so," he said.

"Well," Boyle said philosophically, "at least we know more than we did." He caught a fleeting look of inquiry from Marguery Darp, and nodded, grinning. "I think I should tell you, Lysander, that our linguistics people have picked up a few words of Hakh'hli, here and there. You'll be happy to know that they say your translations seem to check out."

"Did you think I would *lie* to you?" Lysander demanded.

Boyle's face sobered rapidly. "We had to be sure," he said. "This isn't fun, Lysander. It might be survival. We'll do whatever we have to do for the sake of survival." He seemed about to go on, then changed his mind. The smile came back on his face. "Well, that's enough for one day," he said affably. "I'm off."

"And so are we," Marguery Darp said, standing up. "Sandy? If you're really going to take me home—this is the time."

Marguery's apartment was on the thirty-fifth floor of an old high-rise building looking out over what she called Lake Jersey. "That used to be all marshland," she said, "until they filled it in. They built all kinds of things there—look, you can see an old football stadium over there. But when the sea began to rise it all got submerged again."

He nodded, looking around. Even with all Lysander had on his mind, he found room to be astonished that a solitary human being should have so much space for herself. A "kitchen," a "bathroom," a "living room," a "bedroom." He stood in the doorway of that one for a moment, looking around with particular interest. But it was all interesting. It was the first time he had been in the actual home of an actual Earth human—farm-animal herders not counted, anyway.

Marguery said apologetically, "It's a pretty old building. Well, that's why it's a high-rise, of course; we don't build that way anymore. But I'm only in it when I'm not on a mission somewhere. Don't you want to sit down?"

He did. He looked around, estimating the carrying capacity of all the chairs in the living room, and was unsure of most of them. Marguery saw what he was doing and smiled. She patted the couch next to herself. "This ought to be strong enough to hold you," she said. When he sat down next to her she looked up at him in an expectant way. He couldn't be sure, but he really thought she looked as though she intended to be kissed.

He did what was expected of him. Apparently it wasn't satisfactory, because after a moment Marguery drew back and asked, "What's the matter?"

Lysander leaned back. He thought over all the things that were the matter and selected one. "I'm hungry," he said.

"I'm not much of a cook, but we could send out for a pizza." She looked at him closely. "Is that really what's bothering you?"

"It's one of them. Plus about a million others, including betraying the people I grew up with. The people who saved my life in the first place."

"You haven't betrayed anything," Marguery pointed out.

"You mean I couldn't help you. That just makes it worse. I'm not even a *useful* traitor!"

Marguery thought that over. Then she said, "Lysander, you're pretty useful to me." She hesitated, then added, "There's something I haven't told you. I didn't know how you'd take it."

"Oh, *hell*," he groaned. "You've decided we shouldn't be sweethearts after all?"

She laughed at him. "No. Different. Just—well, you know all those tests they kept me overnight for? They weren't tests on me, honey."

"They weren't?"

"They were waiting for the results on you," she explained. "The samples they took in the hospital? The results came back and they showed what I was allergic to. Sandy, dear, I was violently allergic to *you*."

He stared at her in horror. Then he shook himself and began to pull away. She stopped him.

"You weren't listening," she accused. "The word I used was *was*. I *was* allergic to you. But that's something they can deal with, you know. They've given me all these histamine blockers and things. I don't think you can even make me sneeze any more."

Then she sat there, looking placidly at him. Lysander frowned, trying to understand what she was driving at. She didn't give him any clue. She just sat silent for a while. For long enough for Lysander to realize what she was being silent for; and when he did reach out for her, and they kissed again, it was all very clear to him.

She moved her head away to gaze into his eyes. "I think the pizza can wait," she said judiciously. "I wonder just how strong my bed is. But I think we ought to, you know, make sure those histamine blockers really work."

The blockers worked. So did the bed. So did the pizza delivery service that Marguery phoned, and though Lysander did not much like the cheese-tomato-oil mixture, he did like the company.

checked them out. Do you remember what the other pictures were, Lysander?"

He scowled. "There were *hundreds* of them! Let's see. Well, I remember one called *The Battle of the Bulge*. It was all full of tanks and prisoners being shot. And *All Quiet on the Western Front*, and *The Young Lions*—and, oh, yes, there were some that weren't American. They were in other languages; there was one that was called *Hitler Youth Hans*, about killing Russians and American because they were such war criminals—"

"Lysander," she said gently, "weren't they all *war* movies, every one of them? Did the Hakh'hli show their people any movies at all that didn't depict human beings as war-crazy?"

He gazed at her. "Well, in our own cohort quarters we saw all kinds of things. There were a lot with dancing, and family situation comedies—"

She brushed that aside. "I don't mean the ones they just showed you. I mean what they showed the whole ship. It sounds to me as though they were propagandizing them, Lysander. Trying to persuade them that human beings were mad killers. And so I ask you again, Lysander: What kind of people do the Hakh'hli think *we* are? And if they think we're killers, wouldn't they maybe consider it only prudent to get in the first punch?"

He stared at her in horror. Then he said slowly, "I cannot believe that the Major Seniors would do anything like that."

"Can't you? Or is it just that you don't want to?" She looked at him furiously for a moment. Then she jumped up and leaned across the table to fling her arms around him. She kissed him hard, and he felt the dampness of the tears on her cheek.

He pulled away and implored her, "Marguery? What game are we playing now? Is it the I-spy game or the we-love-each-other game?"

"Sometimes," she said grayly, "the games get mixed up."

They looked at each other silently for a moment. Then Lysander sighed. "I'd rather play the we-love-each-other game."

She didn't hesitate. "All right," she said. "Let's talk about making love." Lysander scowled, more puzzled than ever; the expression on her face didn't match the choice of subject. "I have some questions about that, too," she went on. "About the way the Hakh'hli do it. You told me that the females are ready any time; whenever one of the guys is ready they hop to it."

"That's right," he said, torn between embarrassment and anger. To discuss love-making when they had just been doing it was fine, but why did she have to be so clinical?

She became more clinical still. "Do the male Hakh'hli have the same kind of joystick you do?"

He flushed, unwilling to believe he understood her. "Joystick?"

"All right. The same kind of penis, then."

"Oh, the sex organ. Well, I've never really studied one close up, you understand—" But, actually, when one of the males was in season nobody around had any trouble in seeing what it looked like. When he told her, Marguery wanted to hear every physiological detail. All the details. About the everted male organ. About the fleshy crater of the females. About the act of amphylaxis itself, and what it looked like while it was happening, and how long it took, and how every female on the ship was always willing and always able, because the laying of fertilized eggs was their greatest joy.

Marguery looked definitely disapproving, but still queerly determined. "And how do the females know when the male is in heat? Pheromones? Just seeing he has a hard-on?"

When the terms had been explained to him Sandy shook his head doubtfully. "I don't think it's either of those," he said. "I think it's more they're always ready. I mean, it isn't any trouble for them, you know? I mean, for the females.

240

They don't have to get ready or anything. They just do the amphylaxis, and the girl's eggs get fertilized, and half an hour later she lays them, and that's that."

She said, "I can see why it's great for the males, but what do the ladies get out of it?"

"But I told you! They lay the eggs," he explained.

Marguery looked pensive. "It almost sounds like the egg-laying is more important than the scr—the amphylaxis, I mean."

"Well, I suppose it is. The eggs are what count—for the girls, anyway, you know." He chuckled. "The worst thing you can ever say to a girl is, like, you'll steal her eggs and flush them down the toilet. They'd get really mad. You wouldn't even say that, unless you were pretty mad yourself. You wouldn't dare. If you said it to somebody like Polly she'd kick your belly in."

She pondered that for a moment, then seemed to relax. "Well," she said, "that's all very interesting."

Lysander didn't respond. He was waiting for the next curve to be thrown, but Marguery's odd urgency seemed to have left her. She grinned at him. "Would you like some more coffee?" she asked. He shook his head. She didn't take any either. She was looking thoughtful. "In some ways," she decided, "I think sexual intercourse is better for human women."

"Do you?" Sandy asked. That seemed a doubtful proposition to him, considering what he knew of the human burden of raising children as against the Hakh'hli system of freezing and professional nurturing. "How's that?"

"Well, you said it's only the eggs that matter to the female. So she has to wait until she has a new batch before she can, well, do it again."

"Yes, but it isn't that long. It's all up to the male, really. For the females, a few eggs form every day; anytime from a week to a year after amphylaxis she does it again."

"Whereas human women," Marguery sighed, "can do it

all over right away. I mean, if the human male can manage
it, that is."

She looked at him in a way that caused him to tingle. All
the abrupt changes in subject had made him wary. Still, he
thought, nothing ventured, nothing gained . . . "Well," he
said, "if you're curious about this particular one, you know,
I wouldn't be surprised if he could."

Actually, he could, all right. In fact, he proudly did; but
first Marguery made him wait for what seemed an inter-
minable time while she was in the bathroom. It struck Lysander as odd that she stayed there so long. He could hear
the water running; he could also, he thought, hear her voice,
very faintly. But who knew what private things Earth females had to do before, during, or between amphylaxis? He
resolved to ask her, grinning; but when at last she came out
she looked so breathtakingly lovely—no, that was the wrong
word; the right word was not "lovely" but "ready"—that he
forgot all the questions.

Then there was a surprise.

Among the many things that Lysander Washington
hadn't known about human sexual practices was that once
they were done it was often the custom for the male and the
female to sleep in each other's arms all the rest of the night.

What made him realize it was discovering that he had
drowsed off. When he opened his eyes he saw Marguery Darp
lying there beside him. When he started to move she muttered, "Don't go," and threw her arms around him.

As a more or less inevitable consequence, they made love
again, hardly awake but enjoying it all the same, and when
he woke again it was broad daylight and Marguery was already in the kitchen.

She turned to him. She was smiling, but it was a diffident
smile. Still, she put her face up to be kissed, as though they
had been doing this sort of thing forever.

"There's a package for you," she said, pointing to the table.

He looked at it curiously; sure enough, it was a thick brown envelope with his name on it. "It came this morning," she told him. "It's tapes and the transcripts of the translations you did yesterday. Ham would like you to play them over and double-check that you got everything right. I'll show you how to run the machine."

He picked it up without pleasure. It was heavy. He had hoped for a more interesting day. "Maybe I'd better go back to the hotel first," he said tentatively. "Polly will be worrying."

"No," she said somberly. "Polly won't be worried." She glanced at her watch. "Look at the time! I have to make a phone call," she said abruptly.

There was a phone on the table, but Marguery didn't use it. Instead, she disappeared into the bathroom and slammed the door.

In a moment Lysander heard water running. And there was another surprise, and once again an unpleasing one. So she hadn't been singing to herself in the bathroom the night before. It was where she kept another telephone—obviously a private one.

When Marguery came back out he was already prepared for something bad.

He got it. "I've got to go do some things," she said, her face without any expression at all. "I'm afraid I might be gone for some time, but please don't leave. Here, I'll show you how to work the recorder."

And before he could quite believe it was happening she was gone.

She hadn't lied. It was definitely "some time"—time enough for Lysander to have played nearly all the tapes, as ordered, and to have made any number of pointless, fiddling little corrections on the transcripts. He had been hungry three times and had found nothing more than bare subsistence in her refrigerator.

But he stayed. He did as he was told. He was, he told himself, pretty *tired* of always doing as he was told, by someone or other.

By the time he heard her key in the door he had passed from angry to depressed. By the expression on her face as she came in, Marguery was depressed enough herself. She came in silently, holding her sun hat and glasses in her hands. She didn't put them down. She looked at him thoughtfully for a moment before she spoke, and then said sadly, "Oh, hell, Lysander. I wish you'd known more than you did."

"What's the matter?" he cried, suddenly alarmed.

"I'm afraid it's the I-spy game we're playing now," she sighed. "Come on. We've got to go to headquarters. There's something Hamilton has to show you."

Chapter
◆ 21

The process of coming of age is not easy for any organism, anywhere in the universe. Insects cocoon themselves and emerge winged, their larval stages forgotten. Crustaceans painfully molt and often enough are eaten by predators before the new shells form; snakes shed their skins, birds leave the safety of the nest, young carnivores are driven from their dams. It is usually painful. Sometimes it is fatal. It is not much better for human beings, even though the change is only partly physiological for them. When a human child ceases to be a child his rites of passage are as painful, and as dangerous, as for any softshell crab. The process of maturing is difficult for anyone, but maybe most difficult for those who—like Lysander Washington—have thought they already were mature, all along.

Lysander was not surprised to find them approaching the InterSec building. "Are you going to show me some more pictures of what the Hakh'hli are building?" he demanded.

"Not this time," Marguery said, flashing her badge to the guard. "They're still doing it, though. Fast."

"And do you still think it's a weapon?"

She gave him an impenetrable look. "No, I don't think *that* is a weapon any more. Give it a rest, Lysander. You'll hear it all. Here's Ham Boyle."

The strange thing about Hamilton Boyle was that, this time, he wasn't smiling. The champion smiler had a set, determined, unyielding expression on his face. He didn't say anything until they had gone through the ritual of the passes, the unlocking of doors, and the elevators. Lysander noticed that this time the elevator went down instead of up, and for quite a distance. Both Marguery and Hamilton Boyle watched the numbers flick across the indicator as though they were stock-market quotations on a bad day.

"Here we go," Boyle said at last, ushering them into a small room. It was not much larger than a cell, Lysander noted as warily he entered. "Sit down," Boyle commanded, waving Sandy to the strongest-looking of the chairs. There was a smaller one right next to it that Marguery could have taken, but she ignored it. She walked across the room without looking at Sandy, to take a stand by a desk with a keyboard and a video screen; behind her was a slatted thing of the kind they called a venetian blind. The slats were tilted so that no light from the other side came through. But no light could, Sandy thought, since the building had no outside windows.

Sandy frowned. His senses were all tensely alert. This was a hostile place. There was an almost inaudible sound now and then, like a distant keening. It made him uneasy, but he couldn't be sure of what he was hearing.

"So what are these secrets you don't want the Hakh'hli to know?" he demanded.

Boyle blinked at him in surprise. "You've got it backward. We're talking about secrets the Hakh'hli didn't want *us* to know. Like their plans to attack us."

246

In spite of everything Marguery had said to him, the idea remained preposterous to Lysander. "They don't have any plans like that," he said positively.

"But, Sandy," Marguery put in reasonably, "they do. They want to stay here. They want to take over the continent of Africa. They're going to propose that they will settle for building habitats in orbit around the Earth, but that's only a stall; what they really want is to live here. In Africa—for openers, anyway."

"What do you mean, habitats?"

"Big metal shells in space, Lysander," Boyle said somberly. "Like spaceships, but immense. They've got all those millions of eggs waiting to be hatched. They want a place to hatch them."

"I don't believe one word of that!" Sandy shouted, leaning forward. His chair creaked alarmingly. He paid no attention. He added, "Even if it were true, what's wrong with it? They wouldn't hurt anything on Earth as long as they stayed in orbit, would they?"

"But, Sandy, dear," Marguery said gently, "they aren't going to stay in orbit. Once all those unhatched eggs grow up, they'll move in. Polly told us so."

Lysander stared at her in total shock. That was the most preposterous thing either of them had said yet. He tried to make them understand. *"Polly?* No way! She wouldn't *ever* tell you anything she wasn't supposed to—if there were any secrets to tell in the first place, I mean."

"She didn't have any choice," Marguery said somberly.

He glared at her. "What are you talking about? You couldn't make her. What would you do, threaten her? Torture her? But I told you that wouldn't work!"

Marguery sighed. "But you also told us what would," she said, in a leaden tone. She got up and pulled a cord on the venetian blind.

247

Behind the blind was a window, apparently of one-way glass. Behind the glass was Polly.

Lysander stared incredulously. Polly! Alive! But it was Polly as he had never known her before, crouched bedraggled and whimpering before a communications screen. Marguery turned up a sound control, and the almost inaudible pleading voice Sandy had heard before grew louder. It was Polly's voice. Begging. In Hakh'hli and in English: "Please! My eggs! Don't let them spoil!"

Lysander shuddered in horror. The arm of his chair splintered as he pushed on it to rise. Half-stumbling, he glared up at them. "You *bastards*!" he shouted. "How could you?" He couldn't find any other words; so Marguery, too, had betrayed him; so there was no one at all Sandy could trust!

Boyle flinched momentarily before Sandy's rage, but stood his ground. "We had no choice," he said sharply.

He denied nothing. Sandy listened, appalled at what they had done. To threaten a Hakh'hli female with the destruction of fertile eggs—it was cruelty inconceivable! And how had they managed to make them fertile, without a Hakh'hli male to do the job?

Marguery, face white and expressionless, gave him the answer. "But we did have a male, Sandy. We had your friend Obie."

It was getting crazier—and worse! "But Obie is *dead*!"

She nodded. "But we had his body, you see. We didn't tell you the truth at the time. We didn't cremate his body. We gave it to a laboratory for investigation. All right, for dissection, then! What else could we do? We had to know all we could!" She was looking pleadingly at Lysander, but he had no compassion left to give her. She went on, "And we saved all the tissue samples, frozen. Including his sperm. When Polly was in stun time we—we took her prisoner. And then we brought her here and inseminated her."

"Show him the tapes," Boyle ordered.

Imagined horrors were not worse than real ones. What Sandy saw as the screen began to light up was nastier even than he had guessed. First they showed Polly waking up, impregnated. She was already beginning to lay her clutch of eggs—half-dazed from stun time, bewildered, confused—it was by all odds the most unhappy egg-laying Lysander had ever witnessed.

Then he heard Boyle's voice, speaking to her through a microphone. "Hippolyta, listen to me. You are our prisoner of war. You cannot leave this room. You will be fed, but you can't leave and you can't communicate."

Sandy tore his eyes off the screen and stared at the unhappy reality behind the one-way glass. "Polly!" he shouted. "I'm here! I won't let them do this to you!"

"She can't hear you," Boyle said coldly, "and you can't help her. Listen!"

On the screen she was saying bravely, ". . . my people will know at once!"

"Your people," said Boyle's disembodied voice, "will be told you insisted on going skin-diving by yourself and drowned, and your body was lost."

"They won't believe that!"

"They'll believe you do foolishly risky things, Hippolyta. They won't doubt it. They'll remember Oberon."

On the screen Lysander could see her shaking with fear and rage. Frantically she cried, "My eggs!"

Hamilton Boyle's icy voice: "There is a supply of nutrient fluid by the freezer. You may do whatever is necessary for them, and then store them in the freezer. We believe the system is as good as the one on the ship. The eggs will be all right—if you tell us what we want to know."

"Turn it off!" Sandy shouted. "Marguery! You're a *shit!*" He glared at her, cold and furious. She returned his look without speaking, but Boyle spoke for her.

"What she is, boy," he said heavily, "is a human being. Aren't you? don't you want to protect the human race?"

249

"Against what? The Hakh'hli aren't going to hurt you!"

Boyle shook his head. "Before you make a bigger fool of yourself than you already have, listen to what Polly says. Get to the important part, Marguery."

The picture flickered and whirred forward; and then Sandy did listen. With mounting horror.

It was not simply that she confirmed everything Marguery had suggested. Yes, the Major Seniors were determined to have Africa for their own; yes, all those frozen eggs were to be allowed to hatch to fill the continent. Yes, if that were not feasible, then they would insist on building a lot of great orbital habitats out of asteroidal materials; but, Polly confessed, that was only a temporary stratagem. When the eggs were hatched and grown and ready, how could the Earth humans prevent the Hakh'hli from taking whatever they liked? All that was horrifying enough for Lysander to hear . . .

But when she talked drearily of the landers that were being prepared to move into Low Earth Orbit he sat up in shock. He glanced at Boyle, bewildered. "But—what are they going to do there?"

Boyle said succinctly, "Bombardment." He turned off the tape, waiting for Lysander to speak.

"You mean like bomber airplanes over Hiroshima? But the Hakh'hli don't have anything like bombs—I'm sure of that! almost sure," he amended.

Boyle was shaking his head. "They don't need bombs, Lysander. They're there already. Don't you remember, we talked about the possibility at the science center? Eighteen thousand big objects in orbit, and the Hakh'hli can time them so they all hit cities."

"Like Albuquerque," Marguery put in. "Like what almost happened to Perth."

"And if that didn't force us to submit," said Boyle, "you know what they've got in reserve. The entire asteroid belt."

He was silent for a moment. Then he sighed and looked straight at Sandy. "There's a lot more, if you want to hear it."

"I don't think I do," Lysander said bitterly. "I've had enough bad news for one day."

Marguery said diffidently, "It isn't all bad, you know. That thing they're building? It's just a communications antenna. Polly said they haven't heard anything from their home world in centuries, and they're hoping with a big enough antenna they can at least hear if they're still broadcasting."

"They're lost, you know," Boyle said brutally. "They're getting desperate, too. So what about it, Lysander? The ball's in your court now. Make up your mind. Which side are you on?"

"Do I have any choice?" Lysander flared.

"Not much. You can have an accident as easily as Hippolyta. But if you want to help us—"

"Help you how?"

Boyle hesitated. "We have a plan," he said. "We can make it work with or without your help, but it will go better with it. That big ship is pretty vulnerable right now. But we don't have a lot of time. Those Hakh'hli landing vessels could be getting ready to nudge some big pieces into place right now, targeting Seattle or Hudson City."

Lysander looked at each of them in turn, finishing with Marguery Darp. There was nothing to read in her face. She was quite expressionless as she waited for him to speak.

"Tell me what the plan is," said Lysander at last. It was his first venture into adult guile.

Chapter
⋅ 22

Three thousand years is a lot of history. Three thousand years ago on Earth history had barely begun. Civilization was a collection of tiny principalities in the Fertile Crescent, and neither China nor Ancient Greece had been invented yet. The three-thousand-year history of the Hakh'hli is just as long and just as cloudy in its origins. The Hakh'hli know that before that time their remote ancestors lived on one or another of a consortium of planets—four of them, in three separate stellar systems—and deployed immense powers. Powers enough to launch a dozen ships like their own, to scour the Galaxy for new homes for the Hakh'hli race. That was their Golden Age, they know. What they also know is that the history of the three thousand years since the ship first began to swim the spaces between the stars has been not golden at all; it is a history of monotonous voyages and fruitless investigations. It is, to be more exact, a history of three thousand long, uninterrupted years of failure.

The flight back to the lander site was in no slow, comfortable blimp. They were in a hurry. Their plane was a high-energy supersonic jet, and it crossed the North American continent, twelve miles up, in an hour and forty minutes. It was not a pleasant trip. The acceleration as they took off and climbed was enough to push even Sandy back in his seat, and the other human passengers were immobilized until the jet leveled off.

Even then there was not much light conversation. Marguery Darp was lost in her own thoughts. Lysander, sitting by one of the tiny windows, spent most of his time gazing out at what could be seen of country sliding past below.

Hamilton Boyle had donned his InterSec uniform for the job, leather boots, holstered pistol, cap, and all. It was as though he needed to be reassured of his official position. When they were flying almost level he turned to Lysander and demanded harshly, "Do you know what you're supposed to do?"

Lysander turned back from the window. "How could I not?" he asked. "You've told me over and over. My job is to get the Hakh'hli out of the landing craft. You apprehend them. Then I turn it over to you."

"To the human race, Sandy," Boyle corrected.

"What you didn't tell me," Sandy said, "was what you're going to do with the lander after you get it."

"We'll study it, man! We have to find out what kind of technology we're up against."

Sandy nodded as though he had expected that answer. He wasn't signaling acceptance of what Boyle had said, only that he hadn't expected to be told the truth. He pursed his lips, gazing innocently at Hamilton Boyle. "You know," he said, "a suspicious person might think you had a different reason. You might be thinking of using the lander to ram the Hakh'hli ship."

The expression on Boyle's face told him all he had to know. When Sandy turned to look at Marguery Darp her own expression was dismal. "Oh, hell," she said. "We might as well start trusting each other, Ham! Sandy, you're almost right. InterSec has half a dozen fusion warheads hidden away, just in case. Once you turn the lander over to us, Ham wants to put one of them in it and take off. But not to ram it, Sandy! Not unless we really have to."

"No? Then what?" he asked politely.

"Just *threaten* it, Sandy! That's all. They'll have to surrender; the big ship's a sitting duck up there, with its drive motors off."

"I see," Lysander said noncommitally, and stopped there.

Boyle gave him ten seconds, and then demanded, "What's the matter? Don't you think it would work?"

Lysander thought it over carefully. "I never heard of a Hakh'hli surrendering," he said, "but I guess there's a first time for everything. As you say, they wouldn't have much choice, would they? Also," he went on, struck by a thought, "you probably don't have to bother with putting a bomb on the lander. Just crashing into the ship would do it, if you rammed it in the drive-systems area. Imagine strange matter splashing around the ship! Of course, whoever piloted the lander would die, too."

"Do you suppose that would be a problem? There are always human beings who are willing to die for patriotic reasons."

"So I have been told," Lysander agreed. "Only—"

"Only what?" Boyle demanded harshly.

Sandy shrugged. "Only I don't see what your next step is going to be. What are you going to do with the Hakh'hli after they all surrender?"

"We'll take them prisoner!"

"Yes, I see that much. Then what?"

"Then it's up to the civil authorities," Boyle snapped. "Don't worry about it, Lysander! We're not going to shoot them. There are rules about the treatment of prisoners of war."

"Yes, you put them in concentration camps," Lysander nodded. "How long do you keep them there?"

"As long as necessary," Boyle said through his teeth.

Sandy mulled that over for a minute. "There's one other possibility you haven't mentioned," he pointed out. "You could just tell them they had to go visit some other star. Would I be correct if I thought you had considered that and decided it wouldn't work?"

"You would," Boyle said shortly, but Marguery spoke up, ignoring his angry look.

"They can't, Sandy," she told him. "Remember, we said they were desperate. Their drive systems are beginning to wear out. Polly told us that; something about radiation-induced weaknesses in the support structure. She says it's beginning to get serious. The supports might hold up for a few hundred years yet, or they might go in ten."

"So they're stuck here," Boyle added.

"I see," Lysander said, nodding. And then he said, "Poor bastards. Well. Is there anything else we need to talk about right now?"

"Only to make sure you know what you're suppposed to do—"

"I do know, Boyle. You think there'll only be two of the party in the landing craft itself?"

"Usually there are two. They take turns. Two come out and talk to us, two stay in the ship." Boyle hesitated. "At least," he said, "I hope so. There's one little problem."

"Something else you haven't told me?" Lysander inquired politely.

"Something I'm telling you *now*," Boyle said sharply. "They've been out of communication with the interstellar ship for about ten hours now. Interference."

"What do you mean, interference?"

"We've got a high-altitude blimp up there, broadcasting jamming signals," Boyle explained. "They can't talk to the ship; the ship can't talk to them. Don't give me that kind of

255

look, Lysander! We had to do it. We didn't want them stirring up trouble when they couldn't get an answer from Hippolyta or you. It's possible that they'll be so concerned about that that they'll all be in the ship, but probably they'll take it to be some natural thing, like sunspot effects."

"You hope," said Lysander. "Well, it can't be very comfortable for them in there, so maybe they'll get out when they can anyway." He thought for a moment, then added, "I can do what you want me to, I think, although it would be easier if I went in by myself."

"No. It's going to be the way I say. Marguery goes with you."

Sandy shrugged. "And you'll take them prisoner as they come out?"

"Of course."

"All right," said Sandy. "Then there's just one thing left. I'll need one of those." He pointed to the gun at Boyle's belt.

Boyle raised an eyebrow in surprise. "For what? You said yourself you couldn't threaten a Hakh'hli."

Sandy gave him a pleasant smile. "You can kill one," he said. "And now I'd appreciate it if you'd get me a pencil and paper. And don't talk to me for a while, please. I think I'd like to write a poem."

They couldn't see the little settlement that had grown up around the lander as the jet came down; in that heat-drenched, almost windowless jet they had nothing useful to see out of. Only the pilot had any real visibility.

Peering past the pilot's head, Lysander caught a glimpse of cloud, sky, mountain, cloud again; and then the aircraft was bouncing along a runway, the jets screaming louder than ever as the reversed thrust slowed them down. The deceleration threw Sandy against his straps.

Then they stopped rolling.

Lysander unbuckled quickly and reached to open the

hatch, but Boyle put a hand on his shoulder. "You asked for this," he said, offering the gun from his holster.

Lysander turned the flat, heavy thing over in his hand, wonderingly. It was so small and so sinister. "This could kill a person?"

"You mean could it kill a Hakh'hli? It could kill an elephant, Sandy. It's got a shaped charge in the load."

"Show me how to use it," said Sandy. Grudgingly Boyle led him around the far side of the ship, toward the open runway. Sandy got only a glimpse of the lander, fully erected, with its brightly colored shrapnel shroud already in place. More than anything else the lander looked like a praying mantis gift-wrapped for Christmas.

It didn't take long for Boyle to explain safety, sights, and trigger to Sandy. Warned, he braced his arm when he fired it for the first time. Even so the recoil was a surprise. It wasn't noisy, though. The sound of firing was only a sharp *thwuck*, rather than the violent explosion he had imagined, but it made a second, louder sound when the charge struck what it was aimed at (or anyway, where it happened to go by courtesy of his inexpert marksmanship). It blew craters a foot deep in the runway as it hit.

Lysander shook his head, turning to Boyle. "That's no good. I could blow the lander up if I hit the wrong place."

Boyle said, "Well, I suppose we could give you solid rounds instead of the h.e., but I don't know if they would kill a Hakh'hli."

"They won't know that," Lysander said. "Give me the rounds."

Even a dedicated Hakh'hli would not spend days and weeks in the lander if he could help it; it was too cramped, too bare, too uncomfortable—certainly too boring. The humans had obligingly airlifted a sort of cabin in. It was smaller than the common room the cohort had shared back on the big ship. But then, Sandy thought somberly, the cohort was a lot smaller now, too. He saw Bottom peering out of the lander hatch, just above the rodded stick they used for a ladder. Sandy waved to him but didn't speak. He walked to the door of the Hakh'hli dorm and stood there, looking in.

Tanya and Helena were huddled over a television set. Fortunately it wasn't in communications mode; they were simply watching the bland Earth networks, long since censored of any news that might disturb the Hakh'hli. Tanya turned to look at Sandy with surprise. "What are you doing here?"

"I'll show you," he said in Hakh'hli, putting a finger to his lips.

"Show us what? And what was that noise we heard a little while ago?" Helena grumbled.

Sandy said secretively, "I don't know. Something the Earth humans were doing, I guess. Don't waste time." He peered out the door. "Follow me, and don't attract attention. All of you. You too, Tanya. Don't even use the communicator, just come on."

He didn't wait for a response. He went out of the cabin, conspicuously nonchalant as he walked toward the tail of the rocket. It cast a long shadow in the hot, late summer day; and he could see by the shadows beside him that the two Hakh'hli were following him.

Marguery was standing at the tail of the rocket, gazing upward as instructed. Tanya stopped short beside Sandy. "Why have you brought the Earth-female here?" she demanded, licking her tongue out suspiciously.

Sandy said easily, "Look and see." He pointed to a perfectly featureless point on the shroud, and said, "There."

"There what?" Helena grumbled.

Tanya grunted in annoyance, stretched as high as she could on her long, thick legs, and said peevishly, "I don't see any—"

That was as far as she got. She toppled forward on her

face even before Sandy heard the *thwick* of the gas gun. Helena managed to whirl long enough to catch sight of Boyle's sharpshooters, but not in time to do herself any good. It was a fast-acting anesthetic. Both she and Helena were unconscious a moment later.

Sandy signaled to the gunners, crouched at the side of the ship, to take them away and then nodded toward the climbing stick. "Come on then, if you have to," he ordered Marguery.

As they climbed toward the hatch Bottom popped his head out of the door again, staring curiously but without suspicion at Sandy. Then he caught sight of Marguery coming up behind him. In Hakh'hli Bottom called, "Why are you bringing Earth-female aboard?"

"Tanya asked me same question," Sandy replied, already at the door level. "Get out of my way, will you?" He pushed Bottom aside. When Marguery was safely inside, he said, "You can hear for yourself. Listen!" he commanded.

Demetrius appeared behind Bottom just as Boyle's people, hiding under the landing craft, started the tape Boyle had provided. From outside came the recorded pleading, broken voice, sobbing in Hakh'hli, "Please! Please help me!" over and over.

"That's Polly's voice!" Demmy shouted, leaping toward the door. "Come on, Bottom, let's see what's wrong!"

Marguery leaned out the door. "They're down," she reported. "They got them both with the sleep darts. Well, Sandy, I guess we've done what we had to—"

"Get out of the way of the door," he ordered.

"What? What do you mean?" She blinked at him. Then, as he toggled the hatch switch and the door slid shut, she jumped away. "Sandy, what the hell are you doing?"

"I'm strapping myself into this seat," he said calmly. "You can take the one over there."

259

"*Why?*"

"Because if you don't," he said logically, "you'll get hurt when we take off." He turned on the preheater, knowing that almost at once the first faint wisps of hot gas would begin to come out of the thrust jets. He moved uneasily in the pilot seat, hoping the crush wouldn't be too bad in the acceleration when they took off. The seat had fit Polly perfectly. It was, of course, big enough for two or three like him.

It couldn't be helped.

He touched the ignitor and opened the fuel throttle the smallest crack he could manage. He heard the hoarse white-noise hiss of the escaping flame, but the ship didn't even shudder at that low setting. He didn't expect it to. He only wanted to warn Boyle and the others that the main jets would be on in a moment, and hoped they would have the sense to get out of the way—and would drag the anesthetized Hakh'hli out of the way—before he applied power.

"Sandy! Turn that off!" Marguery shouted.

He said, "I told you to strap yourself in."

"Stop it! Do you think I'm going to let you do this? I won't permit it!"

He balanced the flat, heavy gun across his knee. It was pointing in her general direction, and his hand was on the trigger, the safety off.

"You can't help it," he pointed out.

She stared at him in horror. "Would you shoot me, then?" she gasped.

He said, "Not seriously. Only in your pretty, pretty leg, if I had to. Just to keep you from coming at me. But I'm not a very good shot, Marguery, and I might easily miss."

Chapter
◆ 23

Although there are more than ninety thousand trackable objects in Low Earth Orbit, the space doesn't look crowded. Low Earth Orbit, after all, includes a vast volume of space. It is a shell perhaps twenty miles thick, completely surrounding the Earth. The probability that any given orbiting object that is big enough to be detected—say, an expended nuclear pop-up laser— is within a mile of any other—say, an ascending Hakh'hli landing vessel—is very low at any given time. However, the orbital velocities are huge. The pop-up travels that mile in a quarter of a second. And the objects that are too small to be detected move just as fast . . . and there are many more of them . . . and hundreds of thousands of them are just as deadly.

Flying the Hakh'hli simulator was not at all like flying the landing vessel itself. Lysander's inadequate piloting skills were taxed to the utmost. The only thing that saved them from disaster was that there was nothing very hard to do. Taking off was easier than landing. It was the easiest thing in the world: You didn't have to go any place in particular, you only had to go *up*.

Compressed back into the huge kneeling-seat, Lysander could barely reach the Hakh'hli-designed controls. He knew what he had to do. It was just so very difficult to do it. Once they were off the ground he had to release his straps and lever himself forward against the enclosing arms of the seat—forcing every muscle to do more work than it had ever done before—in order to engage the magnetic repellers. Then he let himself drop back, panting.

Behind him Marguery gasped, "What are you doing, Sandy?"

"I am flying this Hakh'hli landing vessel," he said proudly. "Please don't get out of your seat."

"As if I could!"

"Of course you cannot do that now," he agreed, "but once we are at orbital velocity I will cut the thrust. Then you must remain where you are."

"Or you'll shoot me."

"Oh, no, Marguery. It's too late for you to keep me from taking off, isn't it? But if you interfere you may very well crash and kill us both."

She was silent for a moment, panting. Then she called over the distant thunder of the engines, "Would you really have shot me?" He didn't answer. He just smiled at her over his shoulder. She tried a different tack. "What if I have to go to the bathroom?"

"There is no bathroom on a Hakh'hli landing vessel," he told her. "In the cabinet behind you and to the right are waste sacks and sponge materials that can be used for that purpose, if absolutely necessary. But for now I think—*ow*," he cried, as the lander made a sudden sidewise thrust. He rubbed a bruised shoulder. "We must've just dodged a big one! That means we're getting into the garbage orbit, so hold tight!"

It took more than an hour to dodge and bounce their way

through the garbage belt. They were continuously on drive, keeping both of them anchored to their seats. Because they were using the north polar sector of the sky the density of dangerous objects were markedly lower than anywhere else over the Earth. It was still hazardous enough, and definitely a bumpy ride. From time to time alarming noises made Marguery bite her lip, as some microartifact too tiny to dodge splatted against the foil shield and its instant plasma cone clanged against the hull. Some of the clangs were scarily loud . . . but none were followed by the blue-light pressure alarm on the board, or by the hiss of escaping gas.

The little ship's evasive action threw them about mercilessly. But the time they were clear of the worst of the damage even Lysander was nursing bruises, and Marguery was grunting with pain. Lysander calculated the vectors for converting their circumpolar orbit into the equatorial one of the interstellar ship and applied corrections. "I'm reducing thrust," he called, squinting with interest at a familiar face that was silently shouting on the pilot's screen. "You can go relieve yourself now if you need to."

"Thanks for nothing," Marguery snarled. "Who's that looking at us?"

Lysander studied the face. "It's ChinTekki-tho. He isn't looking at us, though. At least, he can't see us, because I'm not transmitting yet. He looks angry, doesn't he?"

"What a surprise!" she snapped. "What are you going to do now?"

Lysander leaned back against the kneeling-seat, rubbing his bruises. "I'll answer him pretty soon," he told her.

"Then what, damn it?"

He looked at her thoughtfully. "Then," he said, "I'm going to do what I want to do. That'll be a novelty, won't it? I haven't had much practice at that. First I did what the Hakh'hli wanted me to do for most of my life. Then I did what you wanted me to do. So this is a new experience, and there's a good chance I'll screw up. But we're going to try it anyway."

"Damn you, Lysander!" she began, and then, in a different tone, she said, "*Please*, Lysander. What are your plans?"

"Why," he said reasonably, "the first thing I have to do is to set course for the Hakh'hli ship. That means there will be a lot of velocity changes, so I'll have to be careful about that; we don't have big fuel reserves. No," he corrected himself, shaking his head, "that's not the first thing. The first thing is to *find* the ship." And, as she started to speak, he finished politely, "Dear Marguery, please shut up. I have to concentrate."

It took a lot of concentration. It took painstaking searching of the three-hour equatorial orbit before Lysander caught his first glimpse of the interstellar ship. He fumbled with the magnification until he got the Hakh'hli ship large in the screen, then worked the course calculators.

Then he sighed and applied a gentle torque, then a small thrust. "It could be worse," he observed. "We should be able to reach it in about six hours. Oh, look, Marguery! They're coming along quite well with that big dish."

"Great," Marguery snapped.

"I'd like to ask ChinTekki-tho when they expect to be able to detect signals," Lysander said cheerfully.

"Go ahead and do it, why don't you? He sure looks like he wants to talk to you."

Lysander hesitated, then reluctantly switched over to transmission mode. "Hello, ChinTekki-tho," he said pleasantly, turning on the sound for the picture. "How are you?"

ChinTekki-tho thundered furiously in Hakh'hli. "John William Washington, why are you doing this thing and not some proper thing? It is that twelfth-day for sleep now! You delay my rest! Your Major Seniors instruct you to cease this conduct which is improper and not as directed!"

"Speak English," Lysander ordered. "I want Marguery to hear everything we say."

ChinTekki-tho twitched his thumbs in furious objection. "But that is unwise and not prudent, Lysander! This Marguery Darp is not only Earth-human who will hear!"

"I said, in *English*!"

"Oh, very well," said ChinTekki-tho, angrily giving in. "Then tell me! Why are you doing this? Where is your gratitude to the Hakh'hli who gave you life? We *saved* you!"

Lysander shook his head firmly. "I don't think I owe you anything for that. You didn't do it for me. You did it for yourselves, and besides you lied to me about it."

"Lysander! You are endangering serious plans of Major Seniors for all our progeny. Think of seventy-three million eggs unhatched!"

"I am thinking," Lysander said harshly, "of seventy-three million Hakh'hli invading the continent of Africa, ChinTekki."

He deliberately left off the "tho" of respect. The teacher winced, but only said, "What are you talking about?"

"That you are invading the Earth!"

"No, no," ChinTekki-tho cried. "We are not 'invading' the Earth. Why do you use that word?"

"Then what do you call what you are going to do in Africa?"

ChinTekki-tho glanced nervously about, as though looking for some Earth-human eye turned in his direction. He licked his lips and said, "We do no harm in Africa. Africa has plenty of room. No Earth-humans are using it."

"But it's their *Earth*. It's their planet. Shouldn't you ask them first?"

"Lysander, you speak without thought. What is the use of asking them if we can live there until we know if it is *possible* for us to live there? No, Lysander! It is not your place to question the decisions of the Major Seniors now! Rather you should explain why it is that you attacked four of your cohort-mates and, without authorization, stole that landing vessel."

265

"Oh?" Lysander said, interested. "How did you know that, ChinTekki-tho?"

"How do you think I know it?" the teacher said bitterly. "They've been telling us about it for the last hour! As soon as your cohort-mates recovered from your foul attack they demanded that the Earth-humans transmit for them. They are speaking to me even now, along with some of the humans. They, too, want you to go back!"

Lysander blinked in surprise; he hadn't expected them to react so quickly. "Why don't they talk to me direct?"

"Because you do not have any receiver for Earth transmissions, foolish Lysander!" ChinTekki-tho roared. "Do you not believe me? Here, wait. I will allow you to see for yourself."

He leaned past the camera to give swift orders in Hakh'hli. In a moment the screen split in two horizontally. On top was the furious face of ChinTekki-tho. Below him were a whole group of people—Boyle and a couple of other humans, and with them Demetrius and Tanya, looking just as enraged. They looked different in other ways, too. Hamilton Boyle seemed to have had his hair cropped short since they saw him last; moreover, he was wearing a burn dressing on one side of his face. Demetrius was bandaged, too, and looked even more resentfully furious. He shouted accusingly: "You endangered our lives, Lysander! If this Earth-human had not managed to pull me out of the exhaust before you applied full power I would have died unnecessarily early!"

"I'm sorry you both got scorched," Lysander said politely. "I see you all survived, though."

"No thanks to you," Hamilton Boyle grated. "Come back at once!"

"Sorry," Lysander said. "I don't have the fuel. Or the desire, either."

"Then come simply and peacefully to the ship, Lysan-

And Hamilton Boyle snarled, "That's not a decision for someone like you to make, Lysander! Forget it! The Hakh'hli have already proved that we can't trust them!"

"It is Earth-humans who have lied!" ChinTekki-tho shouted.

"Oh, stop it," Lysander said wearily. "That's what the, ah, ambassadors are for. Otherwise there's no doubt you'd both lie and cheat." He nodded judiciously. "You are both experts in this matter, of course. You have both lied to me too many times for me to believe anything you say now."

Boyle said earnestly from his half of the plate, "We haven't *lied* to you, exactly—"

Lysander laughed savagely. "'Exactly,'" he mimicked. "And that word is also a lie! Boyle, I know that you lie; I know that Earth people lie easily and well, because I have seen how quickly I myself have learned to do it."

"But you're not—" Boyle began, and then stopped. In the ship Marguery's hand flew to her mouth.

Lysander looked at her, then back at the screen. "I see there are still lies untruthed," he said grimly. "What is it, ChinTekki-tho?"

The big Hakh'hli flexed his thumbs restlessly. "Ask your Earth-female and not me," he grumbled in Hakh'hli.

"I'm asking you! And I want it in English."

"You do not wish it heard in English," ChinTekki-tho said earnestly. "Believe me in this."

"Say it in English anyway! You didn't find my parents alive in a spaceship. I wasn't born of an American woman. The only ones there were Russian, and they were both male!"

ChinTekki-tho said gently, "That is true, Lysander. They were also both quite dead. They had been dead for some time, and there was no air in their ship; there was not enough viable tissue left, really, to salvage."

Lysander flinched but held his ground. To hear it said was terrible, but he had been expecting something of the sort ever since the time in the underwater chamber. "What you mean," he grated, "is that I'm Hakh'hli. You've done genetic alteration on me. Isn't that true?"

But ChinTekki-tho was waggling his jaw negatively. "No, Lysander," he said, "you are not Hakh'hli."

And from behind him Marguery, sitting there almost forgotten, whispered, "No, Lysander. You aren't *even* Hakh'hli."

Of all the tones Lysander had heard in Marguery Darp's voice, he had never heard a tone like that. He turned to search her face. "Is that true? And you knew that?" he croaked.

She nodded. Sadly. Tenderly. "We knew that ever since we checked your tissue samples—first your excretions; we had your toilet plumbing diverted, Lysander. Then the sample they took in the hospital and your sperm—"

"No one ever took a sample of my sperm!"

She managed to smile. "Someone did, dear Lysander. *I* did." He flushed, even in that moment. She went on, "As soon as they began studying your DNA they could see that some of it wasn't human. Naturally we checked it against the Hakh'hli cells from Obie's body; it wasn't that, either, though the Hakh'hli DNA was closer. Yours wasn't anywhere near the DNA from the hawkbees we caught—well, no one expected it would be. But there were other tissue samples—"

He said harshly, "There couldn't have been any other tissue samples! There wasn't anything else alive from the ship!"

She shook her head. "I didn't say alive, Lysander. The other tissue samples were the scraps of food that Polly and the others left over. The—the meat," she finished wretchedly.

He stared at her incredulously, then turned to the screen. "Please, ChinTekki-tho," he begged.

And the old Hakh'hli teacher said somberly, "It is true, Lysander. We had to use other sources of DNA. It was very difficult to splice the genes, preserving as many Earth-human characteristics as we could—and then a surrogate mother was needed to bear you. We borrowed some genetic material from the hoo'hik to make you, Lysander, and it was out of the womb of a hoo'hik that you were born."

Chapter
•24

Considered as housing, the planet Mars isn't the kind of place one can move right into. In real-estate parlance it is what is called a "fixer upper," but it has fine potential for tenants who are willing to do the repairs. The things that are scarce on Mars are air, water, and warmth. The thing it has plenty of is land. It has far more land surface than the planet Earth, because it doesn't spend any precious surface area on oceans. For the Hakh'hli, that is what makes it worth having. Energy beamed down from the strange-matter engines in the big ship can boil water out of crystalline rock, cook air from oxides, smelt ores into steel to build all the habitats they want, and glassify rock to let the sunlight in. The Hakh'hli have the energy. Mars can give them the space to let their seventy-three million frozen eggs thaw, and hatch, and grow.

In the landing craft Lysander was staring blankly at the silent screen. It was only silent at the lander's end of the circuit. Where the people on it came from, both Hakh'hli and human, they were not silent at all. They were shouting. The way they twitched and flung their arms about, the contortions of lips and jaws as they argued with each other made that certain. But Lysander had cut the sound off.

Marguery wasn't even looking at the screen. Her attention was all on Lysander. Her first impulse was to throw her arms around him for solace, for if anyone had ever needed comforting, it was he. She hardly dared. His face was like granite. When she tentatively touched his cheek her fingertips felt the thump of a muscle pulsing under the skin.

Lysander jerked away from her touch, his face averted. He was saying something, but so softly that she didn't realize it until he turned questioningly to face her. "What, Lysander?"

He said, in a voice like lead, "What am I, then? Am I human at all?"

She took a deep breath. "Dear Sandy," she said, "you are John William Washington, and that's all you need to be. The biologists say you can do everything a human being can do. You can think, you can walk, you can make love—"

"And make you sick while I'm doing it!"

She shook her head. "Not if I take my histamine blockers. We tested that out, remember? They even—" She hesitated. "They even said that it was possible you could father a child."

He gave her a look of proud scorn. "That's impossible!"

She said steadfastly, "No. Only, maybe, a little difficult."

"I don't believe you," he said fiercely. "Why does everyone lie to me? Even MyThara did, all those years!" He put a hand to his face and felt something hot and wet. He looked at his hand, and found himself laughing. "At least I'm human enough to cry," he said, his voice unsteady.

"You're human enough for me," Marguery told him. He shook his head despondently. She thought for a moment, and then said, "Sandy? Do you remember on the jet you said you were going to write a poem?"

He looked perplexed for a moment, then fumbled in his pocket. "I've got it here. You might as well see it, I suppose," he said.

"Yes, I certainly want to, but what I was going to say was—"

He wasn't listening. He had already pulled the scrap of paper out of his pocket and handed it to her. It was folded and almost torn, but when she opened it up she was startled at what she saw. "Is that supposed to be a coffin?" she asked.

"It's supposed to be a poem," he said somberly. "Do you know what a poem is? It's how you feel, put on paper. And that was how I felt."

"Yes, I understand that, but Sandy dear—"

"You don't have to read it if you don't want to," he said gloomily. "I don't know if it's any good, anyway."

Marguery gave up. She straightened out the paper and read the poem over carefully:

> Am I womanborn
> or of some strange
> mating in empty space?
> Was I born at all or made?
> Perhaps it is better if I
> never know for what I do
> know of the egg-hatched
> or born does not cause
> me to envy them, even
> less to admire; evil
> they do, unthinking
> but wicked. Shame
> I say & plague on
> both your houses
> & I really hope
> you both lose!

She looked down at him, half-angry, almost amused.

"Lysander, that's *dreary*. What kind of person would write something like that?"

"Any person who took a good, hard look around him would! It's a dreary world. Haven't you noticed? Marguery, look at those people!" He waved a condemning hand at the soundlessly gesticulating figures on the screen.

Marguery looked, but what she saw was puzzling. Boyle was waving his arms across his face. He looked like a baseball fan trying to attract the attention of the grandstand peanut vendor. "What's he doing? Maybe he wants to talk to you," she offered.

Lysander shook his head. "What for? There's no point in talking to me; they need to talk to each other. But they won't." The ship lurched slightly, and then they were floating free. Lysander took a quick look at the board. "We're in coasting orbit," he said. "That'll last for about an hour, but you'd better be in your seat before that. Just before the power goes on again the lander's going to reverse so we can turn around to decelerate." Marguery made a faint noise. He looked up at her, frowning. "What's the matter?"

She said, "I thought you were going to ram the Hakh'hli ship."

He studied her face incredulously for a moment, then laughed. "Why would I do that?" he asked. "We'd get killed."

"Sandy dear," she said sincerely, "I can't tell you how glad I am to hear you say that. But then why did you steal the lander?"

"To keep you people from doing it, of course," he said in surprise. "Then I thought I'd just go back to the ship and try to reason with the Major Seniors."

"With me?"

"I didn't plan on taking you along, Marguery," he pointed out. "But you came."

She began to feel apprehensive. "And now?"

"What else is there to do?" he demanded. "Maybe the two of us can beat some sense into them. And—it would be

275

an adventure for you, wouldn't it? Wouldn't you like to be
the first Earth-human—the first *native* Earthborn human—
to visit the Hakh'hli interstellar ship?''

Marguery thought it over. "It's—frightening," she said.
"But I think I would—with you, Sandy?"

He blinked at her. She went on. "See, I wasn't asking to
see your poem a minute ago, dear Lysander. I was trying to
tell you that I'd written a poem of my own."

"But you never said you wrote *poems*."

She laughed at him. "Maybe I haven't written one yet.
Read it. Then you tell me."

He looked at the piece of paper she was holding out incredulously, then he looked up at her."Oh, my God," he said.

"Read it, God damn it!"

He obeyed.

Sweet   Sandy
the brick   shithouse
torso & the quick, kind
heart. You say that you
love me. I think that
I love you as well.
If you invite me
to marry you
I'll say
Yes!

"Are you *sure*?" he gasped.

"You fool," she said fondly. "Don't ask questions. Just
kiss me."

And it wasn't until he had done it, and done it half a dozen
times more, that Marguery caught sight of the communications screen out of the corner of her eye. The people on the
screen didn't seem to be arguing any more. Hamilton Boyle
was holding up both thumbs. ChinTekki-tho was weeping

amiably, and Demetrius and Bottom, giggling, were acting out shaking hands.

"Sandy," she said shakily. "Do you see what I see? Is it possible that they're trying to tell us that they've agreed on what to do?"

He didn't let go of her, but he craned his neck to see, frowning in bewilderment. "I don't believe it," he said. But his voice was uncertain.

"What else can it be? They're certainly trying to tell us *something*."

He said sincerely, "It is impossible that two such good things could happen to me in a single day. I don't believe that they've decided to cooperate."

"Dummy," she said lovingly. "Maybe they have. Why don't you find out?"

He shook his head. "I don't believe they have," he said stubbornly; but then he turned on the sound . . .

And they had.

Chapter
· 25

At this time John William Washington, often called Lysander, and his wife, Marguery Phyllis Darp, no longer called a "lieutenant," are two of the fifty-four representatives of the human race aboard the big Hakh'hli ship as it orbits the planet Mars. The first settlement is taking shape down on the surface of the planet. The first twelve dozen dozen frozen eggs have been thawed and hatched; as a favor to the Earth representatives, six of them were fathered by Oberon. Marguery and Lysander have been back to the surface of the Earth twice. The first time was a quickie just long enough for Marguery to get her divorce and the two of them to get married. The second time was partly to close up Marguery's old apartment and get rid of her major possessions, because they will not be back on Earth again for many years, and partly to give them a chance to receive some assistance in a breeding project of their own. (It did require a bit of biophysical help, but the results, they are sure, will be worth it.) On Earth, the first two railguns are already in operation, and the project of deorbiting the most threatening *lumps of cosmic junk is well along; the next step will be to launch orbiting vehicles equipped with Hakh'hli-type magnetic repellers to sweep up as many as possible of the smaller ones. It is still not easy for humans or Hakh'hli to traverse the old garbage belt in space; the polar windows are still the only safe places for fragile living beings, but with the railguns everything else can be catapulted past the barrier. The time is in sight when the human-imposed quarantine on space travel will be only an unhappy memory. And as for Lysander and Marguery themselves, they are many things. They are busy. They are useful. They are hopeful. They are expectant; and there is one thing more they are. They are happy.*

About the Author

Frederik Pohl has been everything one man can be in the world of science fiction: fan (a founder of the fabled Futurians), book and magazine editor, agent, and, above all, writer. As editor of *Galaxy* in the 1950s, he helped set the tone for a decade of sf—including his own memorable stories such as *The Space Merchants* (in collaboration with Cyril Kornbluth). He has also written *The Way the Future Was*, a memoir of his first forty-five years in science fiction. Frederik Pohl was born in Brooklyn, New York, in 1919, and now lives in Palatine, Illinois.